Maggie's Hope

Maggie's Hope

Agnes Abrahamson

VANTAGE PRESS
New York

Cover design by Susan Thomas

FIRST EDITION

Copyright © 2001 by Agnes Abrahamson

Published by Vantage Press, Inc.
516 West 34th Street, New York, New York 10001

Manufactured in the United States of America
ISBN: 0-533-13609-1

Library of Congress Catalog Card No.: 00-91569

0 9 8 7 6 5 4 3 2 1

To my daughters, Marguerite Abrahamson and Lynda Murphy, who had faith in this book, and to my darling first granddaughter, Teresa DeLuca.

Also to my half-sister in Canada, Holly Williams, a librarian who helped me with coal mining research early on.

Maggie's Hope

1

Catherine: Winter 1922

The girl picked up the hem of her flannel nightgown and, on bare feet, sprinted down the narrow stairs into the chill kitchen of the company row house. She shivered and hugged herself as she watched her mother pump water into a blue enamel kettle that was dented and sprinkled with black spots of age.

The water trickled out of the pump, and when the kettle was full, Maggie put it on top of the stove, which dominated the small kitchen.

Her mother, slim and dressed in a faded housedress and a baggy, black cardigan, pushed up the sweater's sleeves. She frowned, and minute lines marred her smooth brow. She drew her pale lips into a tight line while she tucked a strand of auburn hair back into the bun at the back of her head.

The girl stood silent and unnoticed by the stairs. She searched her mother's face and tried to push back the thought that maybe this wasn't the best time to bring up the subject of her new dress.

But she was only eight years old, and she could almost see the soft, blue-and-white material sitting on her mother's sewing table in the back room of the house and already pinned to a paper pattern.

Catherine had come down with the flu that raced through the mining community. Soon she would be returning to school, and she could just see herself wearing that dress on the day of her return. Wouldn't all the other girls in the class just stare and stare at her with envy when they saw her in that pretty dress? So...she gathered her courage.

"Ma, are you going to sew my dress today?"

Her mother didn't answer.

Catherine took a step closer, while her mother took a poker from the back of the stove and, with short, quick movements, stabbed at the gray, almost dead, embers.

"Don't just stand there, girl," she finally said. "Great heavens, what's the matter with you? Stop nagging me about that dress. I've more important things on my mind this morning. The dress will be done when I see fit—not a moment before. Why in heaven's name is that the first thing out of your mouth? Get your slippers on your feet, for pity's sake."

She poked vigorously at the coals, willing them back to life until, finally, the few remaining sparks ignited the stray lumps of unburned ones. Then she lifted the coal scuttle and poured the scattered brickets into the stove.

"It's freezing in here. I've told your brother, time and time again, make sure the stove is stoked before you go to bed. He spends his free time with those union people, and it will bring trouble down on our heads."

Catherine waited, still shivering and hugging herself, hoping that her mother's familiar tirade would soon end.

"As it is, he's been on short time, cut down to two or three shifts a week. The pit bosses know who's been mixing with the union trash.

"Lord knows there'll never be any fair play from the company. We have to learn to get along with them. You find that out soon enough when you marry a coal miner."

She looked quickly at her daughter. "God willing we'll be far away from the mines when you're grown. I'd rather see you in your grave than married to a miner. I don't know how, but we'll get away from the mines, my girl. I promise you that!

"The company controls this town, and there's no mercy in them, even if you're starving. Nellie MacLeod told me yesterday her credit at the company store has been cut off. She's near crazy, at her wit's end, and her· with six young ones and her husband crippled, unable to work. Poor things. No good will come from Colie pitting himself against the company. You can be sure of that!"

Catherine said nothing, knowing an answer wasn't expected.

From upstairs, a baby's soft wail drifted down, and beneath the loose bodice of her dress, Maggie felt the familiar tingling sensation as her breasts leaked milk at the sound of her baby. She straightened up and pressed her hands against the small of her back. Then she glanced at her red-headed daughter in the chill kitchen.

Her large, black-lashed, green eyes, looked at her mother.

"Ma," she said, "I can help with the chores. I don't have to take care of Aunt Marion's boys today after all. Her ma's come from the farm for a visit."

"She is, is she? Indeed! And did she bring along a ton of food for that coarse family? Whatever possessed me to marry a dirt-poor miner and let him take me to this miserable town. On my father's farm we worked. We worked hard, but we had food on the table and a roof over our heads that was ours, not the coal company's. I had some pride in those days."

Catherine felt her throat tighten at the mention of her much-loved father, and she was sorry that she mentioned Aunt Marion at all, because any reference to the country brought back to her mother, bitter-sweet memories of her

3

own girlhood and life on her parents' farm in a coastal, fertile valley in Cape Breton.

The baby's crying grew stronger.

"Well," Maggie said, "no use dwelling on what's past. I'd better feed the baby. Catherine, go outside and fill the scuttle. Let's see if I can get some heat from this stove. I've put the bread to rise. This week, we have flour, but if Colie keeps losing time at the pit, we'll be on short rations next week. Make sure you put your coat and boots on. I wouldn't put it past you to run out as you are."

"No, Ma. I'll get dressed first, and I'll be quick about it. Won't take me long, and I'll help you with the chores."

"Yes, girl, you're a good little worker when you put your mind to it. I haven't any dress orders from my ladies of late. I can thank Colie for that! The company wives are in thick with each other. Word gets around. Too bad I don't have a mother living on a nice farm to turn to for help."

Catherine stood, downhearted and defeated. All hope of wearing a new dress to school . . . gone, and she thought, *Ma's going to be mad all day, and it's my fault for reminding her of Aunt Marion's Ma and the farm*.

Maggie sighed and glanced at her daughter. Now mindful of her child's low spirits, she took the time to pat Catherine's thick, shining hair, as red as her own.

"Don't take mind to what I say, dear. I'm just out of sorts this morning. I'll try to get to your dress this afternoon."

Catherine put her arms around her mother's waist and nuzzled up close. Maggie kissed the top of her head, then gently pushed her away.

"Get on with you now. I didn't say for sure I'd make your dress. It will be some time before there's the money for another one. You'll be mighty tired of wearing it by then." Then she turned and climbed the stairs to her baby.

4

Catherine waited until her mother was out of sight before slipping on her brother's boots at the back of the stove. Her own, left out on the back step overnight were sure to be stiff with cold. Her feet slipped around inside the big boots, so she curled up her toes and gripped them tight. She clumped over to the coat hooks on back of the door and removed Colie's heavy jacket that covered her own.

She had grown some since last year, and the coat felt tight, almost too small for her now. Though sun-filled, the sharp, bitter cold December air hit her full in the face, and the wind coming off the ocean took her breath away when she opened the door. She didn't mind the cold. Ma had said that she would try to make her dress. To Catherine that meant she would for sure, for her ma wasn't one to raise false hope. That wasn't her way.

She quickly filled the scuttle and hurried back to the house as a few lumps of the precious coal fell out, hitting the rock-hard dirt of the yard.

Colie sat up in bed, inched over to the side, and tried to stand up. He moaned, held his throbbing head, and thought, *hope that ain't Ma out rattlin' 'round in the shed. She's likely to be tearin'. Clean forgot to stoke the stove. Damn, me head hurts. Drank too much rum. God, hope she don't catch on.*

Slowly, he raised himself from the bed, walked to the window, opened it, and stuck his dark, curly head out. Relief flooded through him when he saw his sister.

"Hey, there, little girl, 'ave a care with that coal," he yelled. "Looks like you've more on the ground than in the scuttle." Then, he leaned further out the window. "What're ya wearin' me boots fer? I got a mind to go down there and give ya a few thumps."

Catherine stuck out her tongue before picking up the stray brickets.

"Better watch out for yourself. Ma's in a real tizzy, she is. She's right mad at you for not stoking the stove before you went to bed. Says your going to get into a lot of trouble for hanging out with those union fellows. The house is as cold as ice, it is, and there's the bread to be baked yet."

"Shut ya mouth. Don't ya be sassin' me. Ma don't understand, that's all. She don't know nothin' 'bout what's goin' on. Get in the house and take off me boots, or you'll know the back of me hand." He pulled his aching head back inside and slammed down the window.

Catherine shuffled back into the kitchen, took off the boots, and put them back behind the stove, thinking, *the big bully, Colie, thinks he's a smart one. Just because that silly Frances James makes goo-goo eyes at him all the time. He's a sneak too, going behind Ma's back to those meetings.*

He wouldn't dare talk of thumping me if Pa were here. My Pa. Nothing is ever going to be the same again. Her throat tightened up and her chest felt as though a huge rock was pressing her down, trying to crush the breath right out of her.

She fought to control the despair that crept over her at the memory of the day they brought her father home. His once-strong body crushed and broken from a cave-in at pit no. Nine.

It seemed only yesterday instead of seven months ago. The Irish-blue eyes staring sightless from his blood-splattered face would never crinkle up and smile out at her again. Never again would he sing only to her the silly little ditties that he made up as he went along.

I won't think about it, I won't! I'll get the stove good and hot. Ma can bake the bread, and I'll take care of baby. I'll rock her in front of the stove. I won't think about Pa. I can run Ma's errands, and she'll sew my pretty dress.

With the back of her hand, Catherine swept away the tears beginning to roll down her thin cheeks. She went into a tiny alcove that served as a pantry and took out a can of kerosene. She thought, *I'll put a drop of this into the stove to get it going good. Ma won't know.*

She lifted the lid of the stove and peered inside, where a few red coals glowed. She tipped the can of kerosene, poured the fuel into the stove, stepped back, and when there was no flare-up, she poured in more of the fuel. Then she leaned over the stove and looked in.

An orange-blue flame leaped up and licked and seared her face before it caught the high neck of her nightgown. She gasped, jumped back, grabbed the stove cover and smothered the leaping flames while they curled and licked their way down her gown to sear and blacken her tender flesh. Pain-filled and terror-stricken, she screamed out.

"Mama, Mama!"

Maggie came out of the room with baby Boydie in her arms. She heard Catherine's screams, raced down the stairs, dropped the baby on a cot by the kitchen window, and caught up with her terrified daughter as Catherine tried to open the front door. She grabbed a patchwork quilt from the back of a chair, wrapped it around her daughter, and they tumbled to the floor.

"Sweet Jesus!" she cried. The air was filled with the odor of burning cloth and flesh, and while Maggie smashed out at the flames engulfing her daughter, they leaped around to sear her own arms and hands. *"Colie!"* she screamed, then her high keening wail filled the small house.

Colie bounded down the stairs two at a time. His eyes, unable to grasp the scene before him, slowly widened in horror.

"Ma, oh, Ma." He grabbed a floor rug and beat at the remaining flames while the acrid stench of smoke billowed out around them.

7

Catherine tried to touch her mother's face with a small blistered hand. Her voice through fire-seared lips was a whisper in the room.

"Don't be mad at me, Mama. I won't do it again. I wanted to help out a bit. You don't have to sew my dress today. I'll wait," and she cried out, "I hurt, I hurt. Make it stop." Then she drew in her breath sharply, her body arched and lifted with a violent shudder. Her eyes, through blistered lids, filled with pain and terror, stared up at her mother, 'Help me, Mama. Make it stop hurting. Oh, please, make it stop hurting."

Maggie rocked back and forth on the floor with Catherine locked in her arms and moaned, "Colie, get help. Run, quick. Get Mrs. Gleason."

Colie, dazed, stared down at his sister, at her blackened face. The sickening smell of burnt flesh filled the room. Tears filled his eyes and ran unheeded down his face, and he didn't seem to hear his mother's plea. He picked up the baby, quietly sucking her thumb, and laid her in the cradle by the door.

"Colie, wake up. What's the matter with you? Run, boy. Dear sweet Jesus, run. Get help. Can't you see your sister's badly burned?"

Colie jolted to life at the sound of his mother's voice. He opened the door and, barefooted and in his long winter underwear, ran next door to the Gleason house.

Maggie tenderly picked up Catherine and laid her on the davenport. She kissed the top of her singed head and spoke softly in Scotch-Gaelic.

"Tha gaol agam ort milis leanabh." ("I love you, sweet child.") Then said, "I'll make your dress, and you'll be pretty as a rosebud wearing it."

2

A small group of women gathered by Maggie McNeil's front door. Huddled together against the cruel December wind, they whispered and shook their heads.

Inside the house, Dr. George Field tenderly covered Catherine's blistered skin with oil then wrapped her in clean white sheets. He could do no more. He thought, *It doesn't seem any more than a blink of an eye since I delivered her into this world. Now, in all probability, I will be seeing her out of it.* There was barely an inch of unburned flesh on her small body. He had given her a sedative and, mercifully, she was out of pain for the moment.

Dr. Field was a familiar figure to the townspeople of Rockhill, Cape Breton. Tall and thin, he looked perpetually underfed and overworked. His thick, untrimmed white hair grew low on his brow and stuck out from his head at odd angles. He had practiced medicine in the coal-mining town for thirty years.

Born and raised in a tiny hamlet in northern Scotland, fresh out of medical school, full of youthful energy, he soon became indispensable to the downtrodden miners and their families. He gave of himself unstintingly, and he imagined that at last he was immune to the harshness, the tragedies of this mining community, but he was wrong. His hand shook as he tended to Maggie's burns.

Maggie, rock-still, motionless, stared straight ahead at the wall in front of her with the picture of Jesus surrounded by little children while Dr. Field dressed her burned hands and arms. From her lap, the blue and white dress material

9

slipped unnoticed to the floor.

Granny McNeil, clean, pink scalp showing through her spare white hair, bent over and picked up the material.

"My little one, my wee babe," she crooned, while her knotty hands caressed the cloth as if the living child was wearing it and could feel her tender strokes.

Outside, dirty, iron-gray clouds floated across the sky and blotted out the sun, turning the once-bright December morning into a world of ashen silver.

Young Colie and his pit buddy, Alex Campbell, sat on the back step of the house. Alex pulled a hunk of chewing tobacco from his pocket. He broke off a piece and passed it to his friend. He looked up at the sky.

"Looks like we'll have a bit of snow," he said. Then he aimed a great glob of tobacco juice high at the family outhouse and watched as the brown spittle crept down the slanted roof. He tore his gaze away and said, "Did you know that they're meetin' off at Johnnie's place tonight? Guess you wouldn't be goin' anyway, would ya? I sure feel bad about Catherine. I sure like that little girl. She'll pull through. Doc'll pull her through." He flung an arm about Colie's shoulder.

"I wasn't goin' to the meetin' even before Catherine—" Colie choked up and couldn't speak. Moments passed, then he said, "Me ma's not been likin' me goin' to the meetin'. Gets her upset. She don't understand 'bout those things."

Alex chuckled and aimed another glob of tobacco at the outhouse door.

"Johnnie Mac's old woman gets a bit upset, too. She chased him down the street, smacking him with a broom. That must have been a sight to see. Big Johnnie being chased by his fat wife." Alex slapped his thigh and glanced sideways at Colie, hoping for a response, but Colie sat with his head in his hands. "Did you hear about Danny MacLoud? Company bullies put his whole family out on the street. It's war now, by God! It's us or them. The UMWA is busy ass-kissin' company bigshots. It don't do nuthin' for us. Meetin' at MacAuley's Creek tomorra' night. On the q.t. Lots of company spies 'round—the rotten buggers. Ya never knows who they is neither—got to keep the lip buttoned up."

Colie listened, thinking, good natured Alex, who loved to talk, could never keep a secret. If there was to be meetin' at MacAuley's Creek, the whole town must know about it by now. He lifted his head and got up.

"Got ta go, Alex. 'Ave to see to me ma. Meet ya at the shaft in the mornin'."

He went back into the house, sat on the floor by his mother's feet, and rested his head in her lap. Maggie absentmindedly stroked his dark head. Except for the soft murmurings of his grandmother, the room was silent.

"Move aside, you bunch of cows," shouted Aunt Marion, pushing her way through the huddled group of women before they could open a path for her. "Don't you have nothin' better to do than stand 'bout gawkin'? Get away now. Go about yer business."

The women scattered like startled birds, only to gather again across the way, keeping watch.

Aunt Marion, tall, sturdily built, with black hair that parted in the middle and hung past her shoulders, carried a heavy flour sack filled with food. She opened the front door and walked past the group in the parlor and into the kitchen.

She emptied the sack on the kitchen table. Jars of strawberry jam, a smoked ham, three loaves of bread, a sack of sugar, a bag of potatoes, onions, and a can of blackstrap molasses soon filled the pantry shelves.

She lifted the stove cover and shoveled in more coal. On noticing the loaves of risen bread in pans on the sideboard, she put them in the now hot oven to bake.

Perspiring in the warm kitchen, she took off her coat and aimed it in the direction of a chair. The water in the teakettle had long boiled away. Aunt Marion refilled it and put it on the stove. Satisfied, she took a quick glance in the mirror over the sink and pushed back loose strands of hair from her face, picked up her coat, and placed it on the back of the chair, then went into the parlor.

Maggie looked up at her sister-in-law with blank, unseeing eyes. Aunt Marion went to her and almost lifted her from the chair. She led her from the room.

"Now, dear heart, you'll have a drop of tea and a bite to eat."

Maggie, who under normal circumstances would never allow herself to be led anywhere by Marion McNeil, went like a sleepwalker, unprotesting, to the table.

One hour later, Dr. Field stood in the doorway, his lanky frame filling the space. He ran a hand through his hair, his face tight with grief.

"It's over. I'm so sorry, Maggie, dear. The child's suffering is over."

Maggie looked up. Then slowly slipped off the chair to the floor in a dead faint.

Across the street, the group of women somehow seemed to know and quietly separated, each to her own home, to bake and cook for the bereaved family. Each secretly relieved that this time, tragedy hadn't stalked them and theirs.

3

The Scotch Presbyterian church, a landmark at the tail end of Main Street, would soon play host and give shelter to the line of somber, thinly clad people who walked silently along the snow-covered road with their arms hugged close to their sides and heads hunched into their shoulders against the stinging, driving snow. Like dark-clad ghosts, their feet made no sound on the soft ground.

Brown shingled, the tip of the church steeple seemed to disappear into the gray, snow-heavy clouds on the morning of Catherine McNeil's funeral. Men, women, and children turned out, and from time to time, a small child would look up and catch a snowflake with his tongue before being pulled along by his father's hand.

The bell in the church tower sounded, a long ominous pealing that filled the stillness like a woman's wail in the frigid air. The people quickened their pace.

Aunt Marion, stately in a black coat, custom-made for her by Maggie, and her thick hair covered by a black shawl, walked beside her husband while he held two small boys by the hand. She stopped, nudged him in the shoulder, leaned over, and stage-whispered in his ear.

"Will yer look at that, now. Right in front there. It's himself, Maggie's brother, John Beaton. Well, it's about time he showed himself. Didn't see hide nor hair of him when poor Jock went to his reward. Maggie, the poor, dear thing surely needs her own kin. Blood seeks its own in times of trouble, but he's here now."

Archie McNeil, almost a head shorter than his wife,

13

looked up and glowered at her from beneath dark, heavy brows.

"Will you button that lip of yours, woman?" he whispered. "Do you think the man's deaf?"

John Beaton, his head lowered, and deep into his own thoughts, didn't hear. He walked in front of them. A small, tight-muscled, compact-looking man, dressed in heavy work boots and a thick, green plaid jacket. The snow fell on his bare head and melted into his fiery red hair and beard.

He thought, *It's been five years since I've laid eyes on my sister. Not since she had the guts to come to Father's wake. Never expected to see her, but there she was, big belly and all.* He didn't like the alien feeling of shame that almost overwhelmed him when he remembered how he had turned his back on her when she approached, timidly holding out a work-worn hand.

He remembered thinking how thin and pale she looked, her swollen belly poking out from beneath her coat. Unknown to him, Murdock had gone into town with the wagon to pick her up.

Her lump of a husband had refused to go with her. She had begged him to, Murdock had later told him. Coward that he was, he didn't have the courage to show himself. Never was good for anything but keeping her in the family way.

Hatred for Jock McNeil still filled him. *He married my sister. Took her to a coal-town. Made a slave of her. Ma and Pa were never the same after Maggie left. Maggie was the sunshine. Jock McNeil took it away. Maggie understood me. The only one who ever did. She went willingly enough.*

John's red beard quivered, and he almost broke into a laugh. *Well, the bastard's gone now, and good riddance. I heard about the accident that did him in. Ned and Murdock went to his wake. They tried to get me to go, but I'm no hypocrite. I hated him*

14

alive or dead, made no difference. I never understood what Maggie saw in him.

That other one. He worked for the coal company, was some kind of manager—sneaky bugger, dallying with my sister. That's what startled the trouble. Well, the pit got him, too. It didn't take her long to forget him. That surprised me. She made such a fuss when Pa gave her a thrashing, made her stop seeing him. I guess that's the way with young girls. The image of a fresh-faced farm girl flashed across his mind. He quickly erased it. *I don't know what I'm doing here. I'm sorry I came. Maggie should have stayed on the farm where she belonged. Henry MacKenzie, a good, hard-working man, cared for her. She could have married him and wanted for nothing.*

Maggie won't want to see me. I didn't know her girl. I feel like a damn fool. Murdock and Duncan wanted to go to the funeral. I should have let them, but their lazy arses, always looking for a chance to get away from the farm. I don't know why I put up with them. They don't know when they're well off. I should send them packing.

John, his scattered thoughts brought back to the present when he reached the church steps, hardly acknowledged the people who nodded sadly to him and to one another before they climbed the church steps. Silent and uncomfortable, he thought, *It's not my place to be here after all that's past. Maggie might turn her back on me. I'll look the fool.* He hesitated on the third step, then turned, only to face Aunt Marion.

She grabbed him and smothered him in a warm hug that knocked him off balance on the step.

"Thanks be to God that you're here, John Beaton. It's a sad sad day. Your poor sister's at the end of her rope. I've done what little I could. I'm putting out a spread for after the funeral. I'd be pleased to have you come by."

He found himself facing the wide church door as Aunt

15

Marion linked her arm in his.

Archie patted him on the back, and they entered the church.

Startled by Aunt Marion's warm reception and held captive by her strong arm, he walked to the front of the church and knelt with Aunt Marion and her family beside a small, white, closed coffin on a trestle.

I'm a damn hypocrite, he thought. *Maggie's daughter's in that coffin, burned to death, only eight years old, yet I never set eyes on her. Now I never will, and here I am, kneeling at her coffin. I should leave.*

An organ played softly, "Abide With Me." John stumbled and fell in front of the trestle as he stood up. Burning with shame, he let Archie help him to his feet and lead him to the first row in front of the altar. He sat beside Maggie and Colie, bowed his head, then reached over and covered Maggie's bandaged hands with his own.

Maggie, Colie's arm protectively around her, deep in shock, was unaware that it was her brother John who sat beside her.

Aunt Marion pushed her way into the row behind them, a self-satisfied look on her face, and sat beside the hunched form of a weeping, Granny McNeil. Granny wouldn't have liked to admit it, but of her many grandchildren, Catherine had been her favorite.

Nine-year-old Kevin asked, tears spilling out of his china-blue eyes, and down his cold-reddened face,

"Ma, is Catherine in that white box?"

Aunt Marion wiped his face with her handkerchief.

"Shush, Kevin. No, she's not there. She's with Jesus now." She bent over Kevin to whisper to Archie, "Did you see himself about to make a run for it on the steps? I was too quick for him. It's time he made peace with his sister. Help her and let bygones be bygones."

16

"Will you shut your trap, woman. Leave the man be."

Six-year-old Sammy, on the other side of Archie, whined.

"Papa, I have to pee."

The organ stopped, and Pastor Ferguson, standing in front of the altar, began to pray.

Catherine was laid to rest beside her father and siblings in the family plot behind the church. It stopped snowing, and the sun came out to shine on the people crowded around the grave site.

More than one let his thoughts travel ahead to Aunt Marion's house and the spread of food sure to line her bountiful table after the funeral rites had ended.

The coffin was lowered. Maggie, silent and dry-eyed, supported by Colie on one side and John on the other, suddenly wrenched free and tried to fling herself on top of the white coffin. Colie and John held her back.

"Maggie, don't take on like this. She's gone. Let me take you home. Back to the farm with me."

Maggie turned and clawed at his face with her bandaged hands.

"Let me go. Who are you? Get away from me. My home is there in the earth with Catherine. Let me go. Take your hands off me. I don't know you! Colie, where's Colie?"

"I'm right here, Ma." Then, "Who the hell are ya, mister? Take yer mitts off me mum."

He punched John hard in the shoulder and grabbed for his mother. John released Maggie, and she almost fell before Colie caught her.

John, irate, pushed Colie, who then bumped into Uncle Archie, who steadied him.

"For the love of God, men," he said, "stop it. Remember where you are."

John's face was now white with rage and humiliation.

"That's the thanks I get. I knew I shouldn't have come to this shit-bag town. You keep your hands to yourself, mister. I'm your mother's brother and damn sorry that I came to pay my respects. Your mother knows where to find me if she cares to." He walked quickly up the snow-covered path and away from the church.

"Now see what you've done, Colie," Aunt Marion said. "The man came in good faith, and you've chased him away."

Colie, fists clenched, glowered at her.

"Who's he think he is, sayin' he'd take me ma home? She's me mother. We don't need him. I can take care of me own mother. I never even heard her talk of him."

"Oh, you're just a boy, you don't know nothing," said Aunt Marion. "I'll go after him." She pushed her way through the crowd, followed John, and caught up with him at the gate. She put her hand on his arm and said, "I hope you don't pay mind to the boy. Maggie is beside herself with grief. The boy, too. He don't know what he's doing either. He's young and upset. I'd like you to come back to the house for a bite and a drop of tea before your trip back. I'd be pleased to put you up for the night if you've a mind to stay."

John shook off her restraining hand and didn't answer. He walked to his horse-drawn wagon at the side of the road and climbed in.

Aunt Marion stood watching as the wagon rattled up the road. She thought, *Now, that is a queer duck, I'm sure.* She hurried back to join the procession leaving the church grounds.

4

Set back high on a bluff overlooking the ever-changing Atlantic Ocean, a row of narrow, two-story, muddy-brown miners' homes stood like sentinels. Connected, supportive of each other, appearing to lean toward the sea as if knowing that far beneath its turbulent waters, sloping ever downward, deep into the bowels of the earth, the male inhabitants of those homes toiled and sweated, digging for its riches—coal.

Each house was an exact replica of the other, drab when pitted against the cobalt-blue sky and vivid grass of a spring day, the house at the very end being the one exception, made bright and colorful by a riot of petunias and impatiens that grew on each side of the front door and along a brick-laid path leading to a patch of backyard and beyond, the end of the bluff, with thick bushes covered with red berries, scrub pine, and hedges of beach roses that guarded the ragged edge and the sheer drop to the rocky beach below.

Toward the back of the house, bent over a round, tin washtub, Maggie McNeil scrubbed a man's shirt. The sun beat down on her kerchiefed head. Tiny beads of sweat formed on her lovely face, and she wiped them away with the back of a burn-scarred hand, then straightened, shaded her eyes, and looked up at the cloudless sky.

Catherine's death had broken her. Each day, like a silent thief awaiting his chance, despair crept about in the shadows of her mind, always there, waiting. *Catherine, My darling girl. How I wish I could take back the terrible words I said that awful morning*, she thought. *Oh,...how could I have said such a thing to a child? To say I'd rather see you in your grave than married to a miner. Dear God, how can you punish me so cruelly for thoughtless words spoken in anger?*

I'm sick and sore at heart, so lonely for my little girl. Are you there in the heavens? Safe in our Savior's arms? You were such a good child. Overcome with emotion, she shook her fist at the sky.

"First Danny, then Catherine. You've taken them from me, my babies. Lord, why are You punishing me? Am I being punished for my sins? For loving Jim those many years ago? I was sinful. I knew it was wrong, but I was young and I loved him. What did I know of life? I loved Jim Boyd and will for the rest of my life. I shouldn't be punished for loving.

"I've paid for my sin, Lord. Oh, how I've paid for my lie, desperate, and no one to turn to, pregnant with Jim's baby.

"Jock wanted to marry me. He never knew Danny wasn't his. I was ashamed, and it was a way out of my trouble. I could never love Jock the way I loved Jim, but I was a good wife to him.

"You were waiting—a God of vengeance. You took my Danny. Gave me stillborn babies, miscarriages, and now you took dear little Catherine. Made sure I had a life of sorrow. You're a vengeful God. Leave me be. I've paid enough."

"Mama, see?"

By her side on the prickly grass sat twelve-month-old Boydie, chubby pink feet bare and dressed in blue rompers, she played in the water from an old dented pot and laughed deep gurgling baby sounds when drops of water splashed up at her. Red-gold ringlets poked out from beneath a pink, lace-trimmed bonnet. "Mama, see?" She looked at her mother, seeking approval of her little game.

Maggie's sudden tirade ebbed. Her body sagged and she felt weary, empty, defeated. She looked down at her

20

baby, then snatched her up in her arms, held her close, and rained kisses on her rosy face.

"Yes, baby, Mama sees." Then she looked toward the sky, and not caring if anyone was listening, prayed out loud. "Forgive me, Lord. I didn't mean what I said. I'm distraught. Don't take Boydie from me, too. I'd be alone. Colie is almost a man now. Soon, he'll be leaving me."

Boydie permitted herself to be held for a moment or two, then struggled to be free. Maggie put her down, remembering Catherine as a baby and how she loved to be held and cuddled, unlike Boydie, who couldn't stand to be confined for more than a few minutes, even in loving arms.

Maggie wiped her face with a corner of a faded blue-checkered apron, and thought, *I'd best stop wallowing in self-pity. The wash won't get done by itself. It should have been hung out long before this. Colie will need a change of clothes when he gets home.*

But, still she stood, and gazed out at the ocean. Pale, gray-blue water, calm and serene for the moment as a peaceful lake. It comforted her, and she prayed. "Lord, please help me to accept my life and not question your ways."

Once free, Boydie resumed her splashing and playing for a few minutes, then, tired of the game, tipped over the pot and scrambled up on her chubby legs. The stiff grass tickled her feet and she clutched her mother about the legs.

"Mama, uppy, uppy."

Maggie picked her up and sat down. She nestled her face in the crook of her baby's sweet-smelling neck. Playfully, she rolled her to and fro in her apron. Boydie chuckled and pulled at the silver chain with the miniature locket, always worn by Maggie, that held a photograph of James Boyd.

"That's enough playtime, my pet," said Maggie, putting the locket back beneath the neckline of her dress. "I

21

can see that it's time for your nap."

Boydie stuck a thumb in her rosebud mouth and her sea-green eyes with their thick black lashes slowly closed.

Maggie gathered her up in the apron and carried her into the house. She placed a thick afghan quilt over the rug with faded pink cabbage-roses on the parlor floor and gently put her sleeping baby down. She kissed Boydie's satiny cheek. "My little beauty. Thank You, God, for blessing me with this child. If I didn't have her, I'd be raving mad by now."

She went back and continued scrubbing the wash. Her burn-scarred arms glistened in the sunshine. Once done, she piled the wash into a wicker basket.

A soft, sweet wind blew off the sea and picked up the scent of the wild flowers that grew along the bluff. She hung the wash on a clothesline that sprang between two knarled, old apple trees.

A man who had been spying on Maggie from behind the curtain of his kitchen window next door came out of his house. He glanced left to right, then walked quickly to Maggie's front door. A cap pulled low on his brow half-covered his ruddy face. He wore a faded work-shirt and pants, was barrel-chested, and had short, stumpy legs. His hand shook as he silently opened the door and stepped into the narrow hallway.

He wiped his sweating hands on his pants and looked around before entering the parlor. He saw the sleeping baby and grinned as he stepped around her. Then he stood quietly in the doorway and watched Maggie. His close-set, bloodshot eyes roamed over her slender form as she bent over the sink.

Sweat broke out along his brow. He took off his cap and twisted it in his hands, then took a step closer to Maggie.

Startled, Maggie whirled around. Her hand flew to her

throat, and the color drained from her face. She saw his eyes and fear made her grip the sides of the sink.

"Mr. Gleason, you startled me. How dare you creep up on me like that!"

Although they were neighbors and Maggie and Jenny Gleason were good friends, Maggie didn't like Sammy, never felt comfortable with him. She didn't like the way he'd brush against her as though by accident, and when he put an arm around her shoulder, her skin would crawl. He'd look directly at her and smile as though they shared a secret.

Now he stared, then smiled, revealing tobacco-stained teeth as he moved toward her. He reeked of whiskey. Revulsion and a sick feeling at the pit of her stomach made her want to gag.

"I just thought you might be likin' a bit of a man's company. Been thinkin' of yer all day, girl."

Maggie tried to regain her composure.

"You mean you've been drinking all day, and don't call me 'girl'. Why aren't you working? The mines are going full tilt. There's plenty of work. Colie's on full time."

"I'm not soft in the head, Maggie, me dear. I'm not about to have a run-in with the strikers. They're a mean bunch and don't take lightly to strikebreakers."

"Colie hasn't had any trouble with them. You can't let a bunch of hoodlums run your life. You've got to stand up to them," said Maggie, her voice firm in spite of her fear. "I'm busy, and you're drunk, and I don't like your sneaking up on me. Your lack of manners is appalling. Get out of my house!"

He ignored her request and took another step toward her.

"Hoity-toity, ain't you sumpthin' now. You think yer better then me with yer big words? You ain't a bit neighborly, Maggie, and yer Colie's gonna get his head knocked off one of these days. He don't let on what's been hapenin'

23

at the pit. Don't want to worry yer.

"I thought the world of yer man, may he rest in peace. We bein' pit buddies, an' all." He licked his lips. "You know, me woman's been with our girl helpin' out with the new baby. I ain't had a bite to eat all day. Sure, you wouldn't be so hard-heartened as to refuse me a drop of tea?"

"I'll offer you nothing of the sort. Jenny wouldn't appreciate your being in my house in your condition. You may have been Jock's pit-buddy for a short time, but as for friendship, there was none, and well you know it. Jock had no use for you. Now go home and sober up."

She tried to quell her rising panic as she thought of her sleeping baby in the next room.

"Now, yer not bein' nice to me, missus." His light-brown, bloodshot eyes turned slinty, mean-looking, and his voice lost its wheedling tone and became tight and harsh. "I thought well of Jock. Even if we didn't see eye to eye on some things. Jock being softhearted like he was, I never held it against him for getting' me in bad with the overman when I was pit stableman. I never hurt the friggin' horse—a little accident, that's all 'twas. Jock had no call to get me in trouble, but I tried to be a good sport about it. Now, c'mon, give me a kiss." He took another step closer to her.

He was so close, she could smell his sour body odor. She thought about running out through the kitchen door, but pride held her back. Shame. She didn't want a scene. One that would have people talking.

"I've been doing a lot of thinkin' about ya," he said. "You must get pretty lonesome, a good-lookin' woman like yerself, bein' a widow an' all. Not havin' a man. It just ain't right. It's a darn shame." His voice was low and sad as he threw his cap on a chair. Sweat poured down his face. He slowly stroked the front of his bulging pants. "I want you to know that I think yer the best lookin' piece in this whole town, Maggie."

Maggie made a break for the door, but he moved quickly, closing the space between them. He grabbed her about the waist, forcing her back against the sink. "Come on girl. I've got something real nice for ya. Can you feel it? You want it. Yer know ya do." He shoved his body up against her, rubbing, pushing, as he pressed his rough face against her cheek. Her kerchief fell to the floor.

They struggled. Maggie wanted to scream out, but the thought of her baby stopped her. With her arms pinned to her sides, she tried to fight him off—they struggled silently.

Then, disgust, anger, and white-hot rage raced through her, and with it, fear left. Calm and in control, she twisted her hand until she found the drawer beneath the sink that held cutlery. She slid it open and grasped a sharp paring knife and held it close to her side.

He pulled her across the room and forced her down on the cot under the window. He tore at her dress, grunting, panting. He opened his pants and fell on top of her.

Maggie raised the knife and aimed the point of it at his fish-white belly.

"Get off me," she hissed and pushed the tip of the knife into his bare, soft gut until blood oozed out.

He gasped, surprised, and pulled away from her. He looked down, and his blotched-red face turned a sickly gray. He released her, rolled on the floor, got up on his knees, then slowly stood up and held his hand over his belly, blood running between his fingers.

"You cut me," he said, disbelieving. Now cold sober, he closed his pants with quivering fingers.

Maggie leapt from the cot, still grasping the knife, which was still aimed at his belly, and moved toward him.

"Get out."

He raised a hand, as though to fend her off, and

moved toward the door.

"No harm done, missus. I didn't mean no harm. Just thought yer might be missin' it. I'll be going along now. Sorry, no harm done." He backed away from her. "You should put that knife away. You might cut yerself." His eyes never left the knife in her hand.

"Get out of my house, you evil devil. If Colie knew what you tried to do, he'd beat you to a bloody pulp."

"Now, there ain't no need to be tellin' yer boy about this or me woman either. I made a mistake, but there's no harm done." He took a soiled handkerchief from his pocket and wiped the blood from his fingers, put it back, picked his cap off the chair, then turned toward the door. His eyes bore into her before he opened it and walked through, past privies, clotheslines, and down a steep path to the right of the house that led to a rocky beach.

Maggie watched him from the window as he slipped, fell, got up, and clutched a scrub pine for support. Then, numb with shock, her legs quivering, she sat down at the table and tried to catch her breath as she straightened her dress. She thought her head would explode, she felt such anger.

Foul man. Sneaking up on me. Thank God, I was able to defend myself. I should tell Colie. He'd give him the beating of his life. He's lying about trouble at the pit. Colie would surely tell me. The union men are always on strike. That's nothing new. Still shaking, Maggie got up, locked the front and back doors and went into the parlor. She looked down at her baby. The sun shone through the snowy white curtain, and sunbeams danced on the wall behind the sleeping child.

Maggie shivered in the warm room. Icy fear gripped her again, and her legs felt too weak to hold her up. She slumped down in Jock's old morris chair and leaned back. Her nails dug into the palms of her hands. Bile rose

26

up in her throat, choking her.

She knew that she had wanted to stick the knife deep into his belly, and it frightened her. She was a Christian, but still, she fought the urge to chase after him and stab him again and again.

His hands on her body made her feel soiled, shamed. *No one must ever know*, she thought. *I'll keep it to myself. This is a mean-spirited town. People would look at me differently. They would snicker and talk behind my back, and more than a few would be quick to say I led him on.*

Jenny, his hard-working wife, was a good woman who kept a spotless house. Maggie was fond of her and valued her friendship, but she wasn't sure how she would keep that friendship and still avoid Sammy.

She went into the kitchen, pumped water into the sink, scrubbed her hands, and splashed water over her face. Then she picked up the kerchief and wrapped it around her tangled hair, struggling to compose herself before Colie arrived.

I have to put it out of my mind, or Colie will know something is wrong. She put a few apples into a pot with a little water to cover them and put the pot on the stove. She thought, *Colie likes applesauce, and it will be good with the pork left over from last night's supper. Not much meat for a growing boy, but I'll put on a few potatoes, and that should hold him along with a few slices of bread and molasses.*

I've finished Mrs. Vincent's dress. She'll be coming for the final fitting tomorrow. I hope she pays me right away. I'll ask for the money outright if she doesn't. It's a cruel world, but Lord Jesus, I will take care of myself and mine. God forgive me, if he ever tries to touch me again, I will kill him though I hang for it!

I have to get away from this town. Somehow . . . Maggie straightened up, rose from the chair, and went into the parlor when she heard Boydie awaken.

27

5

Colie and his pit buddy, Malcolm McGee, pit pails slung over their shoulders, and covered with coal dust and bone-weary, walked out of the bankhead into the spring sunshine. They were accompanied by two company police.

Ahead of them, beyond the fenced-in area of the bankhead and lined up on either side, were the strikers. After each shift, Colie cringed inwardly, knowing he had to pass these men. He looked straight ahead as if unaware of the jeers and curses directed at them and ducked a rock that went sailing over his head.

"Yer old man be turnin' over in his grave, Colie McNeil!" the rock thrower yelled.

One of the guards went for the rock thrower with his billyclub, but Colie put a restraining hand on his arm.

"Never mind, mate." Then he turned in the direction of the rock thrower. "Ya aim's a bit off, man. Ya missed me by a mile."

"You be gutless rats," another man yelled. "You're rotten scabs!"

Colie stopped short. Coal-dust-rimmed blue eyes blazed out in fury.

"Why don't ya' go 'bout yer business. Ya' got nuthin' to do but stand 'bout all day? I got me mum an baby sister to look after. What do ya' want me to do? Let them starve?"

Malcolm tugged at Colie's sleeve.

"For Christ's sake, laddie, don't stop. Let it go," he said.

"Well, I got a wife and six kids to feed, you scummy traitor. They're hungry. You think you're the only one with a family? Bastard!"

A roar went up among the men as Colie started toward them.

Gordie MacRae, one of the strikers, a grizzly bear of a man who had been a close friend of Jock McNeil, pushed Colie back to the road, away from the threatening men.

"Why don't you give it up, boy? Join us. If we stick together, we can win. We'll lick them. The union's working for us now. You were with us once. Come on now. What do you say? You can stand the gaff if we can." Colie shrugged him off, too angry to speak. Gordie yelled out as he was shoved back into the crowd by one of the company police, "Piss on you then. The hell with you!"

They walked past the strikers, who now harassed two other men coming from the mine entrance.

"They're right ya' now, Malcolm," Colie said. "I do feel like a rotten traitor, a scab. Havin' to pass them every morning and after shift is takin' the life clear outta me."

The guards left their side once they were off mine property and went back swinging their billy clubs as a scuffle broke out between the strikers and the two other men.

They walked along the dry, dusty road, hot and weary, too tired for talk. Colie glanced back once or twice half expecting to be followed by the strikers. The wide road suddenly narrowed as they rounded the curve that led away from the mine and into the town.

Colie took off his cap and wiped coal-streaked sweat from his face with a handkerchief that had been snowy white that morning. He put the cap back on.

"Ya' know," he said, "if it wasn't for me mum and baby sister, I'd have taken off long ago."

Malcolm tipped his cap to the worried-faced, sturdy-figured woman with a toddler clinging to her skirt as she

29

stood in the open doorway of one of the houses in the cluster of low, gray-shingled dwellings to the right of them on the treeless road.

"Hot enough for you, Hanna?" he smiled. Then he gestured with his thumb. "Don't worry. Jack's down the road right behind us and all in one piece last I saw of him."

The woman's tight face loosened in a smile, and she unfolded her arms and waved to them.

Then Malcolm turned to Colie.

"What about me?" he asked. "What would I do without the best loader I ever had? Where would you go, laddie?"

"I'd head for Halifax. Alex Campbell's there, been gone three months. Got a letter from him. Wrote he was stayin' with a friend of his sister's. Says he likes city life."

Malcolm kicked at the loose stones and pebbles, sending up a small cloud of dust before them.

"What kind of work did he get? Did he say? Jobs are scarce as hens' teeth everywhere, even Halifax."

Colie, head low, hands deep into the pockets of his overalls, thought for a second before answering.

"He says he's lookin' for work, but no luck as yet. That was awhile ago. I ain't heard from him since, but he's bound to 'ave a job by now. Be back if he didn't. I knows old Alex."

Malcolm looked thoughtful. Ahead of them, a deep blue sky seemed to blend with the road as it reached a crest then dipped and twisted before low, thick, bushes alive with red berries, and stunted scrub pines began to appear. The rich greenness soothed their red, tired eyes and gave release to the ugly brown stain of road.

"Sure, working the pit's no bed of roses," Malcolm said, "but the devil you know is better than the devil you don't. Seems you can't win no matter what. All's I know is if you live in this town, you work in the mines. That's all there is. It's a nice enough town . . . been here all my life. It's home, don't care to live anywhere else. I've been a miner all my life, and my father, and his father. I've seen strikes come and go, and we've never won. The company holds all the cards."

Colie took off his cap and scratched his head.

"Ya, but it sure is rotten havin' yer friends turn on yer. Me poor ma don't know what to make of me. No more sportin' life. Don't go out after dark; somebody might be waitin' to bust me head. Wish I had me a boat. I'd go rum-running, make some good money, maybe enough to take me ma and baby sister and head for the States."

"Sure there's good money to be made, laddie, long's you don't get caught by the Mounties. You could land in Dorchester Prison. The Mounties and police are like fleas on a dog—they're everywhere. I'd stay clear of that sort of thing. I'd rather run the gauntlet at the pit than be chased by the damn Mounties. You have a chaw on you? My mouth's dry as pitch."

Colie reached into his pocket and handed him a plug of tobacco. Malcolm bit off a hunk and handed the rest back to Colie.

"How's your mother?" Malcolm asked. "Keeping to herself nowadays? My Jessie says your mother doesn't go to the sewing guild anymore. Wasn't she club president? But then, it hasn't been long since your poor sister passed on. It takes time to get over a thing like that."

Colie's face, under the sooty coal dust, set in tired, sad lines, the bones, sharply drawn, made him appear ten years older.

"Ma will never get over it. She's not the same, me ma. She sits lookin' off in space a lot of the time. Drags 'roun the house an' never sings no more, even to the baby. I lost me ma when I lost me kid sister."

"It's only been five months, laddie. She'll come back to herself. She's a strong woman. She pulled herself together after Jock's passing, and she will this time. Mark my words."

"No, it's different this time. Catherine was special to ma. To me, too. I miss her. I even miss her sassin' me, and she did that a lot. She had a mouth on her, that little girl. I wish I'd gone down that mornin' and smacked her one for wearin' me boots, before she had a chance to pour kerosene on the stove, but I was hung over." Colie smacked a fist into his hand.

Malcolm reached over and gave Colie a quick, light thump on the shoulder.

"Now, don't place the blame on yourself, laddie. It happened. No one's to blame. A terrible accident, that's what it was."

They reached Malcolm's house, a gray, two-storied square structure, weathered and solid-looking, built high and apart from its nearest neighbors, the squat, ugly-brown company houses that overlooked Rockhill's Main Street.

Malcolm remembered, how, as a young boy, and the only male in a family of four daughters, he helped his father build the house, and he felt proud. He owned his own home. He even had a soul-satisfying view of the sea from his bedroom window. His family need never fear being thrown out in the street from a company house. It was his, free and clear.

Malcolm was kind-hearted and a giant of a man. Sturdy as an oak tree. Thoughtful, self-educated, an avid reader, and he was worried. The striking miners and their families were suffering. Their anger rising, ready to lash out against the men still working the pits.

Malcolm could remember a time, years back, when his

own father lived in a barracks on mine property for weeks at a time, protected by company bullies, fearful for his life and unable to go home. The name-calling by his school-mates, and the shame he'd felt that his father was called a scab and much worse. Being a child, not understanding, he blamed his father for his school miseries. Could it be that his own children were now going through what he had? He didn't think it had reached that point yet, but it was surely coming.

"Papa's home, Papa's home." Two little boys grabbed onto his legs.

"The tub's ready for your wash-up, Malcolm. Say me to your mother, Colie," Jessie called out from the top step of the house.

"I'll do that, Jessie." Colie waved.

"Enjoy your day tomorrow, laddie," Malcolm said. "Meet you at the bankhead Monday morning. Let's show them we can stand their gaff. We won't be scared off."

He walked to the back of the house with two little boys clinging to his pant legs.

6

Colie continued on until he reached a fork in the road. He took the left one that led to the bluff. A fresh cool breeze blew off the ocean. Buttercups and daisies grew tall in the sweet-smelling grass.

Colie sat down by the side of the road and took off his boots and stuffed his socks into them before slinging them over his shoulder along with his lunch pail. He left the road and walked along the side, digging his feet into the cool, stiff grass.

He could see, outlined against the dark-blue sky, the company houses and the slight, dark-haired girl who stood on the front step of the sixth house carrying a laundry basket filled with blinding white sheets, pillowcases, and brightly striped towels unpinned from the clothesline, which stretched from the back of the house to an oak tree.

Now she balanced the heavy basket on one hip and shaded her eyes and looked anxiously down the long road. She wore a loose-fitting, faded blue jumper-dress that hung to her slender ankles.

Her small feet were encased in black, tightly laced up shoes, the sole of the heavy right shoe built up three inches higher than the left. She had straight, thick chestnut hair cut in a Dutch-boy bob that ended at the line of her jaw. She put the clothes basket down and pushed heavy bangs from her pale, moist brow.

Her face was small and heart-shaped with dimples that only appeared when she smiled. She had velvet soft, chocolate-brown eyes that lit up when she saw Colie in the distance as he emerged over a rise in the road. Frances waved and started down the steps, when a thin, high voice sounded from inside the house.

"Frances, gel, where are ye? I want me tea now." Then sounds of a cane thumped against a bare floor, loud, emphatic, and demanding.

"In a minute, Granny. I'm taking in the laundry. I'll make your tea soon, dear," Frances called out. She hurried down the steps and up the road, but her heavy right foot, as always, slowed her progress as it dragged behind her.

Colie saw her and quickened his pace. They met halfway between the house and the road. Colie took her by the hand back down the hill and pulled her to the tall grass by the side of the road and behind the thick branches of a tall oak.

Frances wrapped her arms around his waist and buried her face in the crook of his neck.

"I've waited and waited for you every day for two weeks. Your mother was doing the wash this morning. I waved to her, but she didn't wave back. I guess she doesn't like me. Don't you like me anymore? Is that why I haven't seen you?"

Colie took her arms from around his waist and gently pushed her away.

"Cripes, Franny, look. Now you got your face dirty from me shirt." He started to laugh. Then the sight of her coal-smudged face as she looked up at him, the love that spilled from her soft eyes was too much for him. He took the boots from around his neck and flung them on the ground before he pulled her back into his arms and crushed her slight body against him. The heavy branches enclosed and hid them from view.

"I've missed ya, Franny. I'd of stopped in after shift, but I knows how yer granny hates the sight of me. I didn't want to make trouble for ya."

"That's no reason not to see me. Granny hates everyone." Franny giggled. She snuggled closer to him. "You have another reason, I know. Fear of Granny never stopped you before."

"Ya knows me pretty well. Then, might's well tell ya. Ya know some of the miners' on strike. If it weren't fer me ma, I'd be on strike with them. Things real bad at the bankhead. Haven't ya heard?"

Franny shook her head.

"I knew there's a strike, but there's always a strike of some kind. No one talks to me anyway. How would I know? I go to church with Granny and to the shop to carry home the order on Friday with her. People don't like Granny, so they stay away from me, too. You're my only friend, Colie. You know that."

Frances looked down at her small rough hands and twisted them together. Colie took them and held them close to his chest.

"You're a sweet, funny face. How could ya know how it is at the pit, tied down here, a slave to that old woman. She's old, though, Franny. She can't live forever, then yer free a her."

Frances pulled her hands away.

"Don't talk like that. She took me in when no one else would have me, when my mother ran off and didn't care what happened to me. I owe her. No one else wanted a crippled little girl. They'd have sent me to the Children's Home. She isn't even my real granny, either. She didn't have to take me in."

"She took you in to have a workhorse and for no other reason. You'd mighta been a slight better off at the Children's Home. I 'member me own granny talkin'. She'd say it was a sin how Nora James treated her young. Yellin', screamin', an' thrashin' 'em."

"Well, she never beat me even if she is strict, and I have someone I belong to. Granny needs me." She tilted her head to one side and looked up at him. "Now tell me the real reason I haven't seen you. It's another girl, isn't it?"

"What would I be wantin' with another girl when I have ya?" He stroked her cheek. "It's the mine, Franny. Feelin's runnin' high with the strikers ready to bash me head in for not joinin' up with them. I've been stayin' in after dark. There's more than a few who'd love to do me in if they got the chance.

"I don't want me ma to know how bad it is at the bankhead. She's had enough, but I don't know how much longer I can hold out. I've missed ya, funny face." He tilted her chin and kissed her full pale lips. "God, ya feel good to hold. I'd like to lay you right down now and show ya how much I missed ya." He groaned and pulled her down beside him on thorough grass. His hand slide up her dress.

"Don't, Colie. I have to get back to the house. Granny is waiting for her tea." She pushed his hand away and sat up.

"One more kiss, then." Colie sighed and tried to pull her back down beside him.

They struggled, until Franny broke free and stood up.

"No, I know where one more kiss will lead, Colie McNeil. That's all you care about. You don't care about me. All you care about is doing that!"

Colie sat up.

"All right, all right, don't get mad, funny face." He started to laugh again. "Make sure ya wash ya face before ya give yer old granny her tea. Will ya meet me behind the wharf at Black's beach tonight soon after dark? I'll take me chances with the clowns out gunnin' for me. I got to be with ya tonight, funny face." He ran his hands down her slim body.

37

"I can sneak out after Granny goes to bed, but maybe we shouldn't. You've made me afraid for you. I couldn't stand to see you get hurt." She went back into his arms. He smoothed her hair and held her close.

"Granny is a sound sleeper. When she's down for the night, she stays there until I bring her tea in the morning. I'll let you in my window." Frances giggled again. "I'll put a few spoonfuls of gin in her tea to make sure she stays asleep. Sometimes I put a few drops in her afternoon tea so she'll nod off and I have some time to myself."

Colie threw back his head and laughed.

"Ya little devil, so yer get your granny drunk during the day. What do ya do when yer free of the old witch? Prance into town and flirt with the loafers hangin' 'bout the post office?"

Angry, Frances pulled away from him.

"Don't call my granny names like that! Sometimes you can be cruel. Who would want to flirt with me, anyway?" She looked down at her heavy shoes.

Colie put his arm around her waist.

"Don't be puttin' yerself down, funny face. I didn't mean anythin' by what I said. Ya take things to heart. I flirted with ya in church, and, as I remember, ya flirted right back." He kissed the tip of her coal-smudged nose. "I think yer pretty, and ya me girl. Now, let's see a smile. Show me them dimples."

Frances tried to hide her smile, but Colie cupped her face in his hands and slowly kissed the deep dimples in the now rosy cheeks. He smacked her lightly on the behind. "Ya better get back to the house," he said. He stepped out from behind the tree and looked down the road. "I see ya old granny comin' fast, and she's bangin' that cane of hers like she means business."

Startled, Franny looked also.

"She isn't. You like to scare me, Colie McNeil. Anyway, Granny can't get down the steps unless I help her, poor old thing."

"Well, get back to the house and wash up before she sees ya dirty face. She ain't blind, is she?" He kissed her. "I'll be by tonight soon's it's dark. Make sure ya leave ya window open, funny face. Save me some of that gin ya feed yer granny." He glanced up the road before he stepped out from behind the tree and walked rapidly up the road to his own house.

Frances put her hands against her flushed face as she tried to compose herself and quiet her racing heart. She felt as though she was on fire. She smoothed down her dress and ran her fingers through her hair before she hurried up the road.

He shouldn't talk against my granny, she thought. *He's like everyone else in this town. They don't know her like I do.*

Nora James had kept Frances isolated, away from other children during her childhood. She walked her to school in the morning and would be waiting for her at school's end. Dressed in long, dark, high-necked dresses that covered her small body all the way to her ankles, summer and winter, and dragging her heavy right foot, Frances was judged "crazy" by the other children. They threw rocks, teased and tormented her during school when the teacher wasn't looking. Frances's only refuge was her grandmother. Tearfully, she ran to her at school's end.

Frances led a lonely childhood, but sometimes, when she felt sad, she could imagine soft, warm loving arms around her. A vague, yet familiar perfume haunted her as well as sounds of music and laughter. Then she would think, *maybe I am crazy, like they say I am.*

7

"Frances, Frances, where are ye, girl?" Nora leaned heavily on a thick cane. The bright sun blinded and hurt her old eyes as she stood in the open door. A stiff, starched, gray gingham dress covered her tall, thin frame, and her still-thick white hair hung down her back in a single braid. "I want me tea," she whined before going back into the house.

Nora Murphy arrived in Rockhill from a tiny hamlet in Ireland when she was seventeen years old to become housekeeper to Robert James, a quiet, sorrowful, thirty-five-year-old coal miner still mourning the death of his beloved wife, who left him with four children.

Sold to James by her father in payment of a debt back in Ireland, Nora, a tall, sturdy girl, her thick black hair piled high under a big, feathered, blue-velvet hat, went willingly, for she had seen a photograph of Robert James, and he was a handsome man.

Outgoing and cheerful, she looked forward to a new life in Canada. Eight months after her arrival and heavy with child, she married Robert James, who never let her forget that his first wife was the real love of his life and that Nora could never replace her in his heart.

The years passed. Nora bore James five children, and the big, cheerful, fun-loving girl disappeared, replaced by a dour scold of a woman who seldom smiled or laughed.

One by one, the grown children left the cold, cheerless home as soon as they were able. Robert James died of black lung disease, and Nora bought the company house and lived on a small pension.

When Frances was found sound asleep in a pew of the Scotch Presbyterian Church, a beautiful, but crippled child of about three years old, clean, well cared for, and richly dressed in red velvet coat and leggings, it caused a stir in the town. No one knew who she was, and no one was willing to take a crippled child. She was to be sent to an orphanage in Halifax, when Nora James stepped forward to claim her.

The young, childless wife of the Presbyterian minister, enchanted by the lovely little girl, pleaded with her husband to be allowed to keep her. He refused, and her soft heart nearly broke when she finally had to release the child to the big dour woman.

Nora took Frances home, and the townspeople quickly forgot the little girl except the minister's wife, who took to visiting them until Nora threatened to strike her with a broom unless she left them alone.

They walked the town streets, the little girl's hand gripped tight in Nora's big one. Their dark dresses trailed along the dusty streets. They spoke to no one, and no one spoke to them.

Nora, a Roman Catholic before her marriage to James and excommunicated from her church, attended the Presbyterian church services every Sunday. They arrived late, left before the benediction, and sat in the last pew on the left side of the church.

Frances was sixteen when Colie became aware of her. Although they were the same age and had gone to the same school, Colie never gave her a thought. She was just the plain crippled granddaughter of that crazy old drunk, Nora James.

He used to feel sorry for her when the other children would chase her, throw rocks, and call her names, and he often took her part and gave a few blacks eyes to the school bullies.

41

But nine months ago, sitting beside his mother and Catherine in church, he noticed how pretty Frances was. He kept sneaking peeks at her when he thought she wasn't looking. He was surprised when she shyly lowered her head, then turned toward him and smiled, showing the full force of her dimples.

Colie couldn't get her off his mind, and on a restless, moon-filled night, Colie told his mother he was going to a friend's house, but instead went to Frances's. He could see her silhouetted against the curtain of her bedroom window. He threw pebbles at the windowpane until she heard him.

She opened the window and leaned out. Colie took a harmonica out of his pocket and began to play. Frances, alarmed, tried to shush him. Colie gestured that he wanted her to come out. She shook her head and started to close the window.

Colie quickly shimmied up the trunk of a young maple and climbed in before she could close the window.

He made love to her that night for the first time, while Frances moaned and whimpered and her grandmother snored loudly in the bedroom downstairs.

Nora, seated at the kitchen table, looked up when Frances opened the door. She grasped her cane and struggled to her feet, still tall in spite of her eighty-odd years. She held onto the edge of the table and shook her cane at Frances.

"Where have ye been, ye wee rascal of a gel?" she shouted in her high, tinny voice. "I should take the stick to ye, leaving me alone and that parched I am for me glass of tea." Her voice trailed off into a whine as she sank back down in her chair.

Frances putdown the clothes basket and went over to her grandmother. She picked up the cane, which had fallen to the floor, and propped it against the wall. Then she took a big white apron that lay on top of the basket and wrapped it around her slim waist, hoping it would cover her coal-dusty dress. She pumped water into the sink and wet her face with her hands.

"Granny, dear, the water will be hot for your tea soon," Frances said as she filled the kettle and put it on the stove. "I made some biscuits to go with your tea. It's so beautiful out, I sat down for a few minutes and breathed in the salty air. I dozed off, can you imagine?"

Nora peered up at her with filmed-covered, rheumy, blue eyes.

"You're red in the face, wee gel. Splash some water on yerself, and then get busy with me tea. Stop dillydallying now. Ye got the ironing to do, and I want a good hot supper tonight. You hear me, lass?"

"Yes, Granny, I hear you."

Frances went into their small narrow pantry. Took a thick white mug and a saucer from the shelf, then bent down and found the bottle of gin hidden behind the potato bin. She took a tablespoon, measured four tablespoons, and poured the gin into the cup, paused, then poured in another spoonful.

She looked at the bottle. It was half full. Frances sighed, "I hope this will last until Mr. Dan comes by. Granny won't be fit to live with if she doesn't get her gin."

Frances didn't think it strange that her grandmother was accustomed to drinking a full glass of gin every evening. As a little girl, she'd watch Nora drink it down, without a pause, every evening at seven. Sometimes later, Nora would be fast asleep, and many times, Frances would have to help her to bed. Nora was a steady customer of Big Dan McNarmara, the local bootlegger.

As Frances grew older, she discovered that putting a

43

few spoonfuls of gin in her grandmother's afternoon tea would result in Nora's drifting off to sleep. Frances loved the luxury of that hour, sometimes two.

Once Nora was asleep, Frances would go to her own room and reach under her bed for her pad of drawing paper and pencils. Sometimes, she would sit on her bed and look out her window at the sky and sea just beyond the edge of the bluff. Then she would take her pencil and try to capture what her eyes saw.

When she finished, most of the time she'd tear up her work, but every once in a while, she would gaze at the paper and then slip it into her drawing pad and hide it back under her bed.

She would have liked to show her drawings to her grandmother but knew that she would regard them as fool-ishness and a waste of valuable time.

Frances came out of the pantry with the mug and saucer.

"I'll brush your hair for you, dear, after you have your tea and biscuits," she said. "Would you like that?"

"Just get me tea, and be quick about it. I guess I won't refuse to have me hair brushed, lass. My scalp is that itchy, and me head aches sorely," Nora said.

"I know, dear. You must be suffering." Frances knelt and started to undo the laces of Nora's sturdy shoes. "Let me get these shoes off your poor feet." She took Nora's worn black felt slippers from behind the stove and slipped them on her feet. "Your toenails need to be trimmed, Granny, but I'll do that in the morning.

"I'm going to boil a nice big potato and make creamed codfish for your supper." She took the teapot from the stove and poured hot, strong tea into Nora's mug. She opened the oven door and took out a pan of brown, flaky biscuits and placed them on the table.

"Be careful, Granny," Frances said as Nora picked up the mug. "The tea is hot. Don't burn yourself." She went back into the pantry for butter and strawberry jam. She buttered a biscuit and spread it with jam and put it on a plate.

Nora, with shaky hands, poured a small amount of tea into her saucer. She slurped the tea-gin mixture, some of the brown liquid running down each side of her white, bristled chin.

Frances watched her grandmother for a few moments, then climbed the steep, narrow stairs to her bedroom. She opened the door and went inside. The sparsely furnished room with its one recessed, wide-silled window and starched white curtain was her refuge. A straight-backed chair was on one side of the bed, and a small table and lamp on the other. A gaily painted washbowl and water pitcher stood on a stand near the door. The floor was bare, and the whitewashed walls empty of pictures or decoration.

The room felt hot and airless. Frances went to the window and pushed it open. A cool breeze blew off the ocean. Frances pulled her dress over her head, stood in front of the window in her white petticoat, and let the sea air wash over her. Still she felt hot and feverish, almost ill. She walked over and stood in front of the oval gilt-framed mirror Nora brought with her from Ireland and stared at her reflection, thinking. *He said I was pretty. Does he really think I'm pretty? I shouldn't let him do the things he does to me. It's shameful the way I feel about him. I wish I could hide it from him. He knows I can't refuse him. Is that why he tells me nice things so I'll let him?*

She sat down on the edge of her bed and stared at her hated feet, her thick ugly shoes. She flung herself across the bed and sobbed. *I'm a cripple. He couldn't love me. Why should he? Colie is so handsome, he could have any girl in town. I'm easy,*

45

that's why he comes to see me. I'm just fooling myself to think he could really care for me.

She sat up and wiped her eyes with the hem of her petticoat. *Well, I don't care if that is the only reason he bothers with me. Tonight he'll hold me and say sweet things to me. He'll belong to me for awhile.*

A slow smile spread across her face, and her eyes took on a glow. *I'll keep him happy when he's with me.* She laughed softly. *I know how to make him happy. If that's the only way I can hold him, I will. Colie is going to belong to me. I'll find a way to keep him.*

8

No longer tired, Colie hurried up the road. He heard footsteps behind him—his heart thudded like a crazed thing in his chest—and he whirled around and drew in his breath when he saw Sammy Gleason stagger, then fall on his face like a rag doll in the middle of the road. Then, in a moment or two, Sammy managed to flatten his hands against the ground, steady himself and raise himself to his knees, only to lose his balance and fall on his face again.

Ya damn old fool. Ya scared the livin' crap out of me, thought Colie as he walked back, slipped his arms under Sammy's shoulders, and lifted him to his feet.

"You sure got a snootful in you, old man," he said.

Blood ran from Sammy's scraped nose and spittle from the corners of his mouth. Colie pulled a handkerchief from his own pocket and wiped Sammy's face. Colie, a foot taller than Sammy, looked with disgust as Sammy swayed back and forth and aimed blows in Colie's direction.

"Who ya think ya callin' old man? Come on, ya young punk. I can take ya. Come on, put 'em up!" Colie jerked his head back as Sammy leapt up and his fist grazed Colie's nose. Sammy danced around, ducking and shadow-boxing. "Ya got a yella streak, just like yer old man, Colie McNeil. He was chicken-shit like ya. Thought himself better'n me. Mr. High and mighty. Fat lotta good it did him." Sammy started to laugh until he sputtered, choking on the bloody mucus running from his nose and mouth.

Colie took him by the shoulders, lifted him off the

ground, and shook him. Sammy's head wobbled back and forth.

"Ya rotten bugger," Colie said, "me father wouldn't dirty his hands on the likes of ya. He'd be afraid he'd kill ya. If ya were sober now, I'd give ya a few lumps."

Sammy tried to shake himself free.

"Take yer mitts off me, ya rotten strike breaker. Better watch ya self, that's me advice to ya. Word is out, ya know."

Colie's temper rose. He hauled back a fist.

"Ya really askin' for it, ya old drunk. How come ya not lined up with the other strikers at the pit, then? Ya lazy drunk. Think ya scarin' me, do ya?"

Sammy cringed, and tried to cover his face.

"Don't hit me. I didn't mean no harm. Just givin' a bit of friendly advice, that's all."

"Ah, the hell with ya," Colie said. He let go of Sammy, who fell to the ground and started to retch. The sickening stench of vomit soon filled the air.

Colie stood over him, his fists still clenched. He began to feel sick. Disgusted, he turned away. He walked a few paces, then turned and went back to Sammy. He thought, *I can't leave him in the middle of the road, much as the old shit deserves it. His wife's bein' Ma's friend. She's a good woman. Don't deserve this stinkin' fool. Thought he was tellin' me somethin' I don't already know. I can take care of meself. Sure don't need his advice!*

Sammy, passed out, lay with his head in the crook of his arm, snoring peacefully. Colie looked down at him. He hated to touch him. Finally, he tried to pick Sammy up by the back of his shirt and seat of the pants, but the shirt began to rip, so Colie slung Sammy over his shoulder and carried him to his house and propped him against the wall by the side of the back door.

Then he wiped his hands on his pants as he went up the path that led to his own back door. A riotous tangle of black-eyed Susans, daisies, and petunias grew on each side of the path, and pink and white hollyhocks grew up the wall on each side of the door, almost reaching the pitched roof of the house.

A salty sea breeze blew over the bluff and mingled with the spicy scent of petunias. He dropped his boots and lunch pail by the side of the door, then took the handkerchief out of his pocket and flung it on top of the boots, along with his shirt. The smell of Sammy's vomit still clung to it. He pushed the door. It was locked.

He knocked on the door, then called out.

"Ma, where are ya? Why's the latch on?" Annoyed, Colie pounded on the door. He felt dirty, sticky with the grime from the pit and knew that the stench of Sammy Gleason's vomit still clung to him. He longed for a cool, soapy bath in the big round tin tub in the shed to feel clean again.

Franny will be waitin' for me tonight, he thought, *all sweet smellin', willin', and eager. She's a bit on the scrawny side, but she's pretty. Life dealt her a rotten deal. But she's got spunk. Has a real temper on her, too. Wonder how she learned how to make a fella' feel so good? I'm glad I found out first. Wouldn't me mates be surprised if they knew what I know 'bout Franny James? They'll never hear it from me. I knows a good thing when I sees it. I'm keepin' this one to meself.*

I'd like ta do it to her at Black's beach tonight. I like to hear the waves crashin' into the rocks when I'm givin' it to her. She likes it, too. I can tell by the sounds she makes.

Well, I'll have her in a soft bed tonight. I'll have to put me hand over her mouth to keep her from howlin'. Sure don't want to wake the old woman. They'd be hell to pay.

Franny is all woman though. Not a tease like Kitty Daly. That one lets ya feel up those big tits of hers to get ya really goin', then hollers blue murder if ya try to go a step further. I wish

Franny had big tits like Kitty's.

"Ma, where the hell are ya?" Colie rattled the door again, then started to go around to the front of the house when he heard his mother's quick light step, and the door opened.

He stepped into the hot kitchen. The air was rich with the smell of roast pork and applesauce. Colie's empty stomach began to growl.

"Geez, it smells good in here. I could eat a horse, I'm that hungry."

"Don't use that word," Maggie scolded. "It's taking the Lord's name in vain. You know I don't like that expression."

"Sorry, ma. Where were you? What ya have the latch on the door fer? I've been standin' there for quite a spell. Was just goin' 'round to the front."

"It must have slipped, I guess. Stop nagging at me. What's the difference. You're in now, aren't you? No need to make such a fuss over the door being locked, is there?"

"Gosh, Ma, I didn't mean to get ya mad. Did ya have a bad day? Was Boydie a handful?" Colie looked at his mother's hot, flushed face, the tendrils of auburn hair loose and sticking to her face, hands hidden inside the folds of her big apron. He had noticed how she kept her hands from view since Catherine's death. It disturbed him. He had always loved to look at his mother's hands. He thought them beautiful. Slim fingered, soft and smooth as a girl's.

Maggie had studied music before her marriage, and Colie remembered how proud he felt when she played the organ during church services. Maggie's hands were her one vanity. Now, the welts and still-red scars were a constant, painful reminder of her young daughter's terrible death.

Maggie smiled at him, revealing small, even, white teeth.

"I didn't mean to snap at you, son. I must have lost

track of the time. I was changing baby. I didn't hear you. I've been outdoors most of the day. The baby fell back to sleep once she had a clean diaper and bottle."

She gazed at her tall, broad-shouldered son, at his red-rimmed eyes and dirty face, and her heart turned over. She said, "You look so tired, boy. The water's ready for your bath. Take the kettle out to the shed, and have a washup, then come sit down and have your supper."

Maggie smoothed the springy curls back into place and went to the stove and stirred the hot applesauce. Colie stepped over to the stove and picked up the heavy kettle.

"I ran into Sammy Gleason on the way home," he said.

"He was drunk and mean as a skunk. Darn fool wanted to fight me. He passed out in the middle of the road pukin' his guts out. I left him at his back door ta sober up."

Maggie's voice hardened.

"You should have left him in the road. He's no good. Lazy, cruel, and a drunkard. It's just too bad we have to have such a man living next to us."

Colie paused at the open door.

"You all right, Ma? Somethin' wrong? Never did hear ya talk so harsh 'bout old Sammy."

Maggie had her back to him at the stove. She didn't turn.

"Well, it's time I did. He's a sorry excuse of a man. Now, don't worry about me. I'm fine, boy. Nothing's wrong. I did a big wash and ironing. I'm tired, that's all. Now go wash, for heaven's sake. Stop fussing at me."

"Okay, I'm goin'. I didn't mean to get ya stirred up, Ma."

He carried the heavy kettle out to the shed.

Groaning to himself, Sammy slowly came to. His encounter in the road with Colie forgotten. He pushed

51

himself to his feet and leaned against the wall for support. He thought, *Oh, megod, me damn head feels like it's about to fall off me shoulders. How'd I get home? I don't remember a damn thing after I left Maggie's place.* He looked down at his shirt. *Frick it, puked over meself.*

He pushed open the door, went inside, up the steep, narrow stairs to the bedroom he shared with his wife, Jenny, sat on the edge of the bed for a few seconds, then bent over and tried to untie his boots. The effort was too much for him. He gave up and sprawled on top of the white coverlet in his boots and vomit-smelling clothes and covered his eyes against the sun's rays that streamed in through the lace-curtained window.

Before he drifted off to sleep, he thought, *Glad the old woman's away 'til tomorra. I'd better get meself cleaned up and join the fellas at the bankhead come mornin' or they'll be coming after me. Hope there's a drop of whiskey left in the jug. Way my head feels, I'll be needin' a hair of the dog.*

Jenny better put the bite on our girl. Her man ain't hurtin', makes good wages with the railroad. She'll see the back of me hand if she don't. Should get somethin' for neglectin' her own chores here at home.

Then he remembered Maggie. How she looked backed up to the sink, white-faced and trembling. He started to have an erection. *Maggie McNeil needn't think she's done with me. No twit of a woman takes a knife to Sammy Gleason. Don't care if she tells her boy. He may be big, but he's just a snot-nosed kid. Gonna get his ass kicked anyway. I see it comin', and I'll be one of the first in line.* He drifted off to sleep, and his snores filled the small house.

Thunder sounded, lightning flashed, brightening up the black sky as Colie climbed out of Frances's bedroom window into the rain-swept night. He slid quietly down the tree as another flash of lightning outlined Frances's slim figure as she leaned out the window, blew him a kiss and whispered.

"I do love you, Colie. Do you love me?"

He wanted to answer, "I love you too," but the words stuck in his throat. Through the long, love-crazed night with Frances clinging to him, begging, "Do you love me, Colie?" The words wouldn't come. Did he love her? He didn't know. Was what he felt when he was with her love? He didn't think so. He knew he loved his mother and baby sister. He had loved his father, Catherine, his grandmother, dead a month after Catherine, her old heart unable to stand the loss of her beloved grandchild.

Franny could make him crazy with want. Tonight, he'd had to pull himself away from her before dawn came creeping over the storm-filled night and caught them still together in her soft bed. *I never had any trouble walkin' away from the others, just Frannie. I hate to leave her.*

He looked up and whispered.

"Get ya head back in the window, funny face. Ya getting' all wet."

"When will I see you again, Colie? You didn't say. Will I leave the window open for you tomorrow night?"

"Yah, sweetheart, soon as it's dark and the old lady's down for the night. Now get back inside. Ya getting' soaked."

He waved, then turned and started toward his own house in his bare feet. He opened the back door and crept inside, past his mother's bedroom and up the stairs. He didn't see her sitting in the dark room in a rocking chair, her hands folded in her lap. Maggie watched him as he went up the stairs, carrying his boots in his hand.

Boydie, in a crib by the bed, began to stir and cry out in her sleep. Maggie got up, went to her, and stroked her silky

53

hair. Then she picked her up, sat with her and rocked, whispering, "Shush, now baby-mine, Mama's here."

She thought, *Well, I shouldn't be surprised. Colie is a young man, and I know boys will be boys. There's not much I can do about that. I don't want to have anything to do with Nora James. She's always been a queer sort, though she's an old woman now. I should have a word with her about these goings on, but she's likely to bite my head off no matter what I say.*

Maybe I should talk to that girl. I won't mention it to Colie. Better to let him think he's been fooling me when he sneaks out at night.

I'm no one to judge the girl. Colie is a handsome boy, and she's a pretty enough girl, crippled or not. Always so shy and quiet. You never know about people. Another thought flashed into Maggie's mind, and she sat up in the chair. *Oh, my, what if she gets in the family way! I'd better have a talk with her, soon.*

Boydie slept. Maggie got up, put her back into bed, then knelt by the side of her own bed to pray.

9

Sweat trickled down inside Maggie's white blouse, and the blue cotton skirt clung to her as she, with Boydie in her arms, walked along the hot, dusty Main Street, past the red-brick post office and the men lounging against the side of the building and on the steps.

Her first thought when she awakened that morning had been, *I must go see Marion. Too much time has passed, and I haven't thanked her for all her help when Catherine—no, I won't think about that day.* She blocked the painful memories rushing to consume her. I must try to get on with life as it is now. Please help me, dear Savior.

Sammy Gleason, looked up, tipped his cap, and started to rise.

"Mornin' to ya, missus," he said.

Maggie stared straight ahead and walked quickly past him. He sat down again.

George MacDougal, sitting beside him, nudged him painfully in the ribs.

"Wasn't that Maggie McNeil? First time I've seen her in town since her girl died. Must be a terrible thing to have a daughter burn to death. Say, don't you live near her on the bluff? She sure turned her nose up at you, Sammy. What've you been up to, no good, I'm sure. Sure is a good-looking woman, Maggie McNeil."

"Ah, she likes to put on airs," Sammy said. "Always been a stuck-up piece. All the damn McNeils think they're better'n the rest of us.

"Well, I wouldn't know about that," said George, "but

55

her boy is asking for trouble. Still working no. 3, him and Malcolm. I always liked Malcolm, but he's going against his mates, and that's bad business for a coal miner. They'll both get what's comin' to them. Colie's not like his father. Poor Jock, may he rest in peace. Now, there was a man!"

"So you say," Sammy said. "Well, Jock McNeil wasn't all he was cracked up to be. I knew a thing or two 'bout him, though I don't want to speak ill of the dead. He thought a lot of himself . . . worked 'long side him in no. 3 many a shift. He made trouble for me more'n once."

George glanced at him sidewise.

"You don't say? I'm surprised to hear that, Sammy. Never heard anyone say a bad word against Jock. He was well liked and easy to get along with. Remember the time he put his foot through the floor step-dancing at Miner's Hall?" George slapped his thigh as he started to laugh. "That was a night!

"Course, never worked alongside Jock McNeil, but I often passed the time of day with him. He sure knew how to tell a joke or a story. No one could go up against Jock McNeil when it came to pitching horseshoes either." George took the pipe out of his mouth, knocked it against the step, and said, "Say, I'm gettin' barnacles on my ass, sittin' here. I'm going to the pit. See what's going on. You coming?"

Maggie walked to the corner of Main and Fraser Avenue. Her head throbbed as Boydie twisted and squirmed in her tired arms. She turned the corner and walked down a narrow street lined on each side with low, mud-colored homes, saved from dreariness by neat front yards aglow with summer flowers, except the one in the center of the dead-end street.

In the front yard, holes had been dug here and there. A

rusted tricycle, toy trucks, empty cans and bottles were scattered about the dirt yard. She hesitated for a moment, then walked up to the front door of her sister-in-law's house.

Aunt Marion, who had been watching from a window, flung open the door.

"Maggie, now ain't you the sight for sore eyes! I been thinking of you, and here you are. It's indeed a treat to see you and the little one." She reached for Boydie. "Here, give me the baby.

"Ain't it hot for June? I mind the heat something fierce. Archie took the boys up to me mother in the country—keep them out of trouble. They ain't saints, ha, they sure ain't, my little fellas. You look done in."

When she took Boydie from Maggie's arms, Boydie reached out and tried to grab a strand of her hair. Aunt Marion laughed.

"My, ain't she strong, and pretty, too." She led the way into her hot, stuffy parlor, put Boydie on the bare floor, and said, "Sit down now. Rest yourself, dear heart. I was telling me man just this morning. It's high time Maggie got out and about again."

Maggie sank gratefully into the depths of a wine-red, plush divan.

"My, what a lovely parlor set. It's new, isn't it, Marion?"

"I thought you'd take notice right off. Archie's buying me a new rug for the floor. I picked it out at Eaton's last week. Then I'm buying new curtains for the windows. What's hanging now ain't good for nothing but dust rags. When we get the house all prettied up, we're giving a party the likes this town ain't ever seen!"

"It's a beautiful set, Marion. Very colorful. I'm happy for you. Everything must be going well for you, then. Is

Archie working a lot of shifts? Colie has been working steady."

Aunt Marion threw back her head and laughed.

"Lord, no, dear heart. Archie ain't been working for weeks now. The miners' on strike. Don't you know? You'd never see me Archie go against the strikers. He didn't see eye to eye with them in calling this one, but no, no one's ever accused Archie of being a strikebreaker."

"Well, you could say my Colie is a strikebreaker then," Maggie said, rather sharply. "He hasn't had a bit trouble, at least none that he told me about. I don't understand. As far as I can remember, there have always been strikes—men trying to make trouble for the ones willing to work."

Aunt Marion shook her head.

"If you mean men willing to work for slave wages and in danger of life and limb, that's true enough. Times are changing, Maggie. The union is making it change. It's high time the company gave the miners a fair shake. They never will less they're forced to, and any fellow going against the strikers nowadays is taking a big chance."

"That's all well and good, Marion, but how can people live? The coal mines are all there is. If you don't work in them, you don't eat. So that's why Mr. Gleason has been at home so much. I've wondered about that. But then, he's a lazy man. Not in love with work anyway, and he would be afraid of getting hurt."

"You know, Maggie, I didn't take to that man a'tall. He got into Archie's rum at the house after the funeral. Swilled it down like he bought and paid for it himself. I was happy to see the back of him when his wife led him out. Oh, I'm sorry, dear heart. Don't want to bring up sorrowful things, now that you're here."

"It's all right, Marion. I have to accept Catherine's death. It's been six long months since she was taken from me. But you're right about Mr. Gleason. I have no use for the man." Maggie looked thoughtful. "Although I would have thought Jenny would have said something. She would know. Wouldn't you think she would tell me that Colie was in danger ? Jenny is the only one I've had any real contact with these past months."

Aunt Marion sighed, and the divan sagged as she sat beside Maggie.

"Well, I would take a guess she didn't want to worry you, knowing Colie was still at it. She seemed like a decent little woman. If you didn't keep so much to yourself, dear heart, you'd know how bad things are. There's bad fighting every day. Colie isn't the only one still working. A few of the miners have been against the strike from the beginning.

"Men are getting hauled off to the hospital every day. Archie's been after me to pay you a visit, to let you know, but I didn't think you wanted to see me after you and me had harsh words." Aunt Marion got up. "But that's all over and done with. I'll put the teakettle on, and we'll have a nice visit now that you're here."

Maggie picked up Boydie and followed Aunt Marion into the kitchen. Shyly she touched her lightly on the shoulder.

"I've been wanting to tell you how sorry I am about my behavior at your house after Catherine's funeral, Marion. It's been on my mind, nagging at me."

Maggie, suddenly, was filled with shame as the memory came flooding back, and she saw herself as she rushed at Marion, overcome with rage, punching, hitting, trying to cause hurt, as she was hurting. Then pulling, pushing people toward the door, screaming at them, that the party was over, go home.

The last thing she remembered of that terrible day, was Dr. Field giving her a sedative and redoing the loosened bandages on her hands. Three days later, she awoke in her own bed to find Colie and Jenny Gleason bending over her.

"Can you forgive me, Marion? You tried to make things easier, I know, but I couldn't stop myself. The sight of all those people, eating, drinking, even laughing, enjoying themselves when my dear little girl lay still and cold in the earth." Maggie choked up and couldn't go on.

Aunt Marion put her strong arms around her.

"Now that's all over and done with, dear heart. No one blames you. You're human like the rest of us. You'd have to be a plaster saint to hold up against all the trouble you've had in the past year, first Jock, then Catherine."

Maggie tried to smile.

"You're a kind woman, Marion. I think you are the only real friend I have in this town, and I want to thank you for all your help when Catherine died. Colie told me how you took the baby and looked after her while I was out of my mind. I don't' know what I would have done if you hadn't bee there.

"The thanks are long overdue, I'm ashamed to say. I'm just beginning to come to grips with losing my girl. Lost in my own grief, I haven't paid attention to anything else."

Aunt Marion patted her on the back, then took a fistful of loose tea from a jar on the shelf over the stove, shook it into a fat, white, enamel teapot and poured boiling water into it.

"Archie and me have been that worried for young Colie, afraid he'd get hurt. The men in town won't put up for long with their own going down the pit while they're on strike." She turned from the stove, and with hands on her hips she faced Maggie. She added, "Well, now that you know, you can put a stop to it."

Maggie put Boydie on the floor, then sat at the cluttered kitchen table with her face in her hands.

60

"My poor Colie," she murmured. "He's just a boy. Oh, how I hate the filthy mines, this town, but what can I do? We don't even own the roof over our heads."

Aunt Marion gave Boydie a sugar cookie, and a tin cup and wooden spoon to play with. Then, as she sat opposite Maggie, her hair hanging past her shoulders, she twisted it into a braid as she talked.

"Well, you can't fault the boy for wanting to take care of his mum. He's a good boy. He don't know the trouble he's making for himself. You make him stop. You won't starve, you know, long as Archie and me have anything. We're blood kin, you know."

Maggie lifted her head and tried to smile.

"Thank you. You don't mind my asking how you're getting by if Archie isn't working?" She looked down the hall to the parlor, "and buying new furniture, too! Oh, I'm sorry, Marion. I shouldn't ask such things. It's rude and none of my business."

Aunt Marion got up, went to the open window, looked outside, then closed it. She came back, pulled her chair closer to Maggie, and spoke in a low voice.

"I'll tell you, but I don't want no busybodies listening." She leaned close to Maggie. "You're kin, and I trust you.

"Archie's been rum-running with Big Dan McNarmara. Dan got himself a motorboat and a dory. He asked Archie if he wanted to help him, said there's good money to be made rum-running. They gets word when there's a ship out there with a load of rum to unload. Archie goes off in the dead of night and comes back in the morning, and no one's the wiser.

"He's making money hand over fist, Maggie. That's how I got me my new parlor set." Smiling broadly, Aunt Marion sat back and folded her arms.

Maggie, taken by surprise, didn't speak for a few

61

moments, but she whispered, although they were alone in the house.

"Marion, I don't understand how you can let him do a thing like that. Can't you see the wrong in it? Archie, rum-running! Granny will be turning over in her grave. Archie, bringing in liquor for the town drunkards. It's a terrible thing to do, dishonest and against the law. What if he gets caught. He'll be sent to prison! What would happen to you and the boys then?"

Aunt Marion's face darkened, frowning. She threw back her head.

"Well, girl, don't get on your high horse. I should know you'd find fault. I don't see as it's any great crime. They'd get their drink whether or not Archie is the one to bring it to them. I'm proud of me man. He's doing right by his own in bad times. Where's the harm in that?

"As for getting caught, Archie will just have to take his chances. Ain't it just as terrible not to have food for your young ones? To see them go to bed hungry? It would break me heart. I love them two rascals of mine. I don't see if it's any concern of yours anyway. Sorry I even told you." Stiff-backed, Marion got up and poured them both hot tea. She cut thick slices of bread and put a plate of sugar cookies and a pot of molasses in front of Maggie. "Eat now. I hope it's good enough for you. I'd have made something fancy if I knew you'd be paying me a visit." She sniffed. Then she picked up Boydie and sat at the opposite end of the table. "The company's been putting strikers families out on the street. Of course, you wouldn't be knowing nothing about that, keeping to yourself the way you do. Archie and I could be next if the strike lasts much longer."

Boydie wrapped her soft little arms around Aunt Marion's neck and planted moist kisses on her cheek. Aunt Marion softened.

"Now, there's a love," she said and held her close. "I wouldn't tell another soul this, Maggie, but you're kin, even though you're a bit stiff-necked. I always looked up to you and can't keep it to myself any longer. Got to tell someone or bust.

"I has got kinfolks in the States . . . in Boston. Archie and me been putting a bit aside. We're going to Boston when we have enough put by. What do you think of that?"

Aunt Marion hoisted Boydie up and went over to Maggie and poked her roughly in the shoulder. Maggie took a sip of tea before she answered. She sighed, then put the cup down.

"That's wonderful news, Marion. I must say I'm feeling envious. I didn't know you had people in the States. I wish I did. Maybe they'd help me. Sometimes, I feel so alone. Imagine having the means to be able to get away from this town, the narrow-minded people, the mines. How wonderful it would be. That's been my dream."

Aunt Marion looked hurt.

"Maggie, you got no call to feel alone. Me and Archie are here."

"I'm sorry, Marion, but I think you can understand what I mean. I've lost a husband . . . children. I feel an aching, a feeling of loneliness deep inside, where nothing on this earth can reach." Maggie looked over at Boydie, "If it wasn't for the baby and Colie, I don't think I could go on. You've been a good sister-in-law and friend. I appreciate that."

"Well, dear heart, we can't help how we feel. You've had a rough time of it, but you're still young and pretty, too. Time does heal, you know. Life does go on.

"Look at me, my father was a Micmac, my mother, a white woman. I was raised Micmac, and it was no bed of roses. A half-breed in neither this nor that. People look down their noses at you, Indians and whites. Granny and Archie's brothers sure didn't like one of their own marrying a big, half-breed, and they let me know it. Oh, no one said it to my face, but I knew they talked, made fun of me and Archie.

"He was a full-blooded Micmac. Joe, that was his name. He was twenty at the time. Well, Joe got himself a job as steeplejack in Boston, made good money, and married an Irish girl.

"A few months ago, I gets this letter addressed to me father, may he rest in peace. Joe passed on and his wife, her name's Moira, wanted his family to know.

"We've been writing regular, and she says jobs are plentiful in Boston. Says she'd put us up when we gets there. She's married again, to an Italian fella. She says they'd help us get settled. We could stay with them until we do."

"Marion, that sounds wonderful, almost too good to be true. But I wish you the best of luck. She must be a fine Christian woman. Now, I must get home. I have to have a talk with Colie. I feel guilty. Because of me, he must be going through sheer hell every day facing the strikers.

"What kind of a mother am I? Why couldn't he confide in me, Marion? What have I done to the only son left to me?" She bent her head and began to weep.

Aunt Marion put out her hand and stroked Maggie's shining auburn hair.

"You stop that now, you hear?" she said. Don't blame yourself. You don't do nothing to Colie. He only does what he thinks he should. He's a good boy. You have a talk with him. Make him stop before he gets hurt. You won't starve. Archie and I will see that. Don't be upsetting yourself, dear heart.

"I was thinking the other day, Maggie, about your

64

brother John Beaton. Now, there was a disagreeable sort. Ever hear from him again?"

Maggie lifted her head. Tears streamed from her eyes. She took a handkerchief from her sleeve and wiped the tears away.

"No, I haven't seen him," she finally said. "I wrote to him and tried to explain that I was in shock and didn't know who he was at the cemetery. He didn't answer my letter. I was going to have Colie take me up to the farm if John had answered. When he didn't, I knew that was the end of it. My brother bears a lot of grudges.

"My young brothers might want to see me, but they're afraid to go up against John. My father left the farm to him, you know. John was the eldest son. I think he would have anyway, even if John wasn't the eldest. John was his favorite. Probably because father could see himself in John. John was a lot like him. My father would surely deny it, but we all knew. John could do no wrong in father's eyes.

"Wouldn't it be wonderful, Marion, if we could go back in time and undo the mistakes we make in life? I know I brought great sorrow to my parents. I've been paying ever since." Maggie blew her nose softly, then looked up. "We've had our differences in the past. I hope you won't hold it against me. Who am I to tell you what you should or shouldn't do? I'm not the one to judge you and Archie. But please tell Archie to be careful. He is the only one left."

Aunt Marion sat down next to Maggie. She dipped a corner of bread into her tea, blew on it, then fed it to Boydie.

"How well I know, dear heart," she said. "When Archie's in his cups, he cries for his four dead brothers. Jock is the one he misses the most. They sure got along, didn't they? No one ever took them for brothers. Didn't they look odd together? I used to laugh at the sight of them. Archie, short and bandy-legged. Jock, tall, wide, and handsome, with that thick, black, wavy head of his and poor Archie already starting to go bald."

Aunt Marion threw back her head and laughed, "Don't worry about Archie. My little run is a smart one. Slippery as an eel. He's not about to let himself get caught. He knows all the Mounties and tells me they often look the other way. As long as you don't get to bragging about how you fooled them and gave them the slip. That gets their dander up, and they goes after you worse than before, Archie says."

Boydie, restless, began to squirm around in Aunt Marion's lap and held out her arms to Maggie.

"Mama, me down, me down."

Maggie reached for her.

"Here, let me take her. I feel so much better, Marion. The lunch was delicious, and talking to you, knowing you don't feel any ill will toward me gives me some peace of mind.

"I don't know how I'm going to handle Colie. We do need his wages from the pit. Colie can be stubborn. He knows the company owns the roof over our heads. I do make some money sewing from time to time, most for the company ladies. Though they do take their good time to pay me."

Aunt Marion got up, went into the pantry of the kitchen, lifted the top of an empty flour can, reached into a large black pocketbook hidden there and took out a fistful of bills. She came out of the pantry.

"Here, Maggie," she said, "take this now."

She thrust the money in Maggie's hand. Maggie pushed her hand away.

"Oh, no, Marion, I don't need money right now, but I do thank you. Don't think I don't appreciate the offer. I can manage for a bit." On an impulse, she put her arms around her sister-in-law. "Please come and see me, Marion. I've missed you and Archie. I know Colie has, too."

Aunt Marion stuffed the money into her dress pocket.

"Well, dear heart, if that's how you feel, I won't argue with you. You know the money's here when you do need it," she said, while thinking to herself, *Missus high and mighty, you'll be singing a different tune soon enough.*

Maggie was grateful for the cool breeze now blowing in from the sea as she walked along the dry, dusty road that led out of town to the bluff and past privately owned, Cape Cod-style homes with green shutters, low picket fences, trim lawns, and laughing, playing, tow-headed children. These homes were owned by merchants, some of the more prosperous fishermen, and white collar workers and town officials of Rockhill. Maggie glanced at them without envy as she walked past.

Pretty houses, she thought, *but if I had a choice of living in a mansion in this town or the means to leave and settle, even in a shack, as long as it's away from the mines, somewhere else with my children, maybe even the States, I'd leave as quickly as I could pack my belongings. I've had nothing but heartaches and sorrow here. I hate this town. God forgive me. My dear children, Jock, Jim, all my loved ones, are buried in the soil here. Oh, what am I going to do?*

Her arms ached, so she put Boydie down, held her hand, and let her toddle along for awhile beside her.

She thought bitterly, *Marion means well enough, but I hope I never have to depend on the dirty money from bootleg liquor.* She remembered times when Jock would come stumbling home from Miner's Hall, singing at the top of his lungs and reeking of rum. How she would try to quiet him so the children wouldn't know that their father was drunk. She would undress him and put him to bed, seething inwardly as she thought of the good money wasted on the devil rum.

Maggie had to admit that it didn't happen often and

the drink never made Jock mean or abusive to her or the children, as it did Sammy Gleason and some of the other miners. Jock never raised a hand to her in anger, drunk or sober.

But she remembered how she would be filled with disgust when he would turn to her during the night with the stink of liquor on his breath, murmuring her name over and over, wanting to make love.

No, she thought, *I will never take a cent of that kind of money. No, I would sooner go to John for help.* She picked up Boydie as she went over the rise in the road, and the row of company houses came into view.

Jenny Gleason stood in front of her open door. She wiped her hands on the white apron that billowed out from her round, short body, and when she saw Maggie, she waved a greeting before going back into the house.

10

The day shift, at last over, the man-rake came to a stop, and the tired, silent miners, ones not honoring the strike against the coal company, climbed out and walked slowly up the sloping incline and out of the dark pit.

"Ah, shit, here we go again," sighed Malcolm, as they came out of the pit into a hot, summer sun that made them blink and pull their caps lower on their brows to shade their eyes.

Striking coal miners awaited them. Unmindful of the barbed wire fence, they pushed up against it and threatened to topple it. They threw rocks, hard-packed mud, and rotten fruit and vegetables over the fence.

"Go home ya friggin' scabs. We're gonna get ya!" a man yelled.

Company bullyboys, swinging thick clubs, rushed up the road, around the fence and into the crowd of roaring men, who raced to meet them, carrying weapons of their own—bats, rocks, clubs, and one man, brandishing a wooden crutch while hopping on one foot.

Strikers and police clashed head-on. Soon the humid air was alive with the sounds of curses, thudding fists, and the crack of clubs on unresisting skulls and limbs.

More bullyboys ran from parked cars, anxious to join the melee. One, a company policeman, got out of his car, casually leaned against it, raised his gun into the air, and fired several times. Surprised and startled by the sound of gunfire, the struggling, bloodied men separated, started to disperse, then tangled again.

Colie, knocked to the ground, kicked out and got free of the man astride him. He got his hands around the man's throat and pressed until he started to gasp and choke. He then released him and jumped to his feet with fists clenched as a man came at him with a baseball bat. Too late. The man swung the bat. Colie heard the sickening crack, and his broken right arm dangled helplessly by his side as the ground rushed up to meet him.

Malcolm swung away from the striker he was pummeling in time to see Colie get hit with the bat. He grabbed Colie before he hit the ground and, still dodging fists and clubs, pulled him to the side of the road.

Bruce MacKillup, runty UNWA shop leader, dragged a heavy soapbox in front of the men, leaped up on it, and hollered.

"Enough! Stop! This ain't the way to win. Go the hell home, men, before someone's killed. We're playing right into their hands by fighting each other. It's what they want us to do. Puts them in the right and makes us look like a bunch of thugs to the rest of the country. Is that what you want? Go home now."

"Go home, yourself, ya silly bugger." Gordie MacRae yelled and threw a fist-sized rock, which hit MacKullup square in the face. Blood spurted and covered his face as he fell to the hard ground. Gordie MacRae pushed toward the soapbox, still waving a thick fist. Blood ran from his broken nose and he yelled, "Yah, sure, go home to what? Hungry kids and naggin' wives? Union's not doin' shit for us. All talk, that's all. It's bullshit. No strikebreaking scabs gonna take the food from my kids' mouths. I'm gonna break their heads!"

The policeman again raised his gun and moved toward the crowd. He fired rapidly. The sound bounced and echoed in the hot air and seemed to calm the hollow-

70

eyed strikers. They backed off.

Then two strikers walked over, looked down at the unconscious form of the shop steward, shook their heads, and walked away.

In the distance, the wail of a siren could be heard, and the injured, bloodied strikebreakers were allowed to limp away. Malcolm half-carried Colie up the road and away from the mine.

Gordie MacRae turned, looked at them, spat on the ground, shook his fist, then bent his elbow in an obscene gesture.

Malcolm, his right eye fast swelling up and turning a purplish blue, supported a dazed Colie and tried to keep him upright. Colie's broken right arm hung limply by his side. Blood, mingled with coal dust, ran down his chin from a deep gash in his lip.

"Son of a gun," Malcolm said, "that didn't last long. No one wanted to get a bullet in him. That's for damn sure. The union had no business calling this strike. We weren't bad off. We've had it worse.

"Most of the men didn't want to strike this time, either. I know that for a fact, never agreed to a sympathy strike at all. Let the steel workers fight their own battles. That's what I say, laddie." Malcolm turned and looked behind him. "Got to watch out for Gordie MacRae. He's a mean one when he's been at the bottle. Laddie, we're in now, into it up to the hilt. And the trouble is, no one wants to back down."

Colie moaned softly as he was being half-dragged along by Malcolm.

"You all right, laddie? I know you're hurting, but hang in there. Don't pass out. I'll have you to home, and once the doctor sets that arm, you'll be right as rain again."

Colie, dizzy from the pain, shook his head to try and

clear it. A small grin played along his split, bleeding mouth.

"It does smart a bit, Malcolm," he said, "but it felt good to finally get me hands around that fella's throat. He was punchin' the crap out of me. Who in the hell were they? Never saw some of 'em before. Did ya? The one that came at me with the bat, never saw him before either. Something fishy goin' on, Malcolm."

"Now that I think of it, you're right, laddie Could be men from out of town, paid by the company to cause trouble, make the strikers out to be worse than they are."

"Malcolm, ya look pretty good. 'Cept for that eye, ya don't have a mark on ya. I'm a bloody mess. I guess I didn't duck quick enough. Wait 'til me ma sees me."

Malcolm chuckled softly.

"I knocked a few heads together, got in a few good licks, and kept out of the way of the clubs pretty good, laddie."

Colie started to say something.

"Oh . . . oh . . . " then slumped forward.

Malcolm stopped, tucked Colie's arm close to him, careful to keep it straight, scooped him up and carried him.

Maggie hovered at Colie's bedside twisting a damp handkerchief in her hands while Dr. Field sat by the side of the bed and carefully put the last stitch in a sleeping Colie's torn lip. He sat up and glanced quickly at Maggie.

"Now, don't worry, Maggie. I've told you, the boy will be fine. He has a bad compound fracture of the arm, but I've set it. He will wear the cast for quite awhile, of course, but he's young and healthy; the bone will mend. His lip will be swollen and sore. Give him liquids through a straw for a day or two. Now that the sedative's taken effect, he should sleep for hours." He stood up, towering over Maggie, and bent his head and smiled down at her. "Now, I could use a hot cup of tea before I'm on my way," he said.

"Oh, of course, Doctor. I don't know where my manners are." Maggie moved quickly to the door. With her hand on the knob, she paused and added, "It won't take but a minute to make a pot of tea." Then she opened the door and went ahead of him down the steep, narrow stairs.

Dr. Field followed, and had to duck his head under the low stairwell as he entered the kitchen. He ran his hands through his unruly, white hair.

"It was fortunate that I came upon Malcolm and Colie on the bluff road," he said.

"Thank God, you did, Doctor! Please, sit down now. You must be worn out from the day you put in. I'll put the teakettle on." Maggie went over to the stove.

Dr. Field, continued.

"I hope that this strike is settled before there is any more blood shed. Bruce MacKillup, a union man, has a bad head injury. He's in the hospital. No one's saying who threw the rock that hit him.

"It's just as well. Tempers fly, and men forget they're fighting against themselves. A company policeman fired a gun. The bullyboys, the dregs from Halifax, and God only knows where else, were having a grand time wielding their clubs, I was told. It's bad business. If they had had guns, these thugs no doubt would have used them."

Maggie turned away from the stove and the fragrant apple pie she was busy slicing. Her voice was made harsh with unshed tears.

"When you and Malcolm came to the door carrying Colie, bleeding and so pale and still, it brought back to me in full force the memory of Jock. I'm sorry. You must have thought that I'd taken leave of my senses. I know I acted like a crazy woman, carrying on the way I did, bringing

73

Jenny, and the rest on the bluff on the run. I acted the hysterical fool. They'll be taking me to the crazy house."

"Don't blame yourself for being human, Maggie. You reacted as my mother would have, seeing her son, the shape Colie was in, being carried through the door! Who has a better right? You've had some terrible shocks this past year. More than anyone should have to bear in a lifetime, but Colie will be fine. You have my word on that."

Dr. Field sighed heavily, pulled out a chair, and sat down. "I had come from the MacDonald house. Delivered a fine healthy boy to Elsie . . . Gordon is on strike. The family's having a hard time of it, too many mouths to feed. I heard the sirens and knew there must be trouble at the pit. I spend most of my time patching up miners' injuries. Colie was a heavy armful, even for Malcolm, who's strong as an ox. He was glad to have me relieve him of his burden."

Maggie shrugged, turned her back to him, and poured tea leaves into a white, enamel teapot.

"Still, Doctor, I wish I hadn't carried on the way I did." She sliced a large piece of pie, put it on a blue-willow china plate, and brought it to the table. "But now that it's over, and I know Colie is safe, my mind is clearer. I do feel better. The water will be bubbling soon. I baked this morning. The apples came from the tree outside. Crab apples, but nice and sweet. They make a good pie and applesauce."

She put blue-willow cups and saucers on the table along with a matching creamer and sugar bowl, then went back to the stove, poured hot water into the teapot, and took the teapot over to the table.

"I'm thankful," she said, "that Colie will recover, but the thought of clubs and guns frighten me to death. No one should have to live this way. Well, no matter, my boy isn't going down the pits again until the strike is over." She sat across from Dr. Field and poured the tea into the cups, then hid her red-scarred hands in the folds of her apron. "It's my fault, you know, that Colie's been hurt. No one wanted to tell me about the strike. People must think I'm too fragile to know such things. I wonder how they got that idea! I've had to deal with hardship all my married life.

"I suppose Colie was trying to give me some peace of mind after Catherine's passing...didn't want me to worry." She stared off into space, then, almost in a whisper, said, "God has taken my husband, my babies, my children. I'm thirty-three years old, and I've born eight babies, four stillborn. All I have left is Colie and the baby. Why? Why has God been so cruel to me?"

Dr. Field gave her a long, level look; his vivid blue eyes seemed to blaze out at her from beneath the heavy white hair across his jutting brow. He struck the table with the palm of his hand.

Maggie jumped.

"Don't give in to it, Maggie McNeil! Don't feel sorry for yourself. You're a courageous woman and a fighter. I've always thought so. You're still young and a beautiful woman. Life isn't over for you."

Dr. Field, coughed, then cleared his throat. His long, gaunt face started to turn a brick-red. "I've admired you for a long time, Maggie, since the day I delivered your first baby. You're not like the other women in Rockhill. You're different, a lady, you have breeding, refinement.

"If you ever need anything, anything at all, you can come to me." He coughed again, still, looking ill at ease. "I know I'm not a young man. I don't have much to offer a beautiful woman like yourself, but if you'd let me, I would take care of you. I lead a lonely life in that rambling old house of mine, Maggie." He lowered his eyes and half-mumbled, so that Maggie had to lean closer to hear what he was saying. "I don't know why I bought the old place. I guess I planned someday to meet a lady like yourself, marry, and have a family." Keeping his eyes lowered he added, "I'm rambling on like an old idiot."

Maggie's gray-green eyes slowly widened as she tried to understand the strange things the doctor was saying. She stood up, rested her hands on the table, and leaned toward him.

"Doctor, you take me by surprise. I don't know quite what to say. What is that you're trying to tell me?"

"Never mind. Don't say anything, Maggie. Not now. This wasn't the right time to talk about an old man's dreams. I hope I didn't upset you, but think about what I said." He stood up, went over to her, bent down, and pressed his big hands gently on her shoulders. He picked up his coat and hat from the chair and, pausing at the door, said, "I won't be able to stay for tea, Maggie. I just remembered I have a call to make. I will come by tomorrow to look in on Colie." He opened the door and walked quickly to his car.

Maggie stood still, listening, as the doctor's Ford rattled up the road and thought, *He didn't stay for tea, and after he himself asked for a cup. I should have seen him to the door. He didn't give me time.* Reaction set in, and she started to laugh. "He bolted out the door like the devil himself was after him. Can you imagine that? The good doctor has a liking for me."

She walked over to the mirror above the sink and looked at her reflection. Her looks didn't concern her, but she hadn't really looked at herself for some time. Now she gazed at the face staring back at her as if she had never seen the gray-green eyes fringed with thick, dark lashes, the small straight nose, and auburn hair piled high in a tight bun while a few tendrils escaped to frame a flushed, smooth-skinned, oval-shaped face.

Maggie's lips turned up at the corners in a tiny smile as she turned from the mirror, pleased with what she saw, until she remembered a saying of her mother's: "Vanity comes before a fall."

I'm getting silly, she thought, *gazing at myself in the mirror, just because the doctor paid me a compliment. I won't let myself turn into a foolish woman with an easily turned head. What was the doctor trying to say? He said he wanted to take care of me. How? Did he mean marriage? Well, it doesn't matter. Whatever he meant, I don't intend to ever have another man in my life. I have Colie and Boydie, and I'll manage somehow. I couldn't stand to have a man share my bed again. I had enough of that!*

I must go next door to Jenny and take Boydie home. Poor baby, she was frightened by the commotion and me carrying on.

Maggie smoothed back her hair, took off her apron, hung it on a hook below a shelf that was lined with the blue-willow dinner plates, then went to the kitchen door.

She opened it and was startled to see Frances James standing there, a determined look on her small, pale face, pointy chin held high, brown eyes round with worry, and hand poised in midair ready to knock.

"Oh, please, Mrs. McNeil, I don't want to bother you," she said, in soft, firm voice, "but I saw the doctor leave. I have to know about Colie. Is he going to be all right?" She chewed her lip. "He looked like he was dead when they carried him in. Please, I have to see him."

Maggie's eyes turned as cold as the Atlantic Ocean behind her. She stared at the girl for a few moments.

"I'm afraid that is out of the question, miss. Colie has a broken right arm and other injuries. Dr. Field gave him a sedative, and he is resting now."

Frances wrung her hands.

"Please, Mrs. McNeil, I have to see Colie. I won't wake him. Just let me see him for a minute, then I'll leave."

77

Maggie stood, silent and hard-faced. She folded her arms in front of her. "I'm curious," she said. "Just when did you and my Colie get to be such good friends that you come here and demand to see him? What gives you that right, young lady?"

Frances stood straight, a slim, but defiant figure.

"I know Colie from school, Mrs. McNeil. He used to talk to me sometimes. We were friends. He was kind to me. He took my part when the others made fun of me. We . . . we know each other. Can I see him?"

Maggie sighed, stood aside and beckoned her in.

"Oh, well, I suppose it'll be all right. Come in, girl. I've been wanting to have a talk with you, anyway. I suppose this is as good a time as any. Come in." She motioned her to a chair by the table. "Sit down, miss. Wait here until I come back. I was just on my way to pick up the baby. Mrs. Gleason has been taking care of her for me while the doctor was here."

Frances stood in the doorway clasping and unclasping her hands together. Maggie frowned.

"For heavens sake, girl, I said, come in. That's what you came for, wasn't it? I'm not going to bite you! Come in and sit down." She took Frances by the arm and led her to a chair. "Now, don't go near Colie until I come back, you hear? I'll take you upstairs then, and you can see for yourself that he's very much alive."

A faint pink came into Frances's face.

"Thank you, Mrs. McNeil, for letting me come in. I promise I won't go near Colie until you get back." Then she added, "I watch you when you're playing with your baby sometimes. She is so pretty. I love babies. Your baby has the best laugh I ever heard. When I hear her laughing, the sound of it makes me feel happy, too." Frances put her hand to her mouth and made a small sound. She looked up at

Maggie as she stood in front of the open door. "Oh, oh, I don't mean I spy on you, Mrs. McNeil—nothing like that!"

Maggie tried not to smile.

"I know what you mean, Miss James. There is nothing more precious in this world than the sound of a baby's laugh. Stay here now. We'll have that talk when I get back."

Jenny Gleason greeted Maggie at the door.

"Sh, sh, the baby just fell asleep," she whispered. "What did the doctor say? How is the boy? Will you have a drop of tea?"

"He has a broken right arm, Jenny. He got hit with a baseball bat. The doctor set the arm and stitched his lip. He's bruised, has a few scrapes and scratches, but thank the dear Lord, he will be all right. I can't stay long. I want to get back to Colie. And that James girl is sitting in my kitchen."

Jennie, lifted an eyebrow.

"She is? I'm surprised she could get away from Nora. She likes to keep that poor girl by her side. I didn't know her and Colie were friends. I always felt kind of sorry for the girl, being crippled an' all."

"They know each other from school, Jenny," Maggie said. "I don't hear Boydie. Is she asleep?"

"Yes, I played with her for a bit. Then she stuck her thumb in her mouth and nodded off. She's in here." They tiptoed into the small bedroom that led off the kitchen.

Boydie lay on a narrow cot, covered with a pink and white baby blanket. Damp ringlets of red hair clung to her rosy, sweaty little face. Her thumb was held fast in her mouth, and she lay on her stomach with her tiny rump raised in the air.

Maggie felt her heart swell as she looked down at her baby. She picked the blanket up off her and handed it to Jenny.

"My goodness, it is hot in here, Jenny," she said softly. "Poor baby. She's covered with sweat." She bent down and picked her up, careful not to wake her.

Jenny's round face flushed. She looked down, twisting the narrow gold wedding band on her finger.

"Well, . . . I didn't want the little thing to get a chill, Maggie. It does tend to get cool this time of day, you know. I thought it best to cover her."

Maggie looked quickly at Jenny.

"Of course. You did the right thing in covering her. The weather changes rapidly. I wouldn't want her to catch a cold."

Jenny's eyes grew soft as she looked at Boydie asleep in her mother's arms.

"Isn't she the bonny one, though. I do love her. I'll take her anytime. She's good company for a wee baby."

Jenny Gleason's father was German. He had come, alone, from a tiny hamlet in Germany when he was twenty-four, to get rich by digging for the "buried sunshine," in what he had been told were the busy, bustling, prosperous, coal mines of Cape Breton.

Housed, along with other immigrants, in a boarding house, forced to share a bed on a shift basis with another man, with the cost of his food, shelter, and other expenses deducted from his pay envelope at the end of the week, he soon realized that it would be a long time, if ever, before he had the money saved to send for his wife and little boy in Germany.

He deeply regretted his decision to come to this strange land, unable to speak the language and bewildered by the people and the customs. Visions of riches soon faded. Sad and lonely, his only solace was found in drink.

His widowed landlady had more than a passing interest in the big, blond, good-looking German. She waited her chance, and one night, when he was in his cups, she seduced him and became pregnant with Jenny. She was able to talk him into going through a bogus marriage ceremony, and they lived together as man and wife until Hans Heinrich, in a drunken depression, hung himself from the rafters of their bedroom.

Jenny grew up and helped her mother run the boarding house until Sammy Gleason rented a room and started to court her.

Jenny Gleason was round; everything about her was round, from her round, ruddy, cheerful face, round, bright-blue eyes to her short, round body, and feet in the loose black slippers. Her blond hair, mixed with silver strands, reached to her buttocks which she wore in braids wrapped around her head.

Unlike Maggie, Jenny had borne only one child, a girl. Jenny was proud of her daughter, Anna, a pretty girl who married a man who worked as an engineer for the Canadian Railway. Jenny was proud. Her daughter had escaped Rockhill, the mines, the strikes, and the company stores.

Anna and her husband, Mike Monahan, owned their own small home outside of Rockhill, in the town of Fairhaven. Three months ago, Anna gave birth to Jenny and Sammy Gleason's first grandchild, a girl. Her birth had made Jenny happy. It gave her a new lease on life, something to live for, and reason to get away occasionally from Sammy and his cruelty.

Now she leaned toward Maggie, pecked her on the cheek, and whispered.

"You seem to be feeling better, dear. I hated to see you in such a state of nerves. Not that I blame you. Colie did look bad off. The sight of all that blood must have frightened you out of your wits.

"I expect my Sammy was in the thick of it. He hasn't

come home, yet. Well, he will when he's good and ready and has enough in him. I can always plan on that!

"I've made chicken pies for Colie when he's got an appetite for it. I'll bring them over tomorrow. Colie is fond of my chicken pie. He's a dear boy, that Colie. I do think the world of him, Maggie."

Maggie shifted Boydie up on her shoulder. She leaned down and kissed Jenny.

"Colie will look forward to that. My chicken pies never taste as good as yours no matter how I cook them." She smiled. "You must have a secret that you won't tell me. I do thank you for watching the baby. I don't know what I'd do without you. I'd be lost without you, Jenny. I hope you know that."

"And I, you, dear," said Jenny, patting Maggie's hand. "We've been through a lot together." She chuckled. "But still and all, I don't give my cooking secrets away."

Maggie nodded.

"And well you shouldn't. I'll just have to find out for myself when you're not looking." They both started to laugh until Maggie said, "I'd better go or that girl will take it into her head to wake Colie."

Frances gripped the sides of the chair, willing herself not to dash up the stairs to Colie. She thought, *I said I'd wait here until she comes back. What's taking her so long? I feel so nervous. Colie frightened me; he looked pale and all bloody. He must be going to be all right. His mother wouldn't lie to me. She is so beautiful. I wish I could look like that. She wants to talk to me. About what? Why does she want to talk to me when she never even speaks to me when I see her outdoors hanging the wash. She pretends not to see me and turns away.*

The little girl that died was friendly. At least she'd wave to me, even if she wouldn't come near. I think she was afraid of Granny. All the little kids think she's a witch.

Frances made a little gasp and put her hand to her mouth. *Oh, dear, could his mother know about Colie and me? Has she found out that Colie comes to me at night? Colie said that she's asleep when he leaves the house. He told me he's careful. He knows I'll be in terrible trouble if Granny knew. Oh, please, God, don't let it be that.*

Maybe I should leave. I can't face her. What can I say to her? She'll think I'm a bad girl. No, I can't do that. I have to see Colie. I have to see for myself how badly hurt he is. Please, God, let him be all right.

Frances couldn't sit still. She got up, started up the stairs, then changed her mind. She sat down again and looked around the small, neat kitchen, the clean, sparkling windows with starched, white ruffled curtains and fat vivid, red geraniums on the wide sills. One window faced the back of the house and the blue Atlantic, and the other two looked out over the flowered, red-brick walk and the dusty bluff road. The aroma of apple pie still hung in the room.

Too restless to sit still, Frances got up, walked to the front window and looked out and saw Maggie coming up the walk with Boydie, still asleep, cradled in her arms.

Frances sighed, sat down again and folded her shaking hands in her lap. Then she lifted her chin and thought, *All right, Mrs. McNeil, maybe you found out about Colie and me. I'll have to face you.* She took a deep breath and tried to quiet her racing heart, thinking, *Well, I don't care if you do know.* Then *But I do care. She might make Colie stop seeing me. He would listen to her. I know that. I'd lose him. I couldn't stand to lose Colie. He's all I have, and I love him so.*

Frances stood up when Maggie entered the room. Maggie seemed almost surprised to find her still there. She put her finger to her lips, then went into the parlor, laid

83

Boydie on the davenport, took an afghan quilt from the back of the morris chair, spread it out on the faded, cabbage-rose carpet, and placed Boydie on top of it.

Then she went into the kitchen, walked over to Frances, and stood in front of her with her arms folded.

"Now, Miss James, I think you know what I'm about to say, don't you?" Maggie's blazing green eyes bore into the girl's liquid brown ones until Frances lowered her eyes to the floor.

"You know, . . . you know then, about Colie and me."

Maggie, tight-lipped, nodded.

"Yes, miss, I do, and it's a shameful thing to know that my son's been creeping out at night to your bed."

Frances tried to brazen it out. Indignant, she raised her eyes and looked at Maggie.

"That's not true, Mrs. McNeil. We don't do anything wrong. He just visits with me for a while—"

Maggie cut her short.

"For a while, is it? When I know that he comes creeping back in the wee hours of the morning, sometimes not until dawn is nearly breaking, almost in time to get ready for his shift. I've wanted to drag it out of him many a morning, but held back, waiting, hoping it would stop and he'd get his fill of you." Maggie gave a short, bitter laugh. "I thought it was finished when he took to staying in at night. That lasted a week or two. Then it started up again. Are you trying to tell me, girl, that a young boy like Colie is just visiting all those hours? You must take me for a fool." Maggie paused. "I'm no fool, girl."

Frances said nothing, but looked down at the floor and flushed a deep rose.

"I hope you know you're doing something very wrong. Sinful and disgusting! No decent girl would allow a young man to take such liberties."

Frances felt light-headed, dizzy. The floor seemed to be moving in waves.

"Is it all right if I sit, Mrs. McNeil?"

Maggie nodded.

Frances found a chair, sat, and covered her face with small, work-roughened hands.

"I knew you'd think me a bad girl, Mrs. McNeil. Are you going to tell Granny? Please don't tell her. She's old. It would kill her to know that about me."

Maggie walked over and sat across the table from her. She looked at the girl's bowed, shiny brown head, the out of style, faded blue jumper, then down to her heavy black shoes. Maggie felt pity rise within her, and although more harsh, condemning words were on her lips, she stopped them.

Suddenly weary, Maggie stood up.

"We will talk about this situation later, miss. You know, of course, it can't continue. Sit there, collect yourself. Rest a minute."

"Please, Mrs. McNeil," Frances sobbed, "I'm not a bad girl. I didn't want it to be this way. I don't want to be bad. I love Colie."

Maggie turned to her.

"You love him? Is that what you call it? Stop crying, girl. Tears never solved anything. I didn't say you were bad, but you're certainly a foolish girl. Don't you know that a boy never respects a girl who will allow him to take such liberties? They never marry such girls.

"An unmarried girl is expected to be chaste and pure. Oh never mind! I'm too tired to give you the lesson in conduct and morals that you should have received long ago, and it looks like it's too late now."

Frances sobbed louder.

"Oh, stop sniveling! Come upstairs then. I suppose you

won't be satisfied until you see Colie. Be quiet. I don't want to waken him. He needs rest. That boy is going to get a tongue-lashing the like he's never had before. Colie's had a Christian upbringing. He's been instructed in what's right and what's wrong. There is no excusing him."

Frances followed Maggie up the stairs. She wiped her eyes with a corner of her skirt, and a tiny smile played around her full, pale lips. She thought, *That wasn't so bad. I thought it would be much worse. At least she didn't holler and scream and call me names. I expected her to order me out of the house. She was almost nice to me. She doesn't hate me, I can tell, and she won't tell Granny either. I can tell that, too. She's trying to be hard, but she's really kind. Colie is lucky. He has a nice, pretty mother. But she's wrong if she thinks she can separate us now. Colie belongs to me. She can't stop us. I'll find a way so we can be together.*

They paused when they came to Colie's closed door. Maggie slowly pushed it open.

Colie lay sprawled on his back in a narrow brass bed. His dark, sweat-soaked hair stuck to his forehead in small ringlets, and short, thick, black lashes swept across his closed eyes.

A dressing covered a swollen, blackened lip, and bluish purple bruises stained his jawline. Deep scratches ran along both sides of his face. His right arm, enclosed in a thick cast, lay across his bare, broad chest.

Frances put her hand to her mouth and started to enter the room. Maggie pulled her back.

"None of that now. There's no need to go further. You can see him from here. I don't want him disturbed." Maggie pointed. "You can see for yourself. There he is, all cleaned up and sleeping like a baby. Are you satisfied now? Come, we'll go now." She eased the door shut and led the way down the stairs.

Frances stopped and grasped both sides of the wall.

"No, I have to go to him. He doesn't look like he's breathing. He's all beaten up. Let me go to him, Mrs. McNeil?"

Maggie paused, turned on the stairs, took her by the shoulders, and shook her.

"I told you," she hissed, "there's nothing wrong with my son that time won't heal. He's had too much to carry on his young shoulders. He's worn out. Worrying about me, carrying on with you, and working in that accursed pit!

"He's still a boy, and he's my son. You have no call on him, young lady, much as you'd like to!" She pushed Frances ahead of her until they reached the bottom of the stairs, keeping her arm tight about France's shoulders to the front door.

"I'm tired. You have to leave. Go home to your grandmother, or I'll have her on my doorstep, too. We'll talk when Colie is up to it."

Frances paused, her hand on the doorknob. She turned to Maggie.

"I know you hate me. I was hoping we could be friends. I need a friend, but I was wrong. Thank you for letting me see Colie. I'm sorry if I made a fuss."

Maggie looked deep into her glistening eyes. She shook her head and sighed.

"Hate? That's a pretty strong word, miss. Of course I don't hate you. You've been a careless, foolish young woman. I don't hate you for that. It is what you do in the future that counts now."

Frances spoke in a voice, thin but alive with hope.

"Can I come by tomorrow? Oh, not to see Colie, Mrs. McNeil, just to visit. I promise I won't get in the way. I could mind the baby for you so you could rest. Granny sleeps for hours in the afternoon. It, ... I get lonely."

"Oh, for heaven's sake, all right, come to the door then, when your grandmother's napping, and we'll see."

Maggie shut the door and watched at the window as Frances went limping up the path. She stayed, looking out, until Frances made the turn onto her own walk and could no longer be seen.

Maggie left the window and went into the parlor. Boydie was still fast asleep. She had rolled off the quilt and lay curled up on the bare floor. Maggie bent down, picked her up, and placed her back on top of the quilt.

Then she went into the kitchen, sat at the table, folded her hands, and tried to pray. She looked down at her hands, then turned them palms up so that their red-scarred backs were hidden from her view.

She couldn't pray. Her mind seemed empty, blank; she couldn't seem to find the right phrases. She gazed out across the kitchen through the ruffled curtains, not really seeing the rough green grass of the bluff, scrub pines, her clothesline off the right, with white sheets snapping in a stiff breeze, the dark blue water, and on the horizon, a giant freighter, appearing motionless, silhouetted against a pale blue sky.

Maggie felt guilt pricking at her. She thought, *I was hard on the girl. I came down too hard on her. Who am I to judge? I have no right to judge her.*

She thinks I hate her. Wouldn't she be surprised if she knew that I know all about how it feels to be a young girl and crazy in love with a man. I know all about the pitfalls, too. How it can ruin your life, as it did mine.

What am I going to do about her? There's more to her than appears on the surface. I shouldn't have told her to come by tomorrow. I don't want to encourage her. I've managed to stay clear of that family since coming to the bluff. Now this.

Maggie got up, put the teakettle on to boil, then sat down again and thought, *There will be no wages coming in from*

Colie from now on, but we can get along for awhile from the money left over from Jock's accident, and little enough it was that the company gave me for killing my husband. That along with what I can earn sewing for the ladies, will keep us going, for a time at least. I can't plan beyond that.

Right now, that girl is going to be a problem. She comes from a strange family, indeed! I never was one to listen to idle gossip, but I heard it said that Nora James's daughters became quite wild, loose women once they left home. None of them ever came back to town, and the sons left for who knows where, never to be heard from again.

Nora and her husband were cruel to their children. It's no wonder none of them ever wanted to come back. Not even to their father's funeral. I don't blame them. If I ever get away from here, I'll never come back either.

From the parlor, Boydie began to stir, calling out "Mama, Mama." She toddled into the kitchen on her short, plump legs and held her arms out to be picked up.

Maggie scooped her up. Boydie, well rested and in good humor, cupped her mother's face between tiny, soft hands and said, "My mama."

Maggie smiled, thinking, Well, Lord, I won't borrow trouble. My Colie is safe upstairs in his own bed. He'll not go down the pit ever again. My mind is made up to that. I'll not lose another son to the devil pit! They can't put us out of the house. I lost a son and husband in the mines. That has to count for something.

You took Catherine, but I have this dear little baby of mine. Maggie nuzzled Boydie's soft cheek. As soon as Colie is well, I'll talk to the both of them. God forbid, if she should get in the family way, my son will never escape this town. Though I can see that she's a determined one and has her heart set on my Colie.

I have to find a way to leave here before it's too late for Colie. If it comes to that, I'll go to my brother John for help, beg if necessary. He has to help me. I'm his sister. He can't have forgotten how close we once were.

89

"Cookie, Mama," Boydie pointed to molasses cookies in a square glass jar in the middle of the table.

Maggie put her down, took a fat, brown cookie out of the jar and was about to hand it to her, when, suddenly, against the side of the house, a loud crash, then the sound of breaking glass made Maggie drop the cookie, pick up Boydie and run into the parlor.

A rock lay on the floor with a piece of paper tied to it. Maggie stood trembling, afraid to move. Then she put Boydie down in back of her, away from the broken glass, and with shaking hands, picked up the heavy rock. One word "SCAB," was printed on the yellow-lined paper.

An icy cold chill shot through Maggie. She scooped up Boydie, thinking, *My God, baby was sleeping a minute ago, where that rock landed!* She stood, rooted to the spot, afraid to go near the window.

Sammy Gleason. The name leapt into her mind. *No, Sammy isn't that crazy. He wouldn't be throwing rocks near his own house in broad daylight with his wife at home, unless he was drunk. Dear God, could Sammy be that crazy?*

From the kitchen, the teakettle whistled merrily, unnoticed, as Maggie's rage consumed her. She flung open the door, stood in the doorway, with Boydie in her arms, and screamed at the backs of the two men running away from the house.

"Rotten cowards, may you burn in hell if you ever hurt my children. Devils, filthy cowards!"

Jenny Gleason's plump form rushed out the door of her house to Maggie.

"Dear, Oh, dear," she said, out of breath, "what's happened now. I heard glass breaking!"

Maggie sagged against her as Jenny reached for Boydie.

"Someone flung a rock. Boydie, . . . she'd been lying

there a second or two before the rock came through the window. *There! Look—There they are—it was them.*" She pointed to two men running up the bluff road. Soon they reached the crest and disappeared over the other side.

Frances heard Maggie's screams as she was serving Nora her tea. She rushed out and joined the other women of the row houses, now gathered together at Maggie's door.

Maggie, looking pale and distraught, waved them away.

"I'm all right. Someone flung a rock, broke a window. I'm all right. No one was hurt. It, it, . . . frightened me. I'm sorry."

Mrs. MacKinnon, from the second rowhouse, shook her frowzy, gray head.

"They's got in for you, honey, 'cause of yer boy. Him still workin' an' all. It do make them mad. We all got to stick together in this. That's what me man says." She smiled, toothless, at Maggie. "I do hope yer boy weren't too bad hurt today."

Tall, scrawny, red-headed, and fierce, Mable MacDermott, from the third house, with two dirty-faced children clinging to her skirt, stuck out her long jaw and chimed in.

"We been expecting trouble on the bluff. Our men ain't strikebreakers. Don't see them goin' down the pit. Not when a strike's been called. They's honoring the strike. Our kids are hungry, but we don't back down to the company.

"What's the matter with yer boy? He's a traitor, that's what he is. He got what he deserves, and there's more of that coming if he keeps on!"

Maggie faced them squarely, head held high and hands on hips.

"Not that it's any of your business, but you needn't concern yourselves about Colie. He's had his last day going at the pit. Now you take care of your business, and I'll take

91

care of mine. You're all hateful, spiteful women," Maggie flung the words at them, "Get away from my door!"

Maggie turned and flounced into the house with Jenny and Boydie close behind her.

Mable MacDermott, her face an ugly, mottled red, started toward the door, but Mrs. MacKinnon held her back.

"Never mind now, Mable. Don't get riled up. Maggie McNeil's a changed woman since her girl died in that fire. Ain't none of us able to talk to her no more. Save yer strength." She glanced down at the two children trying to hide in their mother's skirt. "Yer goin' to need it as we all will."

Frances pushed her way past the women blocking the door.

"Please, let me by. I want to help."

But she was too late. Jenny shut the door in her face.

Mable sniffed, then chuckled as she looked down her nose at Frances and put her hands on her hips.

"Well, just look who's wantin' to help? The little gimp. Go on home to yer nanny. It's time for her toddy."

The rest of the women glanced at each other, started to giggle nervously, then dispersed.

Frances stood alone. She looked at their retreating backs, thinking, *Go on, you, make fun of me if you want, but I know I'm better than you. Even if granny drinks, she's still better than all of you. You're all jealous of Colie's mother because she is young-looking and pretty.*

Frances held her head high as she walked back to her own house.

"How you feeling, laddie?" Malcolm, twisting his cap in his hands, stood looking down at Colie in the bed.

Colie struggled to sit up.

"A bit woozy. Whatever the doc gave me knocked me for a loop, Nothin' hurtin' though." He started to swing his legs to the side of the bed.

Malcolm helped him to sit up.

"Well, your face wouldn't take any beauty prizes," he said. "Take it easy, laddie. No need to get up. I'm only staying a minute. Just wanted to let you know the mines shut down. All of them. That's it. They're saying the provincial police have been called in to keep order. That's a laugh. Having those buggers around will fix things for sure. I don't know what's going to happen next, laddie. We'll have to wait and sweat it out."

Colie looked up at Malcolm through glazed eyes.

"What's goin' to happen to us then? What'll we live on? Ma depends on me. Damn! The company'll put us out."

"Let's hope they settle before anything like that comes about, laddie. They have to come to an agreement with the union. They can't keep the mines shut down for long. The company knows that."

Malcolm bent over and patted Colie clumsily on his tousled head.

"Well, you take it easy now. Let that arm heal. You wouldn't be able to work now anyway. By the time your arm is healed, the strike will be over, so don't worry. Remember, we can stand the gaff." He turned and walked heavily down the stairs.

11

No one spoke. Colie sat next to Uncle Archie on the maroon sofa. It was the first time he had visited his aunt and uncle in many weeks. He felt ill at ease and uncomfortable. The room was too warm and seemed airless even though the window was wide open, and through it floated the voices of small boys, yelling and war hopping in a wild game of cowboys and Indians. Colie looked down at his hands and examined his fingernails.

Aunt Marion sat across from them in a matching, over-sized armchair and stroked a big, black and white, tattered-eared, tomcat and, unmindful of the cat's twitching tail, admired the new, peacock-blue rug that covered the parlor floor.

The cat's tail twitched faster.

Archie took the pipe out of his mouth and scowled at his wife.

"Can't yer see the damn cat wants to be let loose, woman? He's gettin' ready to give yer a good scratch. Stop maulin' the poor brute."

"Naw, Archie. Runo loves me. He wouldn't scratch me, the one who feeds and takes care of him. Now, would you, sweet darling?" She ruffled the cat's neck fur until the cat gave a shrill screech, dug his claws into her lap, then leapt, howling, out the window. *"Ouch. You bugger, you!"*

Aunt Marion jumped up in pain and loudly cursed the cat and its ancestry and promised to wring its neck when she got hold of it.

The ice finally broken, Colie and Archie slapped their

thighs and laughed until tears ran down their faces. Archie wiped his eyes with the back of his hand.

"Sweet old darlin', is it? Loves yer, does it? God, I ain't seen yer jump like that since our wedding night. That's the best laugh I've had in a dog's age."

Aunt Marion went over to him and cuffed him roughly on the side of his head.

"I'm happy to be the cause of so much merriment, little man, but better watch your step or you'll be following the cat out the window."

Archie, still laughing, put his hands up to shield his face from further blows.

"Now, now, sweetheart. Colie and me were just having a bit of fun, that's all." He poked Colie in the ribs. "Weren't we, Colie? Now, how about getting yer old man and Colie here a drink of that good rum out in the kitchen?" He flung an arm around Colie's shoulder. "Me and him got some business to talk over."

Aunt Marion threw him a dirty look over her shoulder, on her way into the kitchen.

Colie sat, leaning with elbows resting on his knees and chin in his hand. He shook his head,

"Damn, Uncle Archie, I don't feel right about this. I don't know—sure could use the money. Strike's over, but Ma won't hear of me working the pit again. She's been writing to her snotty brother, hoping he'll help us out, take us in if the company puts us out of the house." Colie ran his fingers through his thick hair. "Hell, I can't think of anythin' worse than havin' to take his charity. He don't care a damn about us. Never did a thing for us before. Why should he now? That's what I told Ma, but she don't listen to me."

He lifted his head and looked at his uncle. "Ten dollars you say, for a night's unloadin'? We're gettin' pretty hard up. Ma sews day and night. It keeps the rent paid and buys a few groceries. Me arm's pretty well healed. I should be workin'. I feel like a useless shit, but Ma would sure have a fit if she knew I'd a part in rum-running, no matter how bad off we got, an' how could I explain bein' gone at night?"

Archie leaned back and rested his shiny, bald head against the high-backed sofa. He puffed thoughtfully on his pipe.

"Aw, you'll think of somethin', smart fella like yerself. Well, what yer say? Yer in? Got to get someone else if yer not. There be a ship due in Friday night with a load of rum." He took the pipe from his mouth and knocked it against the arm of the sofa. "They blacklisted me, yer know . . . .Couldn't go back to work if I wanted to. Nothing left for me in this town. Soon's we can, Archie McNeil an' his old lady . . . brats, too . . . high-tailin' fer Boston."

Aunt Marion came back with two water glasses of dark rum. Silently, she handed one to Colie, placed Archie's on the floor in front of him and went back into the kitchen. Soon they heard the kitchen door slam.

"I think we got Aunt Marion mad when we laughed at her." Colie said. "That old tomcat scratched her good."

"She'll get over it. Drink up now. That's good rum you got in yer hand, straight off the boat."

Colie took a big swallow while Archie beamed at him.

"Yer right. Boy, that's some good, knock me on me ass if I don't sip it slowlike." He put the glass down on the floor and put out his hand. "Okay, let's shake on it. Ten dollars a night, and I'm in." Colie picked up the glass and took a deep swallow. "It's time I was me own man. Ma can't keep leadin' me around by the nose. I got a chance to make some money, and I'm gonna take it! Right, Uncle Archie?"

"Right yer are, boy!" Archie grasped Colie's out-stretched hand, pumped it up and down, reached for his glass and took a long swallow. "Okay, now, here's the story.

96

Be here Friday night, long 'fore midnight, an' I hope to God there's no moon out. Yer'll drive with me and Billy Mac-Dougal. No seats. Have to make room for the kegs, you know. This'll be a big haul." Archie took another swallow and wiped his mouth. "There's nothin' to it. All's we have to do is row out aways, out to the schooner, big mother of a ship, too. Load up the kegs, work fast, and be quiet, then row ashore and unload the kegs. Nothing to it."

"What do we do with the kegs once we unload them? Where do we hide them?"

"Aw, no, boy, that's all you need to know for now. You'll see how it's done Friday night. Yer don't need to know no more than that right now. Just be here full of piss and vinegar."

"What 'bout the Mounties? Do we just row out, help ourselves to the kegs, then row away scot-free? Must be more to it then that?"

Archie took the pipe from his mouth and looked at Colie. "You getting cold feet?"

"Naw, just wondered. What 'bout the Mounties? Ain't they on the lookout for rumrunners?"

"Sure, they is, but they don't know where to look, and it's a big shore line and little coves, places to slip in quiet-like, then slip out again. I ain't had no trouble with the Mounties yet and been at it for months. Making money for the first time in my life, an' not digging coal fer it either."

He slapped Colie on the back. "Don't worry, I'll take care of the details . . . be here Friday night. That's three days from now. I can use a big, strong fellow like yerself. We be partners."

Colie took a sip of the rum. Smooth as silk, it trickled down his throat and, filled with a sense of well-being, he stretched his long legs out in front of him.

"Damn, I feel good. Wish it were Friday night now. He took another sip. "Well, ya don't have to tell me the details if ya don't want to. That's up to ya, Uncle Archie. Yer the boss. Got to think of somethin' ta tell Ma—she be hard to fool."

The rum loosened Colie's tongue and he continued, "I was havin' a fine time nights with a pretty little girl from the bluff 'til Ma found out. Sure as hell, she'll think I'm with Franny if I sneak out at night."

Archie sputtered and started to laugh.

"Maggie always was straitlaced biddy. She put the run on the girl, did she?"

"Ma thinks she has, but me and Franny, we still get together."

"A looker, is she?"

"Well, no, not like that. Well, she's kind of skinny and sort of crippled, but pretty just the same." The heat of the room and the rum made Colie flush a deep red in embarrassment. "Sorry, it ain't right to be talkin' about Franny. She's me girl, now."

"Yer right," Archie said. "It ain't nice." Then he asked, "How the hell can she be kind of crippled? Either she is or she ain't. No matter, yer secret's safe with me." He rubbed his head. "I was a young man once. Had a good head of thick black hair too, just like yers."

Colie looked at him. He grinned foolishly and tried to stop the laughing jag fast overtaking him. The thought of bald Uncle Archie with his black bushy eyebrows that met over a jutting nose, his sweating, shining scalp covered with thick black hair was too much for Colie, and he burst out laughing.

"You got the boy drunk, you damn fool." Aunt Marion came back into the room and stood looking at them as they danced around the room, out of control, slapping their thighs, gasping and choking while tears streamed from their eyes.

"Rum-drunk. You're both rum-drunk. I wish the hell I thought to hide your bottle before Colie got here. Archie,

98

you should be ashamed of yourself for getting young Colie drunk."

"I'm all right. Don't be blamin' Uncle Archie. He didn't pour it down me throat." Colie sat down on the divan, and Archie flopped, like a rag doll, beside him.

Then, staggering silently, Colie stood up again.

"I better start for home," he announced. "Ma will be wonderin' what happened to me. I've been gone all day." He reached for Archie's hand and pumped it up and down. "Sure do thank ya. Be here Friday, with bells on. Me and you, we be partners now, right? I'm not drunk, Aunt Marion. Just havin' a good time." He wiped his eyes. "Time I got home anyways."

"Oh, no, you're not going anywheres 'til you got a few cups of hot tea in you. It wouldn't pay to have Maggie coming down on us for getting you drunk, now would it?" She glared at Archie and pushed him back as he started to rise. "You stay put, old man. I know you're not after tea, and you'll be hard put to find your bottle."

"Aw, now, pussycat, don't be like that." He got up and tried to put his arms around her ample waist.

She shoved him hard, and his head hit the stiff back of the divan.

"Don't pussycat me, you old devil. You're not going anywheres 'til you sober up. You never know when to stop. God knows, I don't begrudge you your right to a drink now and then, but you're not happy 'til you've drained the bottle, then you're after the next one." She turned to Colie. "Come into the kitchen. Let him be. He'll soon sleep it off. That's the fifth glass of rum he's had today, and he is just itching for an excuse to drink more."

Colie glanced at Archie, who was already nodding off, with his head slumped to one side. He shrugged his shoulders and followed his aunt into the kitchen.

12

Colie, dressed in a dark shirt and pants, sat by the side of his bed in the unlighted room. His head cocked to one side, he listened for sounds, but the house was still.

An hour or so ago, his mother and Jenny Gleason were sitting at the kitchen table, sipping tea, as they talked and laughed like young girls, and although it felt good to hear his mother laugh again, he had wished that they would wind down and Jenny go home and his mother to bed.

He could hear his heart beat, even in his ears, as it raced and pounded through his chest, and he thought of the big black touring car soon to be waiting for him on the bluff road.

His thoughts raced back to Tuesday morning and the meeting with Uncle Archie in front of Miner's Hall. They had walked to the rear of the building to talk. Archie seemed gruff, quiet, cranky, and not himself as he said. "Now, I'm tellin' yer, boy, if yer not there, we won't waste time waitin' fer yer. So be there—sharp—and ready to work."

And as a man came around the corner of the building, Archie threw his arm about Colie's shoulder and said, "Let's go get a smoke, young fella." He nodded to the man as he headed down the narrow path that led to the privy used by the miners.

They sat on the grass in back of the hall. Archie rolled two cigarettes, handed one to Colie, and took a deep drag before giving Colie brief instructions.

He was to meet them where the bluff road intersected

with the road into town, then wait to be picked up by a big black car.

"Whose car?" Colie asked, knowing that his uncle didn't own a car.

"Never mind whose car. Listen now, I ain't got all day. Two, maybe three others will be in the car with me. Yer don't have to know no more than that right now."

Colie had thought, *Uncle Archie's actin' like he wishes he'd never set eyes on me. I guess he's had a run-in with me aunt, and she's had second thoughts, knowing Ma and how she hates booze.* But he said, "Cripes, Uncle Archie, I wish ya'd let me in on some of the details. Ya don't have to worry 'bout me. I knows how to keep me trap shut. I hear there's a three-mile limit and the big ships can't come closer. That's a pretty far distance. How we gonna get out that far? Ya gonna use a speedboat?"

Archie didn't answer. He stood up, brushed the seat of his pants, looked sourly down at Colie, and said, "Marion's madder than a wet hen. Won't speak to me, won't cook fer me. Have to get me own grub. She's scared of Maggie and what she'll do if she finds out yer going the rum-row with me. I sure hope I ain't made a big mistake," he said as he walked away.

Colie had flipped his cigarette on the grass and ground his heel into it as he thought, *Aw, the hell with all of yer! Sure, no one cares how I feel, hangin' around with nothin' to do. Ma won't let me work the pit no more. There's no work to be had anywheres.*

Am I to sit on me arse, staring off into space like witless Willie? I planned to get the hell out of here anyway. I'll go to Halifax, or maybe Boston, if something don't break for me soon.

Ma thinks everythin' is just fine. We're getting' along pretty good, I admit that, with her sewin' all the time and the company let-tin' us stay in the house 'long as they gets their rent money, but that won't last if I don't go back to work. Malcom said I could start tomorra. He sure wants me back.

I miss the old bugger. Ma don't know what it's like to have nothin' to do all day. Makes a fella feel damn useless. I need a bit of money in me own pocket.

Uncle Archie said it would only be two or three times a week he'd need me, so she don't ever have to know. What's Aunt Marion got to be afraid of Ma for? Ma can't do nothin' to her. I got a mind of me own. Time I looked after meself.

Colie got up and looked out the open window. The moon drifted in and out from behind floaty dark clouds, and Colie cursed its brightness. Uncle Archie had hoped there wouldn't be a moon tonight.

The moonlight bathed the small room and its meager contents, one small, lace-curtained window, a narrow bed with white chenille spread, a straight-backed wooden chair, a small chest of drawers, and a bare, but shiny, wood floor.

Nearby, an owl hooted, and Colie felt a shiver run through him as he listened for any sounds coming from his mother's room. The house was still.

He put a leg out over the windowsill and leaned far out until his fingers found the chimney. He poked his fingers into the slight depressions, climbed out, and slid until he was a few feet from the ground. Then he jumped, bounced on his bare feet, and crept away from his own silent house and its neighbors.

He picked up the boots he had hidden behind the outhouse, put them on, laced them up, and walked up the dark road with only the busy night sounds of insects for company.

The moon disappeared behind the clouds and the night was black as pitch. He felt bathed in the thick, sticky air as he walked along the deserted road. Once away from the house, Colie straightened up and walked at a fast pace.

He felt the fear of the unknown, but also, with that fear,

a tingling aliveness, almost the way he felt when he made love to Franny.

Franny, he thought. She's sure acting strange. Poppin' in for afternoon tea with Ma, playin' with Boydie, paying me no mind, like I was a piece of shit on the floor. The two of them getting' real chummy.

Two weeks since I've been with her. It's getting' to bother me. I need that skinny little girl. Maybe she don't like me no more? Naw, that ain't it. She's crazy 'bout me. I know that in me bones. Franny's up to somethin', that's all. Suckin' up to me ma, that's what she's doin'. I'll buy her somethin' pretty when I gets me hands on some money. Have her meet me down under the wharf some night soon. It'll surprise her. I never bought her a present before.

Colie's footsteps echoed on the gravel road as if someone was following him. He turned and looked quickly around, then felt shame creep over him. He thought, *who the hell would be followin' me now?* Since the strike, there had been no hard feelings between him and the other men. They were willing to let go and forgive. Most of the strikers, except those few who were blacklisted, were back at work.

Uncle Archie had badmouthed too many of the bigshots. That's why he was one of the few. It didn't worry him. He had a good setup now.

Colie heard a car coming toward him. He stepped quickly to the side of the road and hid behind some bushes, thinking *maybe it ain't Archie, but Mounties on the lookout for rumrunners.*

Archie had warned him not to show himself right away. Then a long, black car with dim lights, slowed down, stopped, and Colie heard Archie's hoarse whisper in the darkness.

"Come on, Colie. Get the hell out from wherever yer are. Show yerself, damn it, and be quick about it."

Colie stepped out from behind the bushes. The door

103

on his side was flung open, and strong arms reached out and pulled him into the car.

It took a few seconds for Colie's eyes to adjust to the car's dark interior. Archie was at the wheel, and Colie recognized Billy MacDougal, another blacklisted miner, sitting on the floor of the car, along with a man he'd never seen before. Colie nodded to Billy.

Archie, without taking his eyes off the dark road, jerked a thumb toward them.

"Yer know Billy. The other fella' is Hank. He's from Balls-Creek. This here's me nephew, Colie McNeil. Strapping young fella' ain't he?"

"Glad to meet you, Colie," Hank reached out a big hand and squeezed Colie's outstretched one. "Now that the formalities are over, let's get the hell out of here."

Archie backed the car rapidly up the road until they came to a narrow lane that was hidden from the road by tall, thick bushes on each side. He turned into it, and the men sitting on the floor in back of the car had to duck to avoid the scratchy bushes poking into the open windows in the rear of the car as it slid and bounced along a lane that was never meant to be driven on by a large car.

The window on the driver's side had glass and was rolled shut. Archie chuckled as Colie and the other men scrunched down as low as they could to the floor of the car and covered their faces with their shirts.

Archie fought to keep the car from hitting trees and bushes as the car rolled down a steep, bumpy knoll, took a sharp corner, then down another long, jouncing stretch of hill, where the lane suddenly widened and came to an abrupt end at a small, rock-strewn beach.

Archie brought the car to a jolting, black-breaking stop just before it hit the water's lapping shoreline.

"Damn it, Archie, what the hell are you trying to do,

drive out to the damn schooner?" Billy whispered as he unraveled himself and got out of the car.

"It always takes me by surprise when I gets to the end of the lane and come upon the beach," answered Archie. "The brakes ain't all that good either. Next time, Big Dan can drive his own frigging car."

Colie, glad to untangle himself from the back of the car, got out and looked out at the seemingly endless black void of a rolling sea.

"I don't see nuthin' out there. Where's the rumboat?"

"Shut up," Archie whispered. "Just do what yer told. Come on, boys, let's get hopping." He led the way behind a crop of broad, black-looking boulders that jutted out a few feet from the water's edge, and to the big wooden dory, with two sets of oars, that lay snugly between the two largest boulders.

Colie, downcast, followed, wondering how the dory got there. Who left it? And why didn't Uncle Archie have a speedboat? *The dory belongs to Big Dan, most likely*, he thought, going over to help.

They groaned and cursed softly under their breaths as they lifted and carried the sixteen-foot dory out from the rocks and into the water. The men took off their boots, put them in the car, then rolled their pants legs up to their thighs as far as they would go.

Colie did the same. No one spoke as they pushed the dory deeper into the water. The dark surf foamed and crashed around them. Silently, they climbed into the rocking boat.

Archie motioned Colie to sit at the stern beside him. Billy had Hank picked up the heavy oars and began to row straight out to sea.

Colie strained his eyes, but all he saw was the dark horizon and starless sky as it came together, seeming to join with the rolling ocean.

"Where's the ship? I don't see no ship out there."

"Shh, shut your trap. She's out there, boy . . . look . . . there now, there she is." He pointed, and Colie saw a three-masted schooner that sent cold shivers along his spine as it crept, soundless, like a ghost ship, into view over the horizon. Archie laughed softly and rapped Colie on the side of the head. "See, there she is, big as life, just waiting fer us. Lying round the bend, she was, and yer worried 'bout rowing three miles out. When it's a night like tonight, she's come in close; the cutters never knows where to look. We'll have our load in jig time."

Hank and Billy rowed faster. Colie felt bile rise in his throat. His hands shook, and he felt sick to his stomach as the schooner seemed to glide over the water toward them. Soon the dory was alongside her.

Two seamen and the ship's captain, their forms shadowy on the unlighted deck, peered down at them. The captain, his voice a croaking whisper in the night air, leaned far out over the deck.

"Nothing doing until I see the sign. Got the sign?" he said.

Archie stood up in the dory. A rope ladder was thrown down. He climbed into the schooner and handed the captain a torn half of a dollar bill. The captain squinted at it, then shook Archie's hand.

"All right," he said, "move fast now. Load up as much as your dory can hold. I'll be looking for you tomorrow night. Two more runs after that should do it. I want to get rid of this load. We're low on provisions. Too bad you don't have a speedboat. We could get rid of the whole load tonight."

"We got one, and it's a hummer, fast as all get out, but don't like to use it much—too noisy and apt to bring the

Mounties out," said Archie. "Can't risk it. We'll be here same time tomorrow if the moon and tide are with us."

Two burly, silent seamen loaded a crane with two ten-gallon kegs, which they hung out over the dory.

Archie scampered back down the ladder, jumped into the boat, climbed over the other men, and sat at the stern giving orders.

"Put yer backs into it, boys. That's good Demerara rum in them kegs fer thirsty Cape Bretoneres."

Billy, Hank, and Colie reached for the heavy kegs and lowered them into the dory. Colie's weakened arm brought him to his knees when he tried to lift a keg across his chest. Hank chuckled as he and Billy shouldered theirs to the bottom of the dory.

"Don't bust your balls, sonny. Easy does it."

The last keg swung over the dory. Colie reached for it, smoothly lowered it to his shoulders, and nestled it among the other kegs.

"Now yer getting the hang of it," Archie whispered from his seat at the stern.

Hank and Billy picked up the oars. The heavily ladened dory sat in the water with only inches to spare at the water line. Colie sat on top of the kegs. The schooner pulled away as the men rowed toward shore.

"Row faster, yer buggers," growled Archie. The damn moon is comin' out again. We're sitting ducks out here. I hope to hell there's no shit-heeled Mounties 'bout."

"Think you can do better? You're welcome to take my place," said Hank. "We'll be lucky if we don't sink. We are carrying too many kegs. We should toss a few over."

"Like hell we will, an' keep yer voice down . . . sound carries over the water . . . come on put yer back into it. We ain't far from shore. I've carried more kegs than this many a time. Thought yer told me yer did this before? What's the matter? Getting cold feet, are yer? Row, damn it!"

Colie was feeling surer of himself.

"Aw, we'll make it," he whispered. "Look, the tide is with us. It's pushin' us right along, right to shore. We won't lose a keg. What'll we do with them once we get to shore, Uncle Archie?"

"You'll see when we get there. Now shut yer trap. Yer getting on me nerves."

"Aw, stop picking on the lad." He ain't never done this before. It's all excited, he is."

"Mind yer own business, Billy. He's me kin . . . stop jabberin'. Get this tub ashore."

"My God," Billy said softly, "you sure have a hair across your arse tonight, Archie."

Hank began to snicker.

Archie shook his fist at them.

"What the hell's the matter with both of you? Think this is some kind of kid's game? For all we know, there's a Mountie hiding behind every rock, waiting to grab us when we gets in. Row, damn it, row!"

Hank and Billy let Archie's outburst pass without further comment. They dipped the oars into the water while their breaths escaped in gasps and grunts. Soon, with the tide's help, they were close to shore. The men jumped out into the waist-high water.

Grunting, panting, and cursing, they managed to push and shove the heavily laden dory until its bottom scraped the rocky beach.

They pulled the dory up on the beach.

"Come on, get those kegs into the car," Archie whispered. "Thank God the damn moon went in. I think we're in the clear." He gave Colie a push. "Okay, boy, time to start earning that ten bucks. Let's load up." He marched ahead of them, pulled open the car doors, and stood with his arms folded across his chest. "Stack 'em up. We got a good load tonight."

"Yes, sir," said Colie. He hoisted a wet, slimy keg onto his shoulders, and it started to slip from his wet hands.

Billy grabbed it before it hit the rocky beach.

"Take it easy, son," he whispered, "You'll get the hang of it."

"Thanks, Billy, I got a grip on it now." Colie shouldered the heavy keg and stacked it with the others in back of the car.

Archie leaned on the front door of the car.

"Never mind the chitchat. This is no tea party. Get yer backs into it."

"We would be loaded up a lot sooner if you put your own back into it too, McNeil," said Billy.

Archie chuckled softly.

"That ain't me job. That's what I'm paying yer for. I didn't take yer along for a moonlight ride, yer know. If yer don't like it, there's plenty more who would be willing to take yer place."

Billy thought of his four hungry boys and thin, tired wife and didn't say anymore.

Colie thought, *Uncle Archie is actin' like a real bastard. You'd think he'd give a hand, since he's so anxious to get out of here. He's actin' like a tin god or somethin'. Well, I'll go along with him. I need the money, but can't say I like him much right now. Sure seein' a different side of him. He ain't like Pa. My pa weren't lazy.*

The men remained silent while they loaded the last kegs into the car. Then Archie, without saying a word, walked over to the empty dory and grabbed hold of the stern end. The others joined him and carried it back to the twin boulders, put it down where they found it, and, still without speaking, went back and got into the rum-loaded car.

Colie crawled to the back, found space on top of the kegs, squeezed in, wrapped his arms around himself, and scrunched down.

Archie pressed down on the aging clutch. The car lurched and jolted back up the hill. He shifted gears, and the car bounced forward. Then after a few desperate twists of the wheel, he managed to turn the car around. The kegs shifted, threatening the little space left to the men. He drove a short way up the lane, then stopped short, got out of the car, stood with his head tilted to one side, and listened for a moment or two.

"All right," he said, "this is where the fun begins. I thank God for the darkness but can't see a damn thing. Hope I ain't forgotten. Pick up a keg and follow me." He pushed his way through the tall, black-looking shrubbery.

The other men, puzzled, looked at each other. Then each shouldered a keg and followed Archie through the scratchy bushes. They ducked their heads as branches and pine needles stung their faces. The ground, covered with parts of dead branches, small pebbles and stones, bruised their bare feet.

"Stop!" said Archie, suddenly throwing out his arms to block their way.

"What the frig you doing, McNeil?" Hank bumped against him and almost lost his balance. "I almost dropped this keg on your thick head."

Archie pulled a flashlight from his pocket, flashed it downward, then got on his hands and knees and groped around the ground. He pushed aside the debris and pine needles until the beam of the flashlight revealed a good-sized, circular cover made of flat oak planks.

"Well, I'll be a monkey's uncle. If that don't beat all," said Hank.

Archie got his stubby hands under the edges of the

cover, lifted it, and then rolled it off into the underbrush. Hank looked down over Archie's shoulder. A dank, musty odor arose from the deep hole.

Archie straightened up.

"Plenty of room for the kegs and tomorrow's load, too, boys. Roll them down easylike, and then let's get the begeezes out of here. It don't feel right. I can feel the hair on the back of me neck risin'."

"What's the matter, Archie? You afraid of the bogeyman?" said Hank before he rolled his keg down the hole. It made a soft thud as it hit the bottom. "I have to say it is a grand hiding place, but I wouldn't want to have to crawl down there for the bottom kegs."

"It ain't yer lookout, is it? Yer sure a gabby one. No more talk."

Silent now, they carried the kegs from the car and rolled them one by one into the pit.

Colie brought the last keg from the car and rolled it easily down the side.

"Got to hand it to ya, Uncle Archie. This sure is a dandy hiding place. How'd yer find it? Where'd the hole come from? It looks like part of an old pit. Is it, Uncle Archie?"

Archie didn't answer as he rolled the heavy cover back in place. The men then got down and pushed branches, dirt, rocks, pebbles, and debris around and over the cover until it was hidden from the beam of Archie's flashlight.

"Go back to the car. Wait for me. I got to do something," Archie said.

"Suit yourself, McNeil," said Hank. "Don't take all night. I got a lady friend waiting for me back in town."

They fought their way back through the bushes. Put on their boots and then leaned up against the car. Time passed.

Colie shuffled nervously.

"Sure is black without the moon," he said. "Hard to see yer hand in front of yer face."

Hank took a cigarette from his shirt pocket and started to light up. Billy put a restraining hand on his arm.

"Wait up a bit for your smoke, mate. We don't want the light to be seen."

"Sure, you're right." Hank threw the unlit cigarette to the ground. Then, not wanting to waste a good cigarette, he bent down and picked it up.

Colie thought, *I could use a smoke meself right now. Wonder what's keepn' me uncle.*

"I don't mean to stick my nose in your business, Hank," Billy whispered, "but I ain't seen you around town before. How'd you get to link up with Archie?"

"That's all right. I don't mind your asking. I was visiting my sister, Sally MacGraw, a while back. She's a good friend to Archie's wife. Archie and Marion stopped one evening. You know how it is. We got to jawing. Archie had a few in him, and he asked me if I would be interested in helping him." Hank laughed softly. "What the hell. It sounded like a good deal. I ain't married. Got no family to speak of except my sister. So here I am. Didn't know then what a prick Archie could be."

"That's true enough. Unless Archie's had a drink, he can be downright sour." Billy chuckled, "As a matter of fact, he can be downright sour with the drink, depends on the mood he happens to be in. So Sally MacGraw's your sister, then?" Billy tugged at his chin. "Could she be Pete Mac-Graw's widow, by any chance? Pete was one of the men trapped in that explosion four years back. Took them a week to dig them out. A real sad time."

"That was him. A fine fellow he was, too. Not having a family of my own, I try to help my sister as best I can."

"Shhh, here's Archie now."

Archie emerged, pulling up his pants. Then he put his hands in his pocket, took out a thick stack of bills, and peeled off three. Two twenties and a ten. He gave the ten-dollar bill to Colie and handed Hank and Billy a twenty each.

"After we drop me nephew at the bluff," Archie said, "I'll treat yer both to a taste of that good rum at me place."

Billy palmed the twenty.

"Thanks, but I'll pass on the drink, Archie. Got to get home. Hey, what took you so long in the bushes? Thought you got lost in the dark. We were getting ready to go looking for you. What were you doing? Taking a leak?"

Archie scratched his head.

"Had to take a shit. Couldn't wait . . . must have the runs."

Colie smiled to himself. He thought, *Uncle Archie is scared of getting caught.* He fingered the ten-dollar bill in his pocket.

"What about me? Will yer be going out tomorra' night?" he said.

Archie was now feeling cheerful.

"Well, we'll see. I'll let yer know in plenty of time. Yer did all right, young fella. Now I better be getting' yer home to yer mama before she finds yer empty bed and thinks yer out bangin' yer girlie."

Colie felt heat rise up the back of his neck and to his face and knew he had to control the temper threatening to overcome his good sense.

He thought, *I'd like to punch him in the mouth, the dirty bastard. Cripes, he was out there in the bushes taking a shit for himself. Hope none got on the tenner he gave me. Well, even if he's a dirty-minded old goat . . . won't give him no lip . . . it still feels good to have a tenner in me pocket, dirty or not. Sure wasn't bad at all. Easy way to make a few dollars. Lots easier than the pit.*

"Let's get a move on." Archie climbed into the front seat, and Colie and the two men climbed into the back. Billy and Colie sat with their legs stretched out in front of them, while Hank sat in the space behind Archie with his knees drawn up and hands clasped on top of them.

"It feels good to have room for those long legs, eh, boy?" Billy said. He took off Colie's cap and rumpled his hair.

Colie reached for his cap and put it back on his head.

"Yer own legs long 'nough, Billy, . . . got some growin' to do before I catch up with yer."

Archie gunned the motor, and the car jolted forward. His nervous, high pitched, almost girlish giggle, filled the car.

"The hell with the Mounties. They can't touch us now. We're in the clear."

He turned on the headlights and drove up the narrow, rough lane until they came to the bluff road. Then he jammed on the brakes.

Colie and Billy braced their feet against the floor of the car to keep from sliding forward.

Archie turned to Colie.

"Out yer go. Straight home now. Yer did good tonight."

"Will yer be wantin' me tomorro' night? I'm willin', Uncle Archie."

"We'll see, we'll see. I'll be letting yer know. Just stay put tomorrow, in case I need yer."

Hank poked a sharp finger in Archie's back.

"Let me out here. I'll make my own way to town," he said and climbed out after Colie.

"Why do yer want to be like that?" Archie whined. "The offer still holds for that drink. Let's be sociable and have a friendly drink or two after a hard night's work. Billy here, now, we knows he has to get home to his woman, but yer ain't married. Yer lady friend won't mind yer havin' a drink with me. What yer say?"

"Thanks all the same, Archie. Maybe next time I'll take you up on that drink. Right now, I feel the need to stretch my legs a bit, and the walk will do me good."

Archie's tone changed.

"Sorry I asked. Nothing wrong with having a friendly drink or two, is there? We'll be partin' company tonight anyway—there won't be no next time. We seem to rub each other the wrong way, mate. Ye're got your money, now piss off!"

Colie and Hank stood and watched the car's taillights disappear as the car turned onto the bluff road and headed toward town.

"Nice to have met you, young fellow." Hank reached out in the darkness to shake Colie's hand. "Guess this is the last you'll see of me. It would seem that your uncle and I didn't hit it off. You take care now. Watch out for that uncle of yours. He's only looking out for himself. I wouldn't go out with him again if I were you. It will lead you into trouble, and you seem like a nice boy."

"Oh, Uncle Archie's not so bad when yer gets to know him. He's a big unstrung tonight." His voice trailed away in the night air when Hank didn't answer him, but stuck his hands deep into his pockets and strode away.

13

A mischievous, hide-and-seek moon poked out from behind slow-moving, dark clouds, and Hank walked briskly until he came to a fork in the road. He turned to the left and took the narrow, uphill footpath that led to Grovner's Beach.

He saw the Ford parked near the shore, half-hidden by scrub pines and boulders, as he neared the beach, and he broke into a run.

The moon shone down on the rippling water and outlined the figure of a tall, thin man who leaned casually against the car, with a cigarette dangling from the corner of his mouth. The man put a hand on his holstered revolver, then took it away as Hank came nearer.

"It's about time you showed up. I was getting real anxious. Well, what happened? How'd it go, eh?"

Hank, slightly out of breath, shook the outstretched hand.

"Good evening to you, Duncan."

"Come into the car. Want a smoke?" Officer Duncan said.

"God, yes!"

Duncan took a rumpled pack of cigarettes from his shirt pocket, took one cigarette out, lit it with the glowing tip of his own, and handed it to Hank. Hank took a deep drag.

"Well, I know where they're hiding the rum," he said. "McNeil didn't take to me this time, though. None of that palsy-walsy stuff like when I met him at my sister's. I'm sure I won't be asked to go on rum-row again, but, that's all right. After tonight, no rum will reach the miners of Rock-hill by way of McNeil and Big Dan."

"The miners are back at work, but it won't last long. They gained nothing from the last strike, and it galls them. Poor devils. We've got to keep the rum away from them, or all hell is bound to break out."

"Yes, yes, sure, I know all that, but out with it, man. What did you find out? Where are they hiding the kegs?"

Hank took another deep drag.

"McNeil is making another run tomorrow night. We can catch him red-handed. His young nephew was with him tonight—grand young fellow—and a man called Billy, an out-of-work miner, nice enough chap, too. Sorry for them, but if they're with him tomorrow, and I think they will be, they need the money, we won't have any choice but to haul them in, too. Wish there was some way I could warn them off without tipping McNeil and Big Dan. I hate to see that young man get into trouble."

Officer Duncan threw the cigarette to the floor of the car and stamped it out.

"Listen here, what's the matter with you? You getting soft? What the hell, you know that it's our job to keep the booze out of town. McNeil's been giving us the slip far too long. I'm damn sick of driving around night after night, not knowing where the hell they're going to land the stuff. They make fools of us."

"I've been trying to catch McNeil and Big Dan for a god's age. There're cagey bastards. No one knows who you are. That's why you were picked for the job. Remember that! Don't go giving the game away."

"Aw, keep your shirt on. Don't worry. I'm not apt to do that. Even my sister doesn't know what I do for a living. She gives me blue hell every once in a while. Thinks I'm a drifter and a bum."

"After tomorrow night, you can tell her. Once we get them, it won't matter. Big Dan and McNeil are the ones we're after. You'll be transferred to another area. So let's hear it. What went on tonight? Don't leave out any details." He started the motor, turned the car, and headed away from the beach. "That young fellow you're so worried about and the other man, if there're with McNeil tomorrow night, it will be the first offense, you know that. They'll get a warning, slap on the wrist, that's all.

"It's McNeil and Big Dan we're after. They've been laughing up their sleeves and giving us the runaround for too long. I want them."

Duncan and Hank MacKenzie pushed their way through thick underbrush and tree branches heavy with rain, which clawed at them and soaked them to the skin.

"You sure this is the place?" asked Duncan as he swatted the mosquitoes that buzzed around his head.

"Positive. Granted it was dark and hard to see last night, but this is where McNeil stopped the car and went into the thicket, and it didn't seem to be far in from the road." Hank got down on his knees and shone the flashlight beam toward the ground.

"You know, we're not going about this in the right way," Duncan said. "This is crazy. All we're doing is getting wet and bitten alive. We should be down at the beach giving them the surprise of their lives. What a hell of a jolt it would be for them if we caught them red-handed with the kegs when they came ashore."

"No. I don't' agree. We can't take the chance of them spotting us and dumping the kegs in the water. It's happened before."

"They won't see us. We'll hide behind the boulders. Scare the livin' shit out of them."

118

"Too risky, Duncan. Let's not take the chance. We've come this far, and I know the kegs are in here."

"It's your show, then. Do it your way. McNeil must be pleased as all hell. A night like this with heavy rain and no moon, just what he's looking for. If it wasn't for the rocks, the ship could land on the beach and not be seen."

Hank stood up.

"You're right . . . mm . . . let's go in a few feet more. Damn these bugs. Shouldn't have left my hat in the car." He wiped the water streaming down his face with the sleeve of his shirt, then directed the flashlight's beam downward as he plunged deeper into the brush, with Officer Duncan following close behind.

Duncan cursed softly.

"Damn it, come on. It's getting late. Find that damn pit before they show up."

"Keep your hair on. What do you think I'm doing?" Hank brushed his feet from side to side, then got down on his knees again. "Hot damn, here we are. Quick, give a hand, I think I found it." He pushed aside the branches, rocks, and ground litter, and a portion of the oak cover came into view.

"Holy smoke," exclaimed Duncan, "we got the buggers."

Together, they lifted the heavy cover and tossed it to the side. It rolled and crashed until it came to a stop alongside the trunk of a big pine.

Hank shone the flashlight down into the pit.

"Shit, oh shit! The cagey bastard." He was looking down into a black, empty pit.

"What, what's the matter?" Duncan looked over Hank's shoulder. He hunched down on his knees. "Son of a bitch. Can you beat that? The runty little shit. He's been tipped off."

119

"No. I don't think so. That's not it. Who could tip him off? No one knew except you and me. He got suspicious, that's all. Damn it to hell."

"Well, if McNeil's got his wind up," Duncan said, "not a chance he'd venture out tonight. Let's get out of here."

"I don't know about that. The captain of the rumrunner was pretty anxious to get rid of the rest of the rum. He's low on supplies, and I can't see McNeil passing on a night like this. After all, he's just going on a hunch, and I'll bet my last dollar it's me he's not sure of. Let's drive around, check out the coves and the gut. There's still a chance we can grab them if they're out there."

"Forget it. McNeil's worried. He won't go out two nights in a row. Doesn't make sense. I'm disappointed as hell. Thought we had him this time. When we do get him, he's going to be one sorry bastard."

They worked their way out of the brush and got into the car. Duncan started the motor, and they drove through heavy rain down the road until they came to the fork.

"Stop the car," Hank said. "I want to go back. I've a hunch the rum is in there somewhere. McNeil didn't have enough time to move it very far."

"What are you talking about? He's had all day to move the stuff. What's on your mind? You think there's another pit? Oh, well, what the hell. Why not give it another try. I'm soaked to the skin anyway."

Quickly, he backed the car, and they got out. Rain pelted them in the face, and the mosquitoes descended on them again. Hank grabbed his hat, and they plunged their way back into the brush.

Hank led the way, flashing the light to and fro. They soon passed the empty pit. Then the ground became softer, swampy, and their shoes sunk deeper into the wet spongy earth.

"We go much further, and we'll be swimming," said Duncan. "This is a fool's errand. Let's turn back."

"No, not yet. Wait a damn minute! What is that?"

Hank shone the flashlight beam to the right, and it came to rest on a low, weather-beaten, shack, which leaned so far to the left that it seemed in grave danger of sinking into the soft ground.

"I knew it," said Hank. "I felt it in my bones. We've hit pay dirt. Come on."

Keeping flashlight beams focused on the shack, they pushed ahead. The brush thinned a bit as they neared the shack. They came upon a door that hung on one hinge. Hank shone the light inside.

Duncan took out his gun, and they went in and looked around. The shack smelled damp, and gamy like an unwashed old man. It held a rusty sink with an aged pump, a cracked cup and plate, a couple of chairs, and a small, rotted table. The splintered boards squeaked under their feet as they moved about.

"Hell, nothing here. Just an old shanty some bum holed up in."

"Don't be too sure of that, Duncan." Hank stopped short, and beamed the light down to the floor. He bounced on the squeaking floor, then got down, grunting as he pulled on a loose board.

"You think the kegs are under the floor?"

Duncan chuckled but got down and helped him pull upon a couple of loose boards. Soon they were looking down into a wide tunnel that twisted to the right and curved downward.

"Will you look at that!"

"Shine your light down. I need more light."

"Sure, here." Duncan leaned over his shoulder with his flashlight. His breath came in short gasps. "I can't believe it! What luck. Who would have thought it? I bet that leads right to the pit."

"We'll find out soon enough." Hank, clutching the flashlight, got down on his knees and lowered himself into the wide shallow.

Duncan stood in the dark shack. A bat whirled around his head. He swung out at it, then shouted down to Hank.

"See anything yet? I'm coming in." He got down on his knees and started to crawl into the cave. Hank's excited, muffled voice reached up through the tunnel. "What? I can't make out what your saying, man. What you find? Are they in there?"

Hank, crawling on his hands and knees brushed up against Duncan.

"Back up. No need to go any further. We hit pay dirt. They are in here, every last one of them."

They climbed out and danced around the tiny shack, slapping each other on the back.

"Great scot," Hank said, "what a night!"

"Sure is. It sure is. We got him by the balls now. Makes you real happy, doesn't it?" Duncan punched him lightly on the shoulder, then shone the flashlight in his face.

Hank's long, lantern-jawed face, broke into a big-toothed grin. He took off his hat and scratched his thinning, blond hair.

"Didn't I tell you? Wasn't my hunch right? I don't mind telling you, I wasn't looking forward to having to suck up to that runty bastard so he'd take me out again. Now we got him."

"*You* got him, you mean. Good thing we followed your hunch. I hope to God they show tonight, but I'm not banking on it. It doesn't matter whether they do or not. We'll be here when they do show."

"Yup, it's a waiting game now," Hank said. "The rumrunner out there can't hang about too long; that's what I heard the captain tell McNeil. So if it isn't tonight, we'll get them tomorrow. "Let's go duck the car."

14

Marion, wearing a red dress, walked into the parlor and looked down at Archie, asleep in the big maroon armchair with his head thrown back and loud snores erupting from his open mouth.

On the floor beside him, an almost empty rum bottle lay on its side. She gave it a mighty kick. The bottle crashed against the wall, broke, and sent glass fragments flying about the room, leaving brown streaks that ran down the wall and ended in a small puddle on the floor.

Archie slept on.

Marion grabbed him by the shoulders and shook him until his head wobbled back and forth and spittle ran down the sides of his mouth.

"Wake up. Wake up or I'll smack you one, drunken fool!"

He opened red, bleary eyes and looked up at her big, square-jawed, angry face, then waved off her rough hands.

"What'n hell is the matter with yer, woman? Can't a man have a nap in his own home? What yer wake me fer?"

"Your home. Don't make me laugh. It's not your house and never was. Now we're to be thrown out like trash. Thanks to you and your big mouth. Or are you too drunk to remember a little thing like that? I'm surprised that they let us stay this long. If it weren't for my mother, we'd soon be on the street or forced to live in a tent, like some poor souls in town."

"Aw, shut your face," he said, ignoring her remarks as he leaned over the fat arm of the chair. "Where's me bottle?

Yer hide it on me? Yer needs puttin' in yer place, woman."

Marion pushed him back against the cushions.

"And do you suppose you're man enough to do it, you drunken pig! That bottle was full when you got into it. You was to watch the boys while I went over to Sally's. Tonight's our bridge game, as you well know. How can I leave them boys to a drunken sod like you?" She looked over her shoulder at Sammy and Kevin, who were peeking into the room from behind the kitchen door. "Get off with you both. Upstairs to bed now, or I'll take the stick to you."

The boys, giggling behind their grubby hands, scampered up the stairs, chanting, "Papa's drunk agin, Papa's drunk agin," then hushing each other, they sat on the top step to listen.

Marion brought her attention back to Archie.

"Colie came by today, looking for you. I told him, and now I'm telling you, for the last time, I don't want him going the run-row. He said you was to go on a run tonight?" She slapped Archie on the side of the head, and he put up his hands to shield his face. "You listening to me? Why didn't you? No, you'd rather sit about swilling down the rum. Big Dan won't put up with that. He'll be looking for a new partner. You wait and see. We ain't been putting by the money we should either. God knows, I haven't minded having to pull up stakes and go to my mother's in the country for a spell and leave the house after I got it fixed up nice, an all, because I thought we'd soon be leaving for Boston. At this rate, I'll be old and gray-headed before we gets there, if ever."

Archie sat up.

"You slap me again, woman, and I'll whop yer back. It's none of yer business what goes on between Big Dan and me. Yer take care of yer job, I'll take care of mine. Changed me mind 'bout goin' out tonight, that's all. And I ain't drunk, so go to yer lousy card party with yer bunch of cacklin' hens. Yer'd think 'twas high society the way yer carry on."

Marion drew herself up to her full height of six feet and looked down on him with scorn.

"You do begrudge me getting any pleasure at all. Don't you? They are fine ladies, and they likes me. Can't stand that, can you? I told you, you finished the bottle, and you'd better not drink no more if you know what's good for you, you hear me? I'm off the Sally's now."

She gestured toward the wall. "There's your a'cursed bottle, what's left of it. Get off your arse and clean up that mess. You ain't done nothing today but lay around swilling rum. I cooked your supper, so you clean up the kitchen. Then get upstairs and see to the boys."

She flounced out of the room. Archie glared at her broad, retreating back, and when he heard the front door slam, he hauled himself out of the chair and went into the kitchen. He glanced at the table, littered with dirty dishes from their evening meal, and at the spindley legged sink, overflowing with soiled dishes, pots, and pans.

"The lazy squaw," he muttered. "Must o' been out of me frigging mind to get tangled up with that one. Tricked me, she did. Got herself knocked up on purpose just so I had to marry her. Was either that or lose me scalp to her brother.

"My own dear, dead brothers. Jock, Kevin, Sammy. They tried to warn me. My cock was calling the tune in those days, with plenty of help from Marion. Big, strapping young girl, she was. Hot as a firecracker. I could make her jump then all right."

He sat down and swept aside the dishes. A plate, cup, and half-full bowl of sugar fell to the sticky, black-and-white blocked linoleum floor, and Archie put his head

126

down and let the crying jag overtake him.

He sobbed out loud, "Me brothers, they cared what happened to their baby brother . . . looked after me. Only ones who ever cared what happened to old Archie. No one left who cares. No one to have a drink with." He wiped his red, streaming nose.

Still crying and feeling sorry for himself, he continued. "Last night, and after I was nice enough to help those buggers out. Gave them a chance to make a few dollars. They wouldn't take a drink with me. Unfriendly as all get-out, and that long-jawed, bucktoothed drink of water, don't trust him. Something funny 'bout him. Broke me damn back movin' the rum under the shanty . . . then again, maybe I sized him up wrong . . . I was goosey as a bridegroom on his weddin' night. After all, he's Sally's brother. Still . . . something 'bout him didn't smell right to me.

"Should've got Colie to help move the kegs . . . Big Dan made me bust me balls stacking them in the tunnel. Got a grand tall stack of kegs. Must be over a hundred kegs down there. Big Dan and his crew'll come fer 'em 'morrow night. Good luck to 'em . . . got me money and a keg or two. I'll have young Colie and Billy with me next time I go on a run . . . take the speedboat . . . get there faster, though it's risky.

"Captain's gettin' itchy . . . don't blame him, stickin' 'round fer a week. He has . . . wants to unload and head back." He pulled a ragged piece of cloth from his shirt pocket and blew his nose, then, feeling better, still talked to himself.

"Marion don't know it, but she's in for a surprise . . . few more runs and I'll have enough. Could leave tomorrow if I wanted to. Not old Archie, though. There's good money still to be had rum-running, and it won't hurt to have a thick bankroll when we gets to Boston. No telling

127

what we'll find there.

"The big bitch. I'll show her. We'll leave this town in the dirt, we will. I don't relish the thought of living with her pipe-smoking hag of a mother. The old woman likes me though. Thinks her 'little' girl came up in the world, snaggin' a white man, when all's her old lady could get was a stinkin' Indian." Archie started to giggle. "Me woman's fault is she's stupid and can't see beyond that big nose a hers."

Archie lifted his head, wiped his eyes, and looked at Sammy and Kevin, who had crept close to him.

Ten-year-old Kevin looked at his father with worried, pansy-blue eyes.

"Ya all right, Pa?" he said, as he reached out to pat his father's bald head. "We heard ya cryin', Pa. Why ya cryin'? Don't feel bad, Pa. Ya don't have to feel bad. Me and Sammy are here. I'll play a tune for ya, Pa. Want me to play a tune?"

Archie hauled himself up. He reached out and hugged the boys to him.

"Me little pals. Yer do care 'bout yer old pa, don't yer? We're pals . . . don't yer ever forget it. Help me clean up the mess before the dirty, old bitch comes home and wipes the floor with all of us."

"Don't call me ma names," said six-year-old Sammy as he sailed into Archie, flaying out at him with both dirty, small fists.

Roughly, Archie pushed him away, then got up and slapped him hard in the face—the sound of the crack reverberated around the room. Sammy lost his balance, fell against the table, then to the floor, and started to cry.

Kevin went over and shut the window. He pulled Sammy to his feet.

"Shut up. Ya want Ma to hear ya? Well, whatcha' hit Pa for, then? Yer own fault yer got hit. Stop bawlin', yer not hurt bad."

128

Sammy put his hand up to his face, touching the sharply outlined red imprint of Archie's hand on his white, pinched face.

Archie reached for him and patted his head, then picked him up.

"Don't ever come at me like that again, pal. Yer just like yer ma, yer are . . . not 'fraid of yer pa a'tall. Yer knows yer can't go 'round hittin' yer own pa, now, don't yer? Ain't I right now? Don't yer think yer had it comin' ter ya?"

Sammy burrowed his face in the hollow at his father's throat, hiccuped and sobbed and couldn't answer.

Kevin looked at them and muttered under his breath, "friggin' brat." Then he picked up the broken dishes, carried them out into the littered yard, hid them in the clump of bushes behind the outhouse, then went back into the house.

"Brat," he glared at Sammy. "Just 'cause Pa hit ya, I s'pose yer won't have to help with the dishes, an' I'll have to listen to yer bawlin' all night, too—baby. Yer nuthin' but a little titty baby. Titty baby, titty baby, Sammy's a titty baby."

Sammy fought to get free of Archie's arms. *I ain't no titty baby! I ain't...I hates ya...I'll get ya...lemme go,*" he yelled.

Laughing, Archie released Sammy, who then pounced on Kevin. They rolled around the floor until Archie spoke up.

"All right, that's enough now. Stop teasing the little fellow. Leave him be." He pulled Sammy to his feet, patted his skinny bottom, and said, "Now you get upstairs to bed, pal." Then he turned and grabbed Kevin by the ear. "Come on. Yer always pickin' on the little fella. I should take the strap to yer . . . warm yer arse fer yer. Start stacking them dishes. I'll give yer a hand, an' we'll be done in jig time." He released Kevin's ear, went over to the sink, and started to pump water over the dishes.

Kevin, slit-eyed, jaw set, and head lowered silently picked a few dishes off the table and carried them to the sink. Archie turned and looked at him, and his jovial mood turned ugly.

"Wipe that look off yer face. I'm warning yer now ... want me to take the strap to yer?"

He walked over to the back door, took a thick, black belt off the hook, and smacked it against his palm.

Kevin turned pale and forced a smile.

"Now, that's better, eh?" Archie said. "No need to sulk." He hung the strap back on the door. "Go dig out the mouth organ, and we'll have us a tune. Liven things up 'round here. That's what we need. Go get the bottle yer mother hid on me. Don't tell yer ma, and I'll give yer a taste."

"Don't drink no more, Pa. We gotta do the dishes. Ma will be right mad if they ain't washed. Let's wash up the dishes, Pa. Then I'll get the mouth organ. I'll play whatever ya want, Pa, all yer favorite tunes, okay?"

"T'hell with the dishes." He gave Kevin a hard push and sent him sprawling. "I ain't washin' no dishes, and neither is yer. That's women's work, boy. Get goin'. Get bottle, and we'll have us a time."

The four women sat around Sally McGraw's white linen-draped kitchen table. A flowered cozy covered the teapot at Sally's elbow, and at each end of the table, mounds of molasses and sugar cookies were piled regally on bone china plates.

Sally, plump and round-faced, glanced at the ceiling and rolled her eyes.

"Well, Marion," she said, "for goodness sakes, do something. We're waiting for you. Minnie bid two diamonds. I opened with a spade, and Doris passed. What are you going to say?"

Marion, her bulk in the red dress overflowing the narrow, straight-backed chair, put down her teacup, pursed her lips, and squinted at her cards.

"Mmm . . . pass. I pass." Then, she picked up a cookie and took a dainty bite before picking up her teacup again.

"Really, Marion! We've got a game on, you know. Can't you bid something? You sure you counted your points?"

Marion slapped her cards on the table and lifted her chin.

"Well, it's sorry I am that I've been dealt such poor cards all evening. Oh, let me look again. Let's see. I'll say two spades then. Does that suit you?"

"For heaven's sake, don't bid a suit unless you have the cards. It sure would suit me fine if you'd pay attention to the game, Marion. What's the matter with you tonight? You're not with it at all?"

Marion picked up her napkin and began to fan herself.

"I don't know, Sally. I guess it's the heat. I've been cleaning out closets and packing. We have to be out of the house in a week, you know, and Archie is no help at all. The heat do bother me . . . carrying all this blubber don't help much either," she laughed and smacked the side of her thigh. The heat makes me sluggish. I can't think straight."

"Well, for heaven's sake, why didn't you say so before this. You don't need to sit there and suffer, for pity's sake."

Sally jumped up and threw open the window, and a soft humid breeze ruffled the curtains before making its way across the stuffy room.

"Ah, that's better," sighed Marion. Through the open window drifted the sound of music. She cocked an ear and said. "You hear that, ladies? That's me Kevin playing. He got a real ear for music. Picked it up all by himself when he got a mouth organ couple of Christmases ago. Don't he sound grand, though?"

131

Minnie sniffed.

"Hi time a youngster his age was in bed and fast asleep."

Marion reached over and nudged her shoulder.

"Aw, what's the harm. School's out. The boy can sleep as late as he wants. Besides, Kevin's a big fellow now—ten years old last week."

"He does play well." Doris said. "We are all going to miss you, Marion, but the countryside is lovely this time of year, and the boys will like running about in the fresh air."

"Really, girls, can we please get back to our game," said Minnie.

"Aw, keep your shirt on," said Marion, nudging her again. "I'll have a drop more tea, Sally, if you please."

Sally leaned over to pour the tea into Marion's cup.

"What' in the world is that?" she said.

From the direction of Marion's house came sounds of glass breaking, yells and thumps, and the tea overflowed the cup, staining the snowy tablecloth.

The women jumped when Kevin pounded on the front door.

"Ma, ma, come quick. Pa's drunk. He's hittin' Sammy!" he was shrieking.

Sally rushed through the parlor to the small hall and flung open the door, with the other women crowding behind her.

Kevin stepped into the hall. Blood poured from his bloody nose and split lip onto the braided scatter rug.

"Dear God in heaven, what has that terrible man done now," whispered Doris to Minnie.

Marion pushed past them, and Kevin threw himself at her and buried his face into her skirt. Marion gripped him by the shoulders and pushed him away.

"Come on, now, you're not bad hurt. Tell me what

happened," she said.

"It's awful, Ma. Pa's crazy drunk. Sammy came downstairs when I was playin'. Pa told him to git back upstairs to bed, and Sammy said he had to go to the outhouse. Pa wouldn't let him, so Sammy messed himself, Ma. He couldn't help it. Pa wouldn't let him go to the outhouse. Then Pa got real mad and shook Sammy like a rat. I tried to stop him, and he hit me—"

Marion stroked his head.

"It's all right, boy. I'll take care of your father. Likes hitting little boys, does he! Come along."

She took him by the hand and pulled him the few feet of dark backyard to their house.

Sally started after them, then had second thoughts, having been involved in some of the McNeil's past squabbles, and decided not to get involved in this one unless she had to.

"Call if you need help, Marion," she yelled.

"Won't be needin' no help with the runt," Marion answered. "Go back to the house, ladies. I'll take care a him. He must a found the bottle, the last one he'll ever get into, you can count on that!"

The dirty brute, hitting little boys, Sally thought. *I hope Marion beats the livin' daylights out of him*. She stood watching the McNeil house for a moment, then sighed and walked back to her own house.

Minnie and Doris stood, huddled together, shadowy figures in the doorway.

"Go back inside," Sally said. "I'll shut the windows. Let them handle their own affairs. Let's have a cup of tea. We won't let it ruin our evening, girls. Guess that's the end of our bridge game. I'll get out the cribbage board."

They went in and sat down at the table. Sally sighed deeply as she poured the tea.

133

"What a shame. Marion was learning to play quite well; that is, when she kept her mind on the cards. I'll ask Elsie Murphy if she'd like to play next week, and Alice Adams said she'd be interested in learning to play bridge."

"Oh, my," Doris said, "I hope there won't be another fight over there tonight. It frightens me when I hear them going at each other."

Sally laughed.

"Don't worry. Archie's deathly afraid of Marion. She's got the upper hand. Besides, he's only good for beating up on his boys."

Minnie sniffed, and the cords in her skinny neck stood out as she tossed her gray head in the air.

"Well, Sally," she said, "though I don't like to say I told you so, but . . . really, you should never have become friendly with the likes of Marion McNeil in the first place. She's common as dirt. I for one am looking forward to the day they're packed up and out of here."

Sally glared at her from across the table until Minnie lowered her eyes and spoke, her voice, dangerously low.

"Minnie Ferguson, you listen good, now. I'm warning you. Don't dare say another word against Marion. She may not be as educated as you, and she may not have the best of manners, but she's a good, kind-hearted soul and a wonderful friend and neighbor. She stood by me when I lost my Pete. I won't listen to another word said against her."

Minnie tossed her head and glanced quickly at Doris.

"Well," she said, "I always say, you can't make a silk purse out of a sow's ear. Isn't that right, Doris?"

"Oh, Minnie, stop putting on airs," said Sally as she poured the tea.

15

Eleven P.M., the rain came down in steady torrents as Big Dan's touring car slid to a stop in front of Maggie's front door. His nickname fit him well, for big Dan McNamara was indeed massive, in height and width, and the sight of him often sent small children scurrying for their mother's skirt.

As a young man in Ireland, he had been a boxer and wrestler, and his nose so flattened that it was hardly recognizable as a human nose. Both ears were cauliflowered, and while the top of his head was quite bald, salt-and-pepper gray hair grew in soft, babylike ringlets around the sides of an enormous head that was supported by a short, bull-like neck.

Big Dan fancied himself a ladies' man. Slyly, he turned to Archie.

"Archie, me bucko," he said, "I hear tell yer sister-in-law's a real looker. She's a widow lady, ain't she? Like to meet up with the piece. What say you to that?"

Archie, slumped dejectedly in the seat beside Big Dan, aroused himself.

"What? Huh? No, sirree. Maggie ain't yer type . . . leave her be. She's a real lady and death against the drink. A spit-fire . . . don't hold with no bootleggers. She'd be apt to bounce a flat iron off yer head. Besides . . . , she ain't here. Gone to see her brother. He's got a farm in the valley. Maggie's a stuck-up bitch, but she comes from good stock."

Big Dan reached over and smacked Archie on the top of the head.

"Yer brainless shit. I wasn't plannin' on meetin' up with

the piece tonight . . . ya silly bugger. We got work to do . . . heh . . . but I know how to tame a spitfire," laughed Big Dan in a booming voice. Yer got quite a woman yourself, bucko. Yer wouldn't call Marion no spitfire . . . a wildcat, she is. What you do to get her riled up like that? Got the worst of it, didn't yer?" He pushed Archie against the door. "Aw, go on. Get the boy. We ain't got all night. I want to move the kegs to the cave and get squared away for the next haul.

"The boat's comin' in with the rum. The MacPherson boys wanted to make a wee bit of change. They's runnin' the speedboat tonight. Make quick work of it, they will. No more foolin' about with the dory. I'm runnin' a business here, so we gotta be businesslike. There's a demand for me product, right, me bucko?"

Archie, sunk in gloom, didn't answer.

Big Dan punched him on the arm.

"Aw, snap out of it. Get a move on. Whatcha waitin' for? Shamed, ain't ya? 'Cause yer don't know how to handle ya old lady. Forget it. No one about on a night like this to see the beatin' yer woman give to yer. Bet to God ya deserved it too, ya little weasel. Yer can't hold yer liquor. That's what's the trouble with yer, and yer been drinkin' too damn much. I don't need a rummy fer a partner, so wise up, bucko."

Archie, cold sober, cringed further down the seat.

Big Dan continued. "We'll store tonight's haul in the cave. I got me some big orders from Lanchester, Frenchville, Coaltown, Halifax, even comin' to get 'em in a truck, mind ya. They know Big Dan can deliver the goods.

"I want to get the kegs outta the tunnel. Don't like to leave them there. Mounties might come snoopin' 'round the shack."

Archie sat up as Maggie's front door opened and Colie, hardly distinguishable in dark pants and shirt, ducked his head, put on his cap and hurried down the walk through the pelting rain. He greeted them, then climbed into the back of the car, and sat down on the floor.

Big Dan turned and extended a beefy hand.

"Dan here. Please to meetcha, sonny."

Colie shook his hand.

"Likewise, Big Dan. Sure glad to meet up with ya." Then he stretched out his legs and leaned against the back of Archie's seat. "We be sure in luck, Uncle Archie. The weather's with us. Don't have to worry about no moon tonight, not with this rain. Be easy goin', don't ya think?"

Big Dan answered for Archie.

"Well, now yer never can count on nothin' in this business. We gets in and we gets out, quick like. That's how the game's played, sonny."

"Heard a lot about yer from your Uncle Archie, here." He gave Archie a nudge, then said, "Heard yer sweet on me old friend Nora James's crippled gal. Nora's been one of me best customers fer many a year, she has to be, sure . . . likes her gin, that old biddy. Delivered a case to her just yesterday. Can't see what yer see in her skinny gal, though." Again he nudged Archie. "Nothin' to that piece but skin and bone, but then, they do say, the nearer the bone, the sweeter the meat, heh? Bet yer'll fatten her up, won't yer, sonny. Got a bun in the oven yet?"

Colie took a deep breath, folded his arms and forced a laugh.

"If ya knows the granny, then ya knows she keeps good tabs on her granddaughter. Frances is me girl, all right, but I ain't got nowhere with her. She's a good girl, and I don't like nobody talkin' against her."

Big Dan laughed.

"Just tryin' to have a little fun, sonny. Don't take it in the neck. Let's be off now. We got work to do."

He put out the car's headlights, and no one spoke as heavy rain pounded against the windshield and the car inched along the night-black road.

A dark hulled, twenty-foot motorboat, hovered offshore, waiting. Two husky young men, miserable in the steady downpour, sat in the rum-laden boat. One at the stern, and the other at the tiller.

Jim MacPherson stood up and cupped a hand to his ear.

"Someone's coming . . . hope it's Big Dan and not Mounties."

Big Dan's car bounced along the path, then onto the rock strewn beach.

"It is them. Let's go."

The motor sputtered to life, and the boat raced ashore. The bottom scraped along the rocks. The men jumped out and started to pull the boat close to the beach.

Harry, youngest of the MacPherson brothers, tripped, fell, and was almost hit by Big Dan's car as he staggered up the beach.

Jim grabbed him and pulled him to his feet.

"Jumpin' blue balls, yer a clumsy bastard. I almost hit yer," hissed Big Dan.

Colie extended a hand.

"Glad to meet ya. Colie McNeil, here."

"None of that crap, sonny," said Big Dan. "No one gives a shit what yer name is. Now, begorra, start loadin' the car. You, too, bucko. Get movin', we got no time to lose."

"Yes, sir, Big Dan. You're the boss," said the brothers, as they saluted in unison.

Big Dan sat in the car and barked orders. The men worked swiftly in the downpour. The car was loaded and Big Dan, dry and comfortable in the driver's seat.

"Okay, me buckos," he said, "that's it, then. Harry, you,

Jim, yer take the boat back to the gut. I'll settle up with yer tomorra—*What the hell is that?"*

A blinding, bright light coming from the direction of the lane shone down on them and outlined them against the darkness.

Spellbound, Harry and Jim MacPherson threw up their hands to shield their eyes. Archie and Colie stood, frozen in place, in front of the two boulders and out of the spotlight's harsh beam.

Colie's heart fluttered in his chest, then seemed to stop beating.

"Oh, me God, Uncle Archie," he whispered, "it's the Mounties." Then he ducked quickly behind the boulders and pulled Archie with him. Archie whimpered and started to tremble. Colie put his hand across Archie's mouth.

"Shhh, shut up . . . come on."

Then, crawling flat on their bellies, they wriggled snakelike to a clump of scrub pines a few feet away. Hearts thumping in their chests and not daring to breath, they paused, listened for a moment, then jumped up and raced from the scrub pines to the marshy woods a few yards away. Panic-stricken, their feet sunk in the mucky underbrush as they struggled to reach the shelter of the denser woods.

"Halt! Don't move—any of you!" Officer Duncan called out.

They kept running.

Spotlight still trained on the Big Dan's car, the Mounties drove quickly onto the beach. Big Dan reached a hand beneath the seat cushion and groped around until his fingers grasped the hidden gun. He whispered to himself, "No, begorra, yer ain't takin' Big Dan to no stinkin' jail."

Back in Ireland, he had killed a man in a grossly mismatched fight and had served four hard years in an Irish prison before escaping. Later, he stood at his mother's grave, before he hid on a freighter bound for Canada, and vowed that never again would he be a prisoner.

Revolver in one hand and flashlight in the other, Duncan and his partner jumped out and approached the car.

"Stay where you are," Duncan said. "Don't move. You're done for, McNamara."

Big Dan hid the gun in his lap and uttered an oath while smoothing the .38 Colt's gun barrel, then, decision made, raised it until it pointed upward toward the open window.

Jim MacPherson, spread-eagled against the car, eyes round with fright, glanced at Big Dan, saw the gun, and yelled.

"Don't be crazy, man!"

With lightening speed, he reached into the car and knocked the gun from Big Dan's hand to the floor of the car.

"I'll be remembering this, yer can be sure of that, punk."

Officer Ward kept his revolver trained on the brothers.

"Steady now," Duncan said, "I don't want you youngsters to get hurt. Don't do anything foolish."

Then he leaned through the window and stuck the revolver snug against Big Dan's florid cheek.

"Fun's over. Pick up the gun slow and careful. Don't give me a reason to put a hole in your ugly face." He pressed harder.

Big Dan squinted against the bright light.

"Aw, now, me Bucko, yer can take the light away. It's damn near putting me eyes out. What's the harm in it? I'm just tryin' to make a livin', that's all. What say yer and me strike a bargain, eh, bucko? What be the harm in that? Somethin' in it fer all of us, eh?"

"Shut up. I'll make no bargains with you. Get the gun,

140

my finger's getting nervous."

Big Dan grunted and reached for the gun, then—decision made—put his finger in the trigger hole and came up shooting.

Officer Duncan took the blast in the chest, and in the same split second, pulled the trigger and blew away Big Dan's face and half of his skull before he slumped against the car, then fell in a heap at Jim MacPherson's feet.

Big Dan's bloody head fell forward, bumped against the steering wheel, and pressed on the car's horn, sending a steady, shrill signal out into the night.

Jim MacPherson, still spread-eagled against the car, almost numb with shock, turned, looked at what was left of Big Dan's head, then staggered away, clutching his stomach, and vomited.

At the sound of gunshots, Archie stopped his mad plunge through the wet, murky wood and stumbled against Colie. He braced himself.

"Ya hear that?" he said.

The car's horn, nonstop, sounded eerily through the thump of heavy rain. Colie's breath came in short, raspy gasps. He pushed Archie ahead of him.

"Keep goin', old bugger. Just keep goin', or I'll leave ya here."

Archie, slumped against a tree.

"Go on, then, leave me. Me legs givin' out. Can't go no further. What I ever do to deserve this, I ask yer? Was just trying to make it right for me family. Planned to take them to the States, to Boston, just to please the big bitch. This is what I gets fer me efforts. Sorry day it was for me when Big Dan came to me door. It's his fault I'm in this mess. Naw, yer go on, boy. I can't make it."

Colie grabbed the front of Archie's soaked shirt and

lifted him. Archie's feet dangled off the ground as Colie held him up close, while tears of frustrated rage ran and mingled with the rain against his drawn face.

"Shut up. Just shut up. Ya always ready to blame someone else for ya troubles. Ya knows damn well I ain't goin' ta leave ya here, much as I'd like. Stop ya whinin', for God's sake. Be a man." He released Archie and said, "Mounties didn't see us. Don't know we was even there, but I ain't never been so scared in all me life, and I ain't blamin' no one but meself. It's me own fault. I should have listened to Malcolm. I hope the shots don't mean someone got killed, 'less it was that big bastard himself."

The car's horn stopped abruptly, and now all they could hear was the drumming rain and the crashing surf. Colie wrapped his arms about himself and tried to stop his trembling. Then he straightened up and pushed a stumbling Archie ahead of him.

"Get movin', or I'll kick ya lazy arse," he said.

"Sure, and have a little respect, boy," Archie whimpered. That's no way to talk to yer dear father's brother. I'll do what yer say, Colie. Yer me own dear Jock's boy. Yer a smart one. Yer'll get us out of this, won't yer? Did I tell ya there's a shack nearbouts? I knows where we are. I knows these woods like the back of me hand, boy. Should be just a short piece ahead. We can hide there. I can't go no further, I'm telling yer, that—"

The rain let up some, and a sliver of moon appeared from behind the scattered cluster of clouds. Colie looked up.

"Cripes," he said, "we gotta get in somewheres, quick." He grabbed Archie by the shirt again. "Who knows 'bout this shack, besides ya? Think it's safe to hole up there 'til mornin'? Tell the truth now, or I'll leave ya to rot here."

"God's truth, Colie, no one knows but meself and Big Dan. We hide the kegs in a sort of tunnel there under the

142

shack. It leads to the pit."

"Ya old bugger. I wondered how ya got at the kegs we buried. God, I wish I knew what the shootin' was about. Maybe we best keep going. We're bound to come out of the woods somewheres near the bluff."

"Sure, we will, boy, and the Mounties will be there, waiting. I'm telling you, the shack's up ahead a piece. Now, let's get to it. Big Dan ain't likely to be shooting off his mouth about no shack where he has all his bootleg rum."

"Ya shut up. Ya not tellin' me a damn thing," said Colie, releasing his hold on Archie's shirt. "Damn it to hell!" he pushed Archie, "Go on then, find the shack. Ya better be right, or I'll throw ya down the bloody pit and let the rats have ya."

They stumbled ahead. The rain stopped, and the sliver of moon became a half-moon.

They quickened their pace, and Colie thought of Maggie and his baby sister. What would happen to them if he were caught? Would he be sent to prison? How could he have been so dim-witted as to think he could make easy money? A rotten ten bucks, that's all he got, and now, here he was, running for his life. His mother's life, too, for he had no doubt what it would do to her if he were caught and sent to prison. He knew his mother. She would die of heartbreak and the shame of it all.

He had to get out of this, and when he did, it was back to the mine for him, no matter what she said. "Please, God," he prayed, "I ain't much, and I got a nerve asking for ya help now, but help me just this one time, and I promise never will I complain 'bout me lot again. I'd give anything right now if that's all I had ta face was goin' down the pit. I knows it's just a mater of time before the company puts us out of the house unless I go back to work in the mine. Help me, Lord, and I'll never do nuthin' dishonest again if ya just gives me another chance."

Archie pointed.

"Right ahead of us, there. Didn't I tell yer?"

Colie could see the dim outline of a small building, and he took a deep breath before he added another prayer. "Lord, there's 'nother thing I been feelin' bad 'bout...I knows it's a sin sleepin' with Frannie. She's never been with a fella' before me. I made her do wrong. I shouda left her alone. She's a good girl. I promise I won't sleep with her no more if you just get me outta this trouble, Lord."

The woods thinned out, and their feet sunk deeper into the mucky earth. Night gulls called out to one another, and their crazy trills and cackles only added to the night's terror as they reached the shack.

The door hung open, and Colie pushed Archie into the blackness. He stumbled up against the table, then found a chair and collapsed into it. Archie swallowed thirstily, then licked his lips and thought of the kegs of rum in the tunnel, and his mouth began to water.

"Colie, boy," he whispered, "what we need right now is a drink of rum to bolster us, and there's plenty to be had right beneath us."

Colie struck a match and looked around the shack. He found the other chair, sat down, then reached over and punched Archie on the shoulder.

"Ya rotten hypercrite. That's all ya can think of, get-tin' a drink? For all we know one of them brothers got shot, and all ya think 'bout is a drink? That's it, then, I don't give a shit what happens to ya. Hope I never have ta lay eyes on ya again. I'll find me way home." He jumped up and ran out into the night.

Archie tried to follow.

"Aw, boy," he whined, "don't leave me here. How'll I find me way? I don't see so good in the dark no more.

Come back. I was only foolin' 'bout the drink."

He peered out into the darkness but could only hear Colie's footsteps crunch against the sodden undergrowth.

Archie thought, *the bloody hell with you then. I don't need yer, shithead...don't need no one...go on then, shithead. Me own flesh and blood...turned against me. I can't see a damn thing in here.* He struck a match and looked around, then thought, *Aw, Colie's got his dander up. He won't let his old uncle down. Colie's soft hearted. I remember the time I took him deer hunting, and he cried like a baby when I shot that doe.* The match went out, and he struck another one.

His thoughts went back to the rum kegs beneath his feet, and he went to the sink, picked up a cracked cup and put it in his pocket, then he got down on his hands and knees and pulled on the floor boards. He tipped over backwards when he came loose in his hands.

Giggling hysterically, he pulled on the other boards, then threw them aside and crawled into the shallow tunnel. He struck another match, then let out a surprised yell as a large, gray rat started to gnaw at his ankle, then crept up his pant leg.

Archie screamed and tumbled all the way down until he bounced against the high-stacked kegs. They toppled over and buried him. The frightened rat ran up the tunnel and out the open door.

Archie lay sprawled under the kegs. Blood poured from his mouth. For several minutes he struggled to free himself from under the kegs. Then he cried out, *"Marion!"* and was still.

Colie stopped, started to turn back, then thought, *Naw, must have been a wild-cat I heard. He's all right. The old goat'll fall asleep and make his way out in the morning. I gotta get away from here...gotta get home.*

16

Officer Hank MacKenzie, dressed in the uniform of the Royal Canadian Mounted Police, parked in front of Archie's house. He thought of going across to his sister Sally, to have her with him when he told Marion.

No, that wouldn't work. Then he'd have two women in shock on his hands. Sally still didn't know he was a Mountie. She'd know after tonight. He pounded his fist against the steering wheel. Could it have been just five hours ago? First to reach the bloody scene on the beach, he cursed his job and his supervisors, their fault, all their fault, the dumb paper pushers.

Hank, an undercover man, had no say in what happened once he blew the whistle on the lawbreakers. And it had grated him. He should have been with Officer Duncan and his partner during the confrontation on the beach. He hid behind a clump of pines in the lane when they attempted to make the arrests.

He thought, *Duncan got careless, too anxious. He'd chased Big Dan and his flunkies for months, and it galled him when Big Dan gave him the slip. Never have happened had I been there. I knew how slippery Big Dan was...too late now.*

Duncan's gone, Big Dan's soul's dancing with the devil, the youngster's in jail, poor lads. That's another thing. They'd gotten clear—first offence—they'd got off with a warning, but the shooting changed all that. Least one good thing came out this black night; young Colie wasn't in on it. Glad I am he's not involved. Must of taken my advice to stay away from run-running and his uncle. Well, get moving...face up to it. Got to tell Marion. Tell her they found

Archie, dead, crushed beneath the kegs, his neck...broken.

I'm asking for a transfer. Can't stand this dirty work. I'll quit if I'm not assigned to another department. I'm tired of uncover work, sick to death of it.

Marion's apt to take a swing at me when she sees this uniform. He unfolded his lanky frame from the front seat and walked to the door.

Marion, flushed and harried, sat on the edge of her bed, dressed in her red dress. She thought, *Here I am, all dolled up, wearing my good dress, ready to give Archie a good time, and the little runt don't come home.*

Always complaining, he is. Says he don't get any. Thought I'd make him happy. Give him a piece...the last time in this house...be the last time ever. Why should I put out for him? He don't appreciate me a'tall.

The room was in wild disorder, with clothes strewn about, half-packed boxes and overflowing paper bags, and blankets and pillows piled high, ready to topple, in a corner of the small attic room.

She bent down and picked up the clock that lay on the floor beside the bed. Three A.M., and Archie still not home. She couldn't decide whether to be angry or worried.

She was thankful that the boys weren't underfoot but settled in happily with her mother and uncle George on the farm.

Maggie had been helping her all week until yesterday, and although she was pleased Maggie was trying to mend the rift that existed between herself and her brother, Marion missed her.

Maggie was brisk and organized. The down stairs swept, cupboards cleaned out, floors scrubbed and polished, and neatly packed cartons and boxes were stacked in the parlor along with the beloved maroon parlor set, soon

147

to decorate her mother's house.

When Marion had protested all the scrubbing and cleaning, Maggie said, "Now, Marion, you know how people talk in this town. You don't want them saying you left a dirty house, do you?"

Of course, Maggie was right. Maggie and Sally were her only friends. Marion was convinced the rest of the women had it in for her because she was a half-breed, though she never did them any harm.

She got up and pulled the red dress over her head and laid it across the foot of the bed. She put on a pink cotton nightgown that reached to her wide, bronzed knees, and then stood in the center of the room with her hands on her hips.

Where is the useless runt? she thought. *George'll be here early, said to be all packed and ready to leave. George hates to dillydally, and there's still lots to be done. Take at least two trips to empty the place.*

Marion's broad face wrinkled up, and her eyes started to fill. She thought, *lived in this house all me married life...boys birthed right in this bed.* Then she shook herself. *Ah, what the hell, what am I getting sentimental for? Never was our house. The company's welcome to have it, and all spruced up at that.*

Wish Archie'd get his old arse home. One day left, that's all. Got to get out of here before the bullyboys show up right ready to throw us out on the street along with everything we own. No sense sitting here like an owl. He'll be here when he gets here. I'm tired.

She stretched out on the bed, dozed off for a minute or two, then was startled awake when she thought she heard Archie call her name.

She leapt off the bed and said, "Thanks be to God. The little runt's home." She smoothed down her hair, adjusted her nightgown and hurried down the stairs.

Puzzled, Marion looked around when she reached the

last step. She went into the empty kitchen. Irritated, she said, "Aw, come on, none of your silly tricks. I suppose you're drunk. Where' the hell you hiding? I'm tired and in no mood for games. Get upstairs to bed. George is coming early, and he'll throw your carcass down the stairs if you're not up and about." She started up the stairs.

Officer MacKenzie took off his hat, paused, took a deep breath, then knocked on the door.

Marion looked over her shoulder and yelled out.

"Damn you, Archie. You're looking for another beating, and I'm telling you that's what you're about to get!" She thumped back down the stairs, flung open the door, and stood with fists ready.

Surprised, she took a step backwards, stumbled and fell against a carton.

Hank reached to help her.

"Sorry to disturb you this time of night, Marion, but I've some bad news."

"Hank MacKenzie! What in the hell you doin' here, and in that get-up? I thought you was Archie?"

"Sit down, Marion, please. I know you don't know what to make of me, and I'm sorry I had to deceive you and my sister. This isn't a get-up. I'm a Mountie . . . been on the force a couple of years, working undercover."

Marion felt her heart squeeze tight, and she moved close to him, closed her eyes, and pounded him on the chest.

"So that's it, eh? You're nuthin' but a spy, a sneak, and a liar. I've met the likes of you before, but not in a Mountie outfit. Where's me Archie? What you do with him? You got him in jail?"

"No, Marion, I wish he were in jail. I never wished a thing like this on him, and I surely hate to be the one to tell you. Archie's . . . Archie's dead."

Marion sucked in her breath.

"No. You're lying, man. Me Archie's sleeping off a drunk some-wheres. I know him."

She tried to push him out the door. He grabbed hold of her hands, and they struggled until the fight left her and she collapsed against him."

"What happened to him? How'd he die? Tell me, damn you," she cried.

"His neck was broken. I don't want to go into details right now. I'm going across for Sally. She'll know what to do. She'll help you, Marion." His arm around her waist, he guided her to a chair.

Marion cried.

"We was going to start fresh, in Boston, soon. I got kinfolk in Boston. You didn't know that, did you? The half-breed's got folks in the States. Nice people, they was going to help us get settled.

"Archie, he wasn't much, and the drink made him ugly, but he was all I had. He's me husband, you know, and him a white man, he married me . . . a half-breed. Went against his own mother and brothers. We had our fights, but I loved him, and he cared 'bout me."

"Yes, he did, Marion. No doubt about that. Now, I'm going across for Sally. You sit here. I'll be right back with Sally." He patted her broad back awkwardly, then hurried out the door, grateful to get away from her raw heartbreak.

Hank went around to his sister's back door, tried it and found it unlocked and went in inside.

Sally, since her husband's death, couldn't bear to sleep in the double bed in the attic room she had shared with her husband, and now slept on an arrow cot in a back room off the kitchen.

Hank, feeling a little foolish, as if he didn't have a right to the uniform he wore, stood in the doorway of the room and whispered.

"Sally, you awake, Sally? Wake up, Sally."

She didn't stir.

He went over to the cot and shook her gently by the shoulder.

She opened her eyes, gasped, then sat up in bed, and, pushing aside the thin blanket, she swung her nightgown-covered legs to the side.

"Hank, what in the world you doing here this time of night and dressed like that?" She put a hand to her mouth, "You've gone off your head!"

"No, I'm not off my head. I'm a Mountie, Sally. I can't stop to explain it to you now. Get over to the McNeils. Marion needs you. Archie's dead."

17

Colie dashed through the woods like a small boy terrorized by dark things in the night. His one thought—home—his room, the safety of his bed, and away from the sounds of gunfire, still ringing in his ears.

Once more, sheets of rain poured down. Colie pushed against thorny branches that reached out and clung to his clothes, holding him back, keeping him prisoner in the hated woods.

Panic stricken, he fought them, and, somehow, the night passed; dawn broke through and turned the sky a sickly gray. The woods thinned into scraggly underbrush, then a clearing that led to a graveled road.

Colie's panic ebbed. No longer lost, he followed the road to the long-abandoned Duchess pit. A mile to Colliery Road, MacDonald's hill, the bluff and home.

Wet and exhausted, Colie walked in back of the row houses until he reached his own. He fumbled with the latched door, then lost patience and kicked it until it flew open. He went inside, closed the door and climbed the stairs to his room. He undressed in the darkness, threw his clothes on the floor, and fell into bed. But sleep eluded him.

He thought, *Maybe I should've taken Uncle Archie...I wanted to punch out his lights; he made me see red...Ah, he's all right. He'd never made it out of the woods. I'd still be there, wallowin' in the muck.*

Good thing Ma ain't home, though I hate to see her kowtow to her brother. I know what she's up to. She's hopin' he'll want to take us in, live with him on the farm.

152

152

Wish Ma wouldn't suck up to him, nervy bastard, all ready to haul me mother back to his place after Catherine's...he could've help Ma after Pa died. Where was the bugger then? I got no use for him, so she better forget it. Anyway, I'm headin' back to the pit with Malcolm... Colie drifted off.

No, Sammy, stop it. Let go of me, Jenny Gleason screamed out.

"I'll fix ya," said Sammy, *"hold out on me, will ya."* He knocked her to the floor and dragged her across the room by her braids.

Jenny's nightgown twisted around her heavy, white legs, and she grabbed onto a table leg and knocked the heavy, cut-glass vase, inherited from her mother, to the floor.

Sammy aimed a kick at her head, but she rolled away from him, got to her feet, grabbed the vase, and held it high over her head.

"Get away from me. Get away."

"Fat cow, I'll kill you!" He grabbed at her.

"No, you won't, not this time," she screamed and brought the vase down on his skull.

Sammy staggered, reached for her again, then crumpled in a heap at her bare feet.

Dazed, trembling, vase still in her hand, Jennie looked down, expecting him to get up and hit her again—he didn't move.

"Oh, God, have I killed him?" she cried.

"Oh, shit, Sammy's at it again."

Colie heard Jenny scream and sat up in bed. He listened for a few minutes, then lay back against the pillow . *That bastard*, he thought, *I'll beat the crap out of him one of these days...should get up...see if Jenny's all right...too tired...fight seems to be over. It's quiet. Hope he's passed out. Don't want to have to go over there...tired...am so tired.*

Colie slept...his last thought, *Ten bucks. A lousy ten bucks. Damn near got caught rum-running for ten bucks...didn't get Franny a present...*

Jenny nudged Sammy with her toe, vase still ready. She felt odd, different, as if she'd climbed out of her body and stood watching a stranger hit Sammy with the vase. Then, a feeling of...peace, even power, swept through her. She'd never fought back before. She put the vase back on the table, sat on the edge of an armchair, and looked down at Sammy.

Once more she nudged him with her foot. Still, he didn't move. Then, bending down, she listened to his heavy breathing. Alcoholic fumes made her back away, and a loud snore erupted from his open mouth.

Jenny thought, *he's passed out. Maybe from the whack I gave him or the rum. Most likely the rum...would take more than a whack from a vase to damage his thick skull, I'm sure.* She went into the hall, took a thin blanket from a closet, looked at him again, covered him, then went upstairs to her bedroom.

Jenny sat on the edge of the bed and looked out the window. The rising sun promised another hot day. *I could go to Maggie's house,* she thought. *He may wake up and come at me again. I never struck him before, might not even remember me hitting him. He was at his worst tonight, in a rage when he found the money I'd hid. I do think he meant to kill me this time.* She examined the purple bruises on her arms and put her hands to her head. Fistfuls of hair came off in her hands.

She thought, *No, I won't bother...what would be the use? Maggie isn't back from her brother's, and Colie's just a boy. I don't want to get him after Sammy. What could a boy do with the likes of Sammy? Except knock him down. No, I don't want Colie mixed up in my affairs. I have to figure a way out myself.*

154

Something happened to me tonight. I know I can fight back. After all these years, I've found out I can fight the wretch. Drunk or sober, he won't beat me again.

Tomorrow, I'll call Anna from the drugstore. I can live with them until I get on my feet. Anna's expecting again. I will be a help to her...earn my keep.

Jenny searched her mind and remembered happier days, why she married Sammy, when she didn't have to...she wasn't in the family way; days long past when Sammy lived as a boarder in her mother's house, a kind, thoughtful, and passionate lover before the rum took hold of him.

She got up and took their wedding photo off the wall. She sat on the side of the bed and gazed at it. *Was I ever that slim and pretty*, she thought?

When did the drink take over? She couldn't remember the first time he'd hit her or for what reason. She always thought he'd change if she just didn't make him angry. But Sammy turned into a brute, and now, Jenny knew he'd never change.

She sighed and put the picture back on the wall. *I'm her mother...Anna has to help me...got nowhere else to go. Maggie would help, but she's about to be turned out of the house herself, a matter of time, that's all.*

Jenny got up, took a chair, and wedged it under the door. Then she went to the bureau, opened the wicker sewing box on top of the bureau, and took out a pair of scissors. She looked down at them in her hands, then thought, *what in the name of God am I doing?* She shoved them back in the box and closed it quickly, then lay down on top of the white bedspread and sobbed.

Downstairs, Sammy came to, sat up, rubbed his head, and complained.

"Heh, ooh, what in the frig? Me head hurts . . . feels like I got hit with a club." A vague memory started to form in his mind . . . *Jenny? Naw* . . . he felt the lump at the side of his head. "Must 'have got in a fight . . . can't remember a thing . . . "

He got up, and a wave of nausea gripped him and made him sway, and the floor seemed to ripple beneath his feet.

He hung onto the walls, staggered out to the kitchen, and vomited into the sink.

18

Lizzie MacKinnon knocked on the front door, listened for a moment, then hollered in a raspy voice.

"Colie, wake up. You in there? It's me, Lizzie!"

Colie was dreaming that Mounties were at the door, coming to take him away, their faces stern and angry under broad-brimmed hats as they reached for him. His heart pounding, he sat up in bed, shook himself, and tried to clear his head.

The knocking continued. He thought, *Bad dream...Mounties don't know a thing 'bout me...must be Jenny...Sammy's actin' up again...* then the horror of the night, the gunfire, the pelting rain, the run through the woods, the shack, Uncle Archie, came back to him in a rush. He leaped out of bed, pulled on his pants, ran down the stairs, and flung open the door.

"Sorry, ta wake yer, Colie...but we just got word 'bout yer Uncle Archie...and the shootin' down at the beach...terrible, terrible, poor Archie...thought yer should be knowin' " She stood in the doorway in her ratty, Indian blanket bathrobe and shook her head, then tried to look inside the house. "Is dear Maggie ter home yet?"

Colie felt like reaching out and shaking her scrawny old neck. Then a wave of dread crept over him, and his legs trembled. He hung onto the door.

"Lizzie," he said, "What...what about me uncle...out with it, woman."

Lizzie, spokesperson for the small group of women standing behind her, screwed up her face, and a few croco-

157

dile tears ran down her wrinkled cheeks.

"He's gone to his maker. They found him in an old pit, a tunnel. Crushed 'neath rum kegs . . . dead . . . sometime last night . . . they did.

"Big Dan MacNamara's dead . . . caught rum-runnin', him an' a Mountie . . . both shot dead in their tracks. Two young fellas, brothers, I think, put in jail." She looked over her shoulder to the women. They nodded encouragement. "We wants yer to know we wants to help out. Poor Maggie'll be beside herself when she hears. Is there anythin' we can do ter help, dear? We knows it'll come as a terrible shock to poor, dear little Maggie."

Colie, unable to find his voice for a few moments, looked down at her, then stammered.

"No, no, but thanks . . . thanks for tellin' me, Lizzie." He looked over at the women. "Thank ya, ladies . . . for ya concern." Then he shut the door.

Colie slumped against the door. He ran his tongue over dry lips, and thought, *Oh, me God, Uncle Archie. Should never left him. Where was me dumb head? What was I thinkin' of ta leave Uncle Archie alone, with all that rum 'neath his feet? The crazy old bugger . . . and Big Dan . . . and a Mountie . . . shot . . . Oh, me God.*

Lizzie . . . go home, old hag. Fat lot ya cares 'bout me uncle or me ma. Come 'round ta gloat, that's all. Couldn't wait ta get over here with ya bad news . . . ya and ya friends. Me fault, never should have left him in the shack. Should've dragged him with me . . . thinkin' of me own hide, and getting' away. Gotta get dressed . . . go to see Aunt Marion, the boys . . . oh, me God . . . Colie moved away from the door.

The door slowly opened, and Frances James entered and shut the door.

"Colie, . . . those women. They said, . . . they said that your Uncle Archie is dead. Oh, Colie, how terrible."

"Franny." Colie reached for her and took her in his

158

arms. He buried his face in her hair and cried. "I need ya, Franny. Need ya a whole lot. Ya been stayin' away from me. Why ya been stayin' away from me, Franny? Don't leave me."

They swayed together in the sunlit hallway.

"I'll never leave you, Colie. We belong together," and she thought, smiling to herself, *no one can keep us apart, not now.*

Mable MacDermott looked at the McNeil house and nudged Lizzie.

"Look at that!" she said, "the crippled slut just went in the house."

Lizzie chuckled.

"Mable, yer know the old sayin', 'when the cat's away, the mice will play.' Those young'uns will waste no time gettin' hard at it . . . if yer knows what I mean."

Mable threw back her head and laughed, then linked arms with Lizzie and went to spread the news to the rest of the town.

19

Maggie stood in the doorway of the barn and watched John begin to milk the first cow in the stall of the ten impatient cows. The sun at her back made a golden halo of her piled-high auburn hair. Her face, smooth and tanned, held no sign of the lines that had begun to mar her lovely face, and she looked young once more.

She rehearsed again what to say to John and prayed that she'd say the right thing. So much depended on his giving Colie a chance.

Oh, she knew how stubborn John could be; when he made up his mind, it was difficult for him to change it.

He has to give Colie a chance, she thought. *It's our only hope. Soon, we won't have a place to live. What will become of us?* Maggie lifted her chin and thought, *this was my girlhood home. I have some rights. Oh, it has been a perfect three weeks. If it could only last. Boydie loves the farm, and it has been sheer heaven for me to be home again. But I must get back. I can't run away from my responsibilities.*

Colie hasn't written...didn't really think he would. I would guess he's spending a lot of time with Frances James, now that I'm not around to keep an eye on them. Maggie sighed, remembering ... *can't do much about the love-making between them, now that it started. Surely I'm the one who knows that.*

Then she put a smile on her face.

"John," she said, "I can't believe I'd forgotten how comforting a barn can be. I even love the cow smells. Guess I'm still a country girl at heart. Let me finish the milking; I haven't lost the touch. I feel useless. Please. Let me help.

160

You have so much to do."

John turned from the stool to look at her. He didn't answer for a moment, then turned back to the protesting cow.

"Didn't ask you here to put you to work. You've done enough. What with cooking, baking, and keeping up the house, don't want you mucking around the barn, too. Where's the little girl?"

Maggie stepped into the coolness of the barn.

"Boydie's sleeping. It's her nap time. John, . . . it's . . . it's been wonderful being with my brothers after all these years, and Boydie's never been so good. She adores the farm . . . and her uncles. It is a real change for both of us to spend time with you and Murdy."

The back of John's neck reddened.

"You're welcome to stay, Maggie, you and the girl. I told you, this is your home if you want to stay. No need of you going back. You need never go back as far as I'm concerned. I'll take the truck and get your things. Don't go back, Maggie. I'll take care of you and the girl."

Maggie frowned and dug her hands into her dress pockets.

"You know I'm grateful to you, but I still have Colie to think about. I wish you would get to know him. He's a good boy. He'd be a great help to you on the farm if you would open your heart. Please, give him a chance to prove himself."

John turned and faced her. He ran his fingers through wiry red hair, peppered with gray.

"Colie and I got off to a bad start, I will admit, but he's a hothead like his father, looks just like him. Cut from the same cloth and, most likely, just as lazy."

Maggie's temper flared, but she bit into her lower lip to cut off the sharp reply, knowing it would only enrage John,

161

and went quickly to his side. Hands on slender hips, she answered.

"There's not a bit of truth to what you just said. Colie's not in the least like Jock, except in looks, and there's not a lazy bone in his body. You don't know a thing about him. How can you judge my son? You can't begin to imagine how it was for him, a little boy, having to go down the pit and him barely twelve years old. A good student, too. I had to take him out of school to work the filthy pit. It broke my heart, but he went without a murmur of protest."

"Simmer down, Maggie, if you hadn't run off like you did, you wouldn't have a son going down a pit for a few dollars. I'm telling you now, Colie's not included in the bargain. I don't want him around the place. I've Murdock. I don't need Colie. He can look after himself. He's grown. He doesn't need his mother to wet-nurse him."

Maggie tried to keep the anger from her voice.

"You seem to forget that I grew up on this farm. We had the same parents. I have some rights here."

John jumped up and knocked over the stool. His squinty eyes held a wild gleam.

"So that's it, eh? I'm to have Jock McNeil's rotten spawn around the place. Rights! Don't talk to me about rights. You have none. It's your fault Ma and Pa died. They never got over what you did. They died from grief, while you lay fornicating with that black Irishman. This farm belongs to me. You have no rights here, madam." He picked up the stool, looked at it as if he'd never seen it before, then sat down with his back to her. "You and the girl can stay. She'll have a good Christian upbringing, but I'll have no truck with the spawn of Jock McNeil."

Maggie, a hand to her mouth, tried to stop the words she knew were coming, then started to laugh.

"That's a strange thing to say. Jock McNeil was my

162

husband in the sight of God and man. I've led a natural life. What about you? Who will care when your life is over?" She gestured toward the cows. "Maybe they will. I've had a husband and children, even if with all the sorrows.

"Are you jealous of who I lay with? Could that be what's behind your crazy anger at Colie? You're willing to have my little girl, but you won't have anything to do with Colie. My baby is Jock's spawn, too. How do you know she won't grow up to be like me? How can you predict the future? You hate me because of what I did when a young girl. Boydie could run off too and marry without your approval. Did you ever think of that?"

John swung around and faced here, red-faced, eyes wide and bulging.

"Yes, yes, I did hate to think of that bugger and you together in bed. His hands all over you. You were too good for him. Why'd you go with him when I needed you—"

She stopped him and put a hand on his shoulder.

"For God's sake, John, stop it. Don't say anymore. We're brother and sister, John. What you felt for me wasn't right. Don't try to make me feel guilty for Ma and Pa's death. I'm not responsible for their death, and I've paid dearly for my mistakes.

"You're a hard man, John Beaton. I'm sorry for you. There's no give to you, and you're wrong when you say you don't need more help. I've seen for myself what work needs to be done. You've let the place run down. Pa wouldn't have left the farm to you if he'd known you'd neglect it so. Pa took pride in his property. Murdy can't do it all—you need another farmhand." Maggie paused and took a long breath. "Colie would work hard for you if you gave him a chance. He is your nephew, after all."

She turned away so he wouldn't see the tears forming, ran to the door and into Murdock in the doorway. He reached out and steadied her.

"What's wrong?" He looked over her head at John. "What you do to her? Why's she crying?" Fists clenched, he stepped up to his brother. "I asked you, why's Maggie crying?"

John stood up.

"Get out! Go back to your chores. This is none of your business."

They were the same height. Murdock moved in close and pushed his face up to John's. John pulled a fist, punched him hard in the pit of the stomach, and Murdock doubled over. With booted foot, John kicked him, and he fell to the barn floor. Murdock covered his head with his hands. John kicked him in the head, then pulled back his foot to kick him again.

Maggie cried out and fell across Murdock's body. She screamed.

"Get away from him. Are you crazy? You'll kill him!"

John, crunched low, straightened up and back away. Breathing heavily, he leaned against the cow. His face pale, spittle forming in the corners of his mouth, and voice low, he spoke.

"Slut, take him with you then. Go to hell. Go back to coaltown. Get off my farm, I'm through with both of you. Go on, get out!"

Maggie pulled at Murdock.

"Quick, get out. Lean on me. He's lost his mind."

Murdock shook his head and stumbled to his feet. Maggie, her arm protectively around her younger brother, turned to stare at John, now a deranged stranger she never knew. In shock, she felt as though ice water were running through her veins.

"Good-by, John. I'm sorry my first visit home after all these years had to end this way," she said and pulled Murdock away through the doorway and up the rutted path to the house.

Murdock straightened, picked up a shovel from the side of the barn door, and pushed her away. He wiped the blood from his nose.

"I'm all right," he said. "Go back to the house, get the baby and your things. I'll get the truck. If he comes at me, I'll be ready this time."

Maggie hugged herself to stop the trembling.

"Be careful. I'll run over and ask Henry to give us a ride into town."

"Nothing doing. I'm taking you back in the truck. Then I'm coming back and having it out with him. He's had it his way right along, but I know Pa didn't sign the place over to him. There's nothing saying John owns the farm except word of mouth. Pa figured it should be his, since he's the oldest. Pa thought John would do right by Ned and me. John drove Ned off, treated him like a slave. Ned couldn't take it. I took it. No more, though, . . . and he ain't driving me away." He grasped her shoulder. "Go on, quick, get the baby."

He left her side, walked to the pickup truck parked by an outbuilding a short way from the house, climbed in, and started the motor.

Maggie looked down the road. John was walking slowly toward them, swinging his hunting rifle. Her heart thumped crazily. She ran into the house to the room off the kitchen, where she and her brothers had been born, picked up a sleepy, protesting Boydie, and ran to the truck.

"Did you see him? He's coming up the road with a rifle!" she gasped.

"Yah, I see him. Get in." Murdock flung open the door and hauled her and Boydie inside.

"The baby's clothes, my things—"

"Come on, I'll get them later."

He gunned the motor and drove the truck around the back of the house. It bounced across a dried-up brook, across a parched field, then back to the road past his enraged, rifle-swinging brother.

John wheeled around and aimed at the truck tires. The whine of bullets pierced the air, and the left rear tire blew up.

Murdock ducked his head and cried out.

"Watch out. Get down." He gunned the motor, and the truck sped up the road. The steering wheel shook in his hands as he fought to keep control while the big green truck wobbled and swayed across the rutted road. He pulled the wheel hard right and missed a ditch by inches.

John kept firing. Shots whizzed by the truck. Maggie, with Boydie held tight in her arms, got down on the floor of truck.

"No, Mama, . . . " the frightened child cried out and struggled to get free.

Murdock regained control, drove a mile and a half, until the corrugated road leading to the farm ended, then he turned left onto the pavement of County road, drove a short distance, and pulled to the side and stopped. He took off his cap and wiped his brow with it.

"Crazy. He's gone plain crazy. I'll change the tire, . . . you and the baby all right?"

"No, I'm frightened." She shook her head. Hair had come undone and straggled across her ghost-white face. She pulled herself up to the seat, and Boydie clambered up on Murdock's lap. Maggie pushed hair away from her face. "Oh, God, what's happened to John? It's beyond belief. He's full of hate. Hate against me and what he thinks I did to him and Ma and Pa. It's made him lose his mind." She sobbed and covered her face with her hands.

166

Boydie, no longer frightened, now that the had stopped, pulled her mother's hands away with her small ones.

"Mama play peek-a-boo?" she said.

"No, you're wrong there," Murdock said. "I know John's not right in the head. Been that way all his life. You don't know some of the things he did when we were kids. It ain't nothing you or anyone's done. He beat up Ned and drove him off, but he ain't driving me away. I'll change the tire. You stay put."

"We can't stay here. He'll come after us. Please, keep going."

"Can't, won't get far with a blown-out tire. Besides, John'll have to hitch up the wagon to come after us, and we'll be long gone before that. Have to get you and the girl back home, then I'm coming back to settle up with him."

Maggie reached over and clutched his arm.

"John's dangerous. Stay with Colie and me. I'm afraid for you—"

"I can take care of myself, don't worry. He took me by surprise in the barn, but I'm going to get him. Ned ran like a scared rabbit, . . . not me. I'm going after what's due me."

He shook off her hand and got out of the truck.

"Me go, too. Me go with Murdy." Boydie tried to get free of her mother's arms.

"Be still." Maggie spoke sharply. Then as Boydie began to whimper, she said, in a softer tone. "We'll play peek-a-boo until Murdy finishes changing the tire."

John stood, spread-legged in the road, still aiming the rifle, though the truck had disappeared from his sight, and talked to himself. "Aw, . . . he'll come back with his tail between his legs, like he always does. He can stay with the slut. Don't need him or anyone. Maybe I'll just burn the place, ha, wouldn't that surprise them! I'll set the damn place afire. That's what I'll do. I'll fix them . . . got to make sure Jock's whelp don't get hold of it. I'll burn the damn place first."

He lowered the rifle and walked toward the outbuilding in back of the barn for the can of gasoline inside.

Henry MacKenzie, a great bear of a man, sat on his tractor. He looked up. Dark clouds rolled across the sky, and the air felt strange, ominous. Suddenly cold, he thought a storm was on the way, then—a muffled *boom*! Startled, he looked to the right, toward the Beaton farm as a fireball lit up the sky. "Son of a bitch!" He jumped off the tractor and ran toward the barn and his truck.

The wind picked up, carrying with it sounds of crackling dried-out wood and black smoke billowing toward him. Henry got into his truck and drove straight across the barren field adjoining the two properties.

John stood and watched the flames shoot up from the burning farmhouse, then started toward the barn and went inside. He stood in the doorway. The cows, with distended udders, turned their heads in unison to look reproachfully at him as they mooed their discomfort.

He thought, *Don't want to do it, but got to. Got to destroy the animals . . . leave nothing for the slut and her whelp.*

Henry leapt from the truck, ran to the barn, tackled John, knocked him down, then kicked the gasoline can away from him. Fumes filled the barn. John reached for the can, they struggled, then John gave up, covered his face, and started to whimper. Henry struck him repeatedly across the face.

"Bugger, cruel bugger, gonna burn the barn, too . . . cows and all, were ya?" He picked John up, shook him, then dragged him away from the barn as neighbors and fire-fighting apparatus arrived.

168

20

Murdock brought the truck to a stop in front of Maggie's door, got out, and went around to the other side to help Maggie, with Boydie heavy in her arms, climb out.

Maggie pleaded with him.

"At least come in for a cup of tea and something to eat before you go back. Please—"

Murdock bent down, kissed her cheek and hugged Boydie.

"No, I have to go back now. Don't worry. I'll come tomorrow with your stuff."

Maggie gazed up at him as if for the last time, at the washed-out, pale-blue eyes in his narrow freckled face, and at the red hair badly in need of a trim. She remembered that she had intended to cut his hair that very day. Slight of build, he was no match for John, she thought, and her heart turned over.

"John won't let you take the truck or the wagon. He'll be waiting for you. You'll be alone with that madman. He has a gun, and he's crazy. Please, . . . listen to me. Come into the house. At least stay the night with us."

"Thanks for the offer." He smiled, revealing large, square, white-looking teeth. "Go on now. Remember, I'm not your little brother anymore. I'm an old man of thirty next month. Go in the house and get some rest. I'll be back tomorrow." He walked away, turned to wave, then climbed into the truck.

"Murdy, me go with Murdy," Boydie, hot and cranky, struggled to be let down.

Maggie watched the truck drive away in a cloud of summer road dust until she could see it no more, then put Boydie down, held her by the hand, and went up the brick walk to her door.

The door opened. Frances James, clutching a dust cloth, her skirt covered with Maggie's blue-checkered apron, stood there with a startled look on her flushed face.

"You're back, Mrs.—"

"Doesn't it look like it? Of course I'm back. What are you doing here?" Annoyed, Maggie thought, *for heaven's sake, she's taken over the house in my absence.* "Where's Colie?" She brushed past her, and Boydie reached out her arms to Frances. "Uppy, uppy," she cried. Frances picked her up.

"He's left, a while ago," she said, "to . . . to bring you home. Mrs. Gleason's daughter and son-in-law were visiting. They gave Colie a ride to the farm. They've only just left. You should have passed them on the bluff road."

"We didn't come by the bluff. Murdock took the gutway. It's quicker."

Frances's face paled.

"You don't know, do you?"

"Know what?" Maggie snapped. She reached out and grasped Frances's arm. "What's wrong? Tell me! Why'd he go after me? Are they putting us out of the house? Colie knew I was to spend another week with my brothers and John was to drive me back. What's wrong now?"

Frances's eyes started to fill.

"I'm sorry to have to be the one to tell you, Maggie, I mean, Mrs. McNeil. You're tired, won't you please come into the kitchen? I've a pot of tea brewing. I know you think it's bold of me to be in your house when you're not here, but I wanted to tidy up the place before you got home, that's all."

"Oh, for heaven's sake, girl, do stop babbling and tell me what's wrong, and never mind this Mrs. McNeil busi-

170

ness. You can call me Maggie. Since it looks like you've taken over my home, you may as well call me by my given name. Go on, pour the tea. I am tired, weary to the bone."

Frances, Boydie still in her arms, busied herself at the stove, while Maggie sipped the hot tea and looked at the girl's slim back, thinking, strange how she's pushed her way into my life, when I always made it a point to stay away from Nora James and her kin.

Frances limped over to the table and sat opposite Maggie. Head lowered over Boydie's bright curls, she spoke so softly that Maggie had to strain to hear.

"Your brother-in-law, Archie, Colie's uncle, he . . . he's dead."

Maggie put down the teacup before it reached her lips.

"What did you say about Archie? Surely I didn't hear right."

Frances lifted her head and spoke louder.

"He's dead, ma'am. They say he fell down an old pit. His neck was broken. That's all I know. The same night they found him, the bootlegger, Big Dan McNamara, and a Mountie were killed, shot down at the beach.

"Lizzie and her friends woke Colie early this morning. Colie went right over to his uncle's house. Colie and George, his aunt's brother, I think, were to go to the farm to get you, until Mrs. Gleason's son-in-law said he would. Colie said his Aunt Marion's in a bad way and needs you. She keeps asking for Maggie."

Maggie stared in disbelief. A thought raced through her mind—*the girl's making it up...an excuse for being here*—then, *that's insane, no one would make up a story like that. I must be crazy*.

"Marion, I must go to Marion. Archie dead. I knew the bootlegging would bring grief."

Her hand then flew to her mouth.

"Oh, God. John! And Colie is on the way to the farm. There'll

be bloodshed." The memory of her older brother as he stood in the road firing at them made her shudder. "He'll be in a rage. I was wrong to taunt him."

Frances looked puzzled. She put Boydie on the floor and went to Maggie's side.

"What can I do to help? What about the farm? Is Colie in danger, Maggie? Please, tell me what's going on?"

Maggie stood up and smoothed her wrinkled dress.

"Yes, you can help by minding the baby. I'm going to Marion. Other things have to wait. There's nothing I can do now about John or Colie or Murdy now. I can't think about anything except Marion. She needs me." She pressed her lips against Frances's cheek in a light kiss. "Pray, dear, pray for John, Colie, Murdy, for Archie's soul, and Marion and her boys. Pray that I can comfort my sister-in-law as she has comforted me."

She went to the sink, drew water from the pump, washed and dried her hands on the towel hanging from a hook next to the sink, and glanced quickly in the mirror at her stark white face and disheveled hair.

"Oh, Lord," she said, "look at me. I can't go walking through town looking like this." Quickly, she took the remaining pins out of her hair, finger-combed, rewound and piled her hair in a thick bun at the back of her head.

"Someone's at the door, ma'm," said Frances, putting Boydie down.

"Well, go see who it is, for heaven's sake. Oh, never mind." Maggie brushed past Frances and opened the door.

Dr. Field stood in the doorway and gazed down at her and tried to keep the love he felt for her from spilling out from his eyes, knowing that that love was not reciprocated. He took off his hat and reached for her hand.

"Hello, Maggie. I'm relieved to see that your back. I heard about your brother-in-law, a terrible way to die."

172

Maggie removed her hand.

"I still can't believe it, Doctor." She turned to Frances, standing behind her. "I just now returned home. Miss James informed me. I'm on my way out the door." She looked around him at his car parked in front of the row house. "Please, will you drive me to my sister-in-law's? I hate to ask. I know how busy you must be."

Dr. Field's eyes glowed under his busy brows. He reached for her hand again.

"I'm never too busy to be of help to you, Maggie. That's why I came by. I hoped you'd heard about Archie's death and had come home. If there's anything at all you need or want done, just tell me, and it's done." He let go of her hand and whispered in his mind, *darling Maggie.*

Maggie turned to Frances.

"Mind the baby. I'll be back as soon as I can. If you need anything, go to Jenny Gleason."

"Jenny Gleason isn't—" Frances started to say, but stopped in mid-sentence as Maggie hurried out to the car.

Frances shut the door and rubbed her cheek against Boydie's.

"Sweet baby," she said, "now, Auntie Frances will get you a cookie." They went into the kitchen. She took a pan of cookies from the stove, sat Boydie in a chair, and sat opposite her at the table. Happily, they munched cookies and grinned at each other. Frances said, "I hope my baby will be a little girl just like you."

Then she thought, *Oh, I should have told Colie's mother that Mrs. Gleason's left her husband and gone to live with her daughter. Oh, well, I can tell her later on. Colie will be a good husband, not mean, like Mr. Gleason. I know, he's kind.* Frances put her hand on her still flat belly. *I have to tell him, soon. Oh, God, help me. Colie has to marry me. What will I do if he won't? I'll kill myself if Colie won't marry me.*

173

21

Sally MacGraw, her face flushed and gleaming with perspiration, rushed into the side bedroom with a damp towel in her hands, slapped it across Marion's brow, and scolded.

"You have your sons to raise. No one's going to do it for you. Get hold of yourself for the Lord's sake."

Sally, hot, weary, and out of patience, had tried to calm her distraught friend all day and couldn't understand Marion's grief. After all, it wasn't as though Archie had been a good husband as her own dear man had been.

Secretly, Sally thought, *good riddance to bad rubbish. Marion and the boys are better off without the brute. If it be me, I'd be jumping for joy to be rid of him.*

Marion lifted her head from the pillow and moaned.

"I can't help it. Oh, Archie, my little runt, I don't want to go on without you."

She thrashed about until the narrow bed threatened to collapse beneath her.

In the seldom used parlor, Minnie and Doris placed Sally's white tablecloth on a hastily set up oblong folding table. Minnie looked down at the frayed red napkins in her hands.

"These are more suited for Christmas holidays than a spread after a funeral. Won't do at all. I'll run home and get my own, though I don't like to use my good linen for—well, this one time won't hurt, I suppose." She looked at the napkins again. "Really these are quite shabby."

Doris snatched the napkins from her and flung them on the table.

"Minnie, will you stop? Get that nose of yours down, and stop putting on airs. No one will give a good damn about the napkins. No one but yourself, I'm glad to say. This is a tragic time. We're here to help a neighbor in need, not to put on a fancy tea to impress God knows who. You're quite exasperating. Do us all a favor and just *go home!*"

Doris shouted out the last two words, then flounced into the kitchen for the platters of hot food donated by friends and acquaintances of the McNeil family.

Across the street, two company bullyboys carried out of Marion's former home the family belongings, then, having nothing better to do as they waited for the truck, sat smoking, laughing, and flicking cigarette ashes over her prized divan.

Sally sat on the edge of the bed. "Get up, dear," she said. "Wash your face and make yourself presentable. Show what you're made of. People will soon be coming by to pay their respects."

"I can't. Leave me be. I don't want to see nobody. I want my Archie."

"Don't think I don't know what your going through. Remember, I lost a good husband. A sight better man he was than Archie McNeil. I learned fast enough that crying and carrying on wasn't going to bring him back."

"Sally, you don't know the lot of it. We had such plans, me and Archie. You knew we was going to Boston. I told you about that long ago, I did."

"Yes, you did. Ha, I found it hard to believe Archie'd stay sober long enough to make the trip."

Marion sat up. She stared at Sally with crazed eyes for

a moment, then leapt out of bed.

"You just shut up a'fore I smack you one!" She pulled back her arm ready to strike, then put it down again. "He's gone, my Archie's gone. Why you running him down? Don't you have no respect for the dead?"

Sally got up, smoothed out her dress, and smiled.

"Sure I have, if the life a person led deserved respect, that is. Now, that's the girl. Get mad. Get good and mad. That's the Marion McNeil I know. Feisty and full of fight, not the whining, moaning lump that's laid on my bed all day. Come dear, into the kitchen. Have a hot cup of tea and a little bite of food. You need to keep up your strength for what's ahead."

Minnie, her feelings hurt, looked up and sniffed when Marion and Sally entered the parlor. The table adorned with red napkins, the frayed edges carefully hidden, looked festive against the snowy tablecloth, and in the center of the table was a glass vase with a riot of summer flowers from Sally's garden.

Marion wiped her eyes with the hem of her dress and glanced at the table.

"It do look nice. Real fancy. You all be good friends. I thank you."

Minnie tilted her head to the side and looked away. Then loud, men's voices sounded from the open parlor window. The women looked out.

Marion stumbled to the door and flung it open.

"Get your rotten arses off my divan!" she shouted.

Sally and Minnie pulled her away from the door as George pulled up in his truck. He got out and, with fists clenched, walked slowly toward the bullyboys.

The man gaped up at him, then leapt to their feet. George, a giant of a man, with coal black hair parted in the middle and reached his shoulders, broadly built, and six

176

feet six inches tall, looked down at them.

One took off his cap and gestured toward his partner.

"Got the whole lot out of the house, and we was restin' a spell. We'd be glad to give ya a hand with the loadin' up." He nudged his partner who stared open-mouthed at George. "Won't we, Eddie?"

George gazed at them for a full minute, not speaking then unclenched, and backhanded the speaker, who fell back on the divan.

Slowly, George picked him up by the lapels, lifted him into the air, let him dangle for a second or two, then swung him around before tossing him into the stiff hedges bordering Minnie's front yard.

Eddie cringed and backed away.

"Hey, take it easy now. Ya know, we don't like to do this. Think we like puttin' folks out on the street? We ain't done nuthin' but what we're paid for doin'. Only did our job."

"Get another job." George said softly. He picked him up by the seat of his pants, and Eddie soon joined his partner in the hedges.

"Good for you, George!" Marion cried. "You give it to them shit-heels. Give 'em one for Archie!" She turned from the door. "You see that? Did you see my brother? Didn't he show them who's boss? He always took my part when we was young. Now look at him. Ain't he something, though?" He's still looking out for his sister, he is." She wiped her tear-stained face again. "If I didn't feel so bad I could laugh at the sight of them company stool pigeons on their arses on the bushes. My Archie'd split a gut, laughing. He'd laugh himself sick. He sure loved a good laugh."

Sally put a hand to her mouth and giggled.

"Will you look at them now. They can't get away fast enough. Oh, what a sight. The fat one's pants are dragging about his backside. Ha, he's about to lose them. Oh, my

177

gosh, cover your eyes, girls."

Dr. Field pulled to a stop in front of Sally's door and got out and walked to the passenger side. Maggie, too quick for him, already out of the car, charged up the walk into Marion's open arms, which enfolded her.

"So, you here, dear heart. Oh, Maggie, he's gone. My Archie is gone. All our plans. What'll I do? I'm scared. I'm that scared. My man's gone, all the plans we made. I'm all alone."

"Now, none of that talk," Sally stiffly, "We'll help you. You have friends, after all."

"Of course," Minnie chimed in, "and you have family. Soon you will be with your mother and brother in the country, away from this town. Won't that be nice?"

Doris glared at her.

"Come on, Minnie, we've work to do in the kitchen," and she edged her out of the room.

"I never wanted to live back there with me mother," Marion sobbed. "The company put us out 'fore we was ready to go to Boston. Had to go somewheres. Never let on to Archie, but I hated the thought of livin' off me mother. Back there, I feel like the half-breed I am.

"When Ma and Pa got married, he had some land and a few cows and hogs. Pa made a real farm from that backland, good as any in that neck of the woods. People still looked down their noses at us. Indian squaw they called me. Here, I'm the wife of a white man. No one dares call me 'squaw' to my face."

She looked past Dr. Field's lanky form and across the street at George as he loaded her furniture into his truck, while the bullyboys ran in fear of their lives up the street.

Then she raised her arms and ripped her fists into her black hair until it fell in a dark cloud around her shoulders and down her back. Crying out, she shook her fist toward the house.

"Look, all of you, look! That's my home, where we lived, me and Archie. Had me babies there. Got it fixed up nice inside. Then the letter from kinfolk in Boston. Me and Archie, we put our heads together, figured out a way to get money together, were going to pull up stakes, settle in Boston with Archie's kin." Marion reached for Maggie again. "You was right, dear heart. Shouldn't of let him go in with Big Dan, never . . . never. 'Easy money,' he said. Sure, now my Archie's gone."

Maggie shushed her.

"Don't be hard on yourself. I know. Sally knows. We lost our men. We know how it hurts. God knows it hurts, but you'll get through it. One day at a time. Now you're tired. You need to rest."

Sally nodded.

"She's been carrying on something wicked. Sleep, she dearly needs sleep."

Maggie beckoned to Dr. Field as he stood by, waiting to be summoned, ever-present black bag in his hand.

He approached Marion, his voice calm, soft, and soothing.

"So now, then, Mrs. McNeil. There, there, you've had a great shock. You're distraught. Let me give you something to calm you. It will help you sleep."

"No, don't want to sleep, want to die, want to be with Archie." She broke away from their restraining hands and made a dash for the door.

In one stride, Dr. Field wrapped his arms around her waist and pulled her back into a chair.

"What kind of nonsense talk is that? You have two fine boys. That's plenty to live for."

Sally stood, waiting, a glass of water in her hands.

"Maggie, I want Maggie."

"I'm right here, Marion." She took the pills from the doctor's palm and the water glass from Sally. "Here, swallow these, dear. You and Archie planned to go to Boston? Well, don't give up your plans. Hold on to your dream. It isn't so far-fetched. I have dreams, too. Who knows? If we plan together, maybe our dream will come true. I've made no secret that I plan to leave here, and Boston is as good a place as any."

Dr. Field turned and looked squarely at Maggie.

"I hope I can change your mind about that." He took the glass from her, tilted it toward Marion's mouth and said, "Come on, drink this now."

22

The truck rumbled along the country road. Murdock, conscious of the hollow feeling in the pit of his stomach, wished he'd taken Maggie's offer of tea and food. His feet felt almost too heavy to lift from the gas pedal, and he dreaded the showdown, long overdue between him and his brother. Fights that always left him cowed, bloodied, and beaten. He never won a fight with him, and now, without Maggie and the baby by his side, he felt his courage desert him.

He went over in his mind what he would say to John. *John, I tried to get along with you, and it hasn't been easy since Ned left. Just more work and no thanks ever coming from you. Give me my share, and I'll get out of your way. I only want what's due me for working my arse off, never getting nothing but room and board and the few bucks you'd throw me from time to time. Give me what's mine, and I'll be off. I'll stay with Maggie until I get something going for myself...mmm, won't tell him that, only get him riled. God, I hope he's put the gun away and come to his senses.*

Murdock's clothes, damp with sweat, clung to him as he turned off the country road. Dark clouds gathered, and thunder sounded in the distance. Lightening zigzagged across the sky, and the wind carried acrid smoke into the truck, which stung his eyes and caught his breath . . . then rain, heavy with hailstones pinged off the windshield.

He leaned forward and squinted as he stuck his head out the window, thinking, *something's wrong here. John—God, what's he done now?* Chills coursed through him. He shivered, then stepped hard on the gas, taking a short cut. The

181

truck shuddered a protest as it climbed a bank, shot around a bend, bounced down an embankment, then back to the road that led to the farm. Up ahead stood a group of farmers, and trucks and wagons blocked the road.

Murdock shouted to them, then jumped from the truck, stumbling as he hit the ground . . . .Still on his haunches, he stared at what was left of his house. He ran toward the men as they stood, defeated, letting the rain and hailstones pelt them while the farmhouse collapsed into a smoldering heap. A horse whinnied in the field, and in the barn, the cows mooed their distress.

Murdock grabbed Henry's arm.

"John, he did it, didn't he? Where is he, the black-hearted devil?"

Henry put big hands on Murdock's shoulders.

"Easy son. God, Murdock, we couldn't save the house. He's done it this time, the crazy son of a bitch! He set fire to it, his own house . . . intended to burn the barn as well, but I stopped him . . . got here in time to save the barn, boy." Henry gestured toward his truck. "He's hog-tied . . . had to knock him out, but he came to, screaming like a woman, so I gagged him. Sorry about that. I had to quiet him until they got here."

Murdock started for the truck.

"No, don't go near him. Won't do you any good to see him like that. He's out of his mind, a raving maniac if I ever saw one . . . but . . . he's your brother, after all. I called the State Hospital. They're coming for him. Let him be."

Colie, watchful, stood by, then stuck out a hand.

"Colie here. Guess ya be me uncle," he said. He gestured to Mike, the bantam-sized man beside him. "This be Mike Monahan. He gave me a ride here. Been a death in me pa's family . . . me uncle Archie, so I came ta get me ma. Gotta tell ya, me heart was in me mouth when I saw the house burning. Damn near scared the crap outta me. Thought me baby sister and ma was in there. Wish we got here sooner . . . coulda stopped him. Damn sorry, man. Things in a mess back home, what with me uncle dyin', but Ma would want ya ta come back with me, no matter what."

Henry reached out and pressed Murdock's shoulder.

"Don't want to tell you your business, son," he said to Colie, "but we look out for each other here. I know you're Maggie's boy, and family an' all." Henry looked toward the neighboring farmers. "We talked it over. We'll have the house up in jib time for Murdock here, soon's we get the lumber. No time to waste. Murdock will want to stay and help with the building of course." He pressed harder.

Murdock winced and shrugged him off.

"Maggie's clothes, the girl's, didn't have time to get the clothes. All burned, I guess," he said.

Henry pointed toward the barn.

"First things first. There's them cows bellowing to be milked. Get a move on. Take care of your livestock." None to gently, he pushed Murdock toward the barn.

Murdock, dazed, obeyed and went into the barn. The cows, their udders swollen, turned and looked at him accusingly as he approached them. He picked up the milking bucket and sat down beside the first cow in the stall.

Henry spoke.

"Have to keep him moving, keep him busy. Don't give him time to think."

Colie took off his cap and scratched his head.

"Ma won't like it a damn bit if I don't bring him home with me, I'm sure a that. She'll blame me. What'll I tell her? He's gotta come back with me, Mr. MacKenzie. I'd like ta stay an' help, but Ma'll be worried if I don't get back soon. Don't seem right to leave, though." He glanced toward the truck. "Think he'll be all right 'til they come fer him? Ya might need help with that one."

"There's enough manpower here to handle him if that happens." Henry said. "You get yourself back to town. Tell your mother Henry MacKenzie's taking care of things. Your mother's known me all her life, knows she can trust me. Go back to town. Murdock'll be around to see her in a few days. I'll bring him myself right to her door."

He put a hand on Colie's shoulder. "Nice to finally meet one of Maggie's offspring. Sorry it had to be at a time like this. Give my condolences to your mother and your uncle's family." Henry bowed his head. "God rest his soul."

Colie put his cap back on.

"Okay, then, we'll be leavin'. Remember, I'm takin' yer at yer word 'bout me uncle. Ma will be high tailin' it out here anyways once Uncle Archie's buried."

They shook hands all around, then Colie and Mike got into the car and drove away.

Henry thought, *good looking boy...don't see Maggie in him...must take after the father. If I play my cards right, maybe Maggie come back to live. Big strapping boy like Colie, just what the place needs. Between him and Murdock, they'd make the place look the way it used to. I never wanted any woman but Maggie...hope it's not too late.*

Get a proper house up, give Murdock a hand fixing things up, now that the crazy arsehole's out of the way...might be a chance for me. Maggie'll need a man to look after her.

A black and white ambulance, sirens wailing, pulled into the lane and jerked to a stop. A few of the farmers hesitated, then strolled over to meet it. Henry went into the barn for Murdock. They walked up to the ambulance.

The doors flew open and two no nonsense-looking husky men in white coats jumped out and walked swiftly toward them. The farmers kept their heads lowered. Rain poured down and they shifted their feet and sweated in the heavy, wet air. No one spoke.

23

Frances sat in the rocking chair with a squirming Boydie on her lap. Usually happy and sweet natured, Boydie, all that long afternoon had whined for her mother. Now, dusk had fallen, and Maggie hadn't come back. Neither had Colie.

"Shush, baby. Oh, why won't you go to sleep? Please . . . please stop whining." Frances thought, *I've got to get home to Granny. She'll want her supper. Maybe I'll ask Mrs. Gleason to mind the baby . . . oh, no, I forgot, she's gone to her daughter's. Oh, what's keeping Colie's mother.*

"Mama . . . me want Mama . . . ," Boydie cried, her teary face red and sweaty.

Frances sighed and got up.

"I'll get you some milk and a cookie, baby. Please be good for Auntie Frances."

"No, no want cookie, want Mama!" Boydie pushed Frances away, then butted her head against Frances's tender breasts.

"Ooh, . . . stop that . . . you hurt Auntie Frances."

"Go 'way . . . bad girl . . . Mama . . . me want Mama."

Frances put her down, then sat on the floor beside her.

"Okay, let's play a game until your mama get here. We'll play patty-cake, baker's man. Be good for Auntie Frances. I'm tired too, and I don't feel good." Frances touched her tender breasts, "and my tummy feels sick." Frances tried to stop the tears puddling in the corners of her eyes.

Boydie, surprised, stopped crying and reached over and patted Frances's cheek.

"No cry . . . girl . . . no bad. Baby kiss girl." She put her arms around Frances's neck and plastered her face with moist kisses.

They didn't hear Maggie come into the room until she had heaved a sigh and flung herself into Jock's chair.

Frances put Boydie down and got up.

"Mrs. McNeil, I didn't hear you come in."

"Mama, my mama . . ." Boydie toddled over and climbed into her lap.

Maggie's eyes were ringed with dark circles, and she looked close to exhaustion. She picked up Boydie.

"Doctor drove me home. What a day! Hope never to see another like it. Can't remember when I've been this tired," she said.

"I didn't plan on leaving the baby with you all afternoon, girl, but my sister-in-law clung to me like glue. Marion's taking it harder than I'd have expected. She cared for that man, scoundrel that he was. Never knew a couple to fight like those two. Well, it's done—Archie's gone—Marion'll have to make the best of it, as I've had to do." Maggie, sat with eyes closed for a few seconds, then with Boydie still held in her arms, went over to Frances. She put a hand on her shoulder. "You look done in too, girl," she said. "Did the baby give you a time of it? I appreciate your minding her. Did she fuss after me?"

"Well, she cried quite a bit. I didn't know what to do. I thought of going to Mrs. Gleason's, but them remembered she'd gone to visit her daughter. Oh, dear, excuse me." She covered her mouth, turned, ran into the kitchen and vomited in the sink.

Maggie followed, trying to crush the thought gathering in her mind as she handed her a towel. Frances kept her head down, took the towel, wiped her mouth, and clung to the sink. Maggie felt it like a blow to the stomach. She put

186

Boydie down on the floor, dug her fingers into Frances's shoulders, and whipped her around. Sparks flew out of Maggie's green eyes, and they bore into Frances's brown ones.

"What's wrong? What's wrong with you, girl? Tell me, tell me, damn you! You're caught, aren't you? You're in the family way, girl?"

Frances waited a few seconds before she answered, then lifted her chin and looked squarely at Maggie.

"All right . . . I'll tell you. Everyone will know soon enough anyway . . . all the biddies on the bluff . . . Granny, too. The whole town will know. I'm going to have Colie's baby." She smiled and lifted her chin higher. A tiny smile lurked at the corners of her mouth. "And there's nothing you can do about it. I'm two months gone. Colie loves me. He'll marry me. I know he will, no matter what you try to do."

White hot anger swept over Maggie. She sucked in her breath, then pulled back her hand and slapped Frances stingingly in the face. Maggie's voice rose to a shout and with Boydie clinging to her skirt, she pushed Frances toward the door.

"Get out, you tricked him. Think you're pretty clever, don't you? Well, Colie's too young for marriage, and you'll be sent to the home for unwed girls. He'd never marry you. You're trash, like the rest of your family!"

Frances fought back at the door. She whirled around and shouted.

"You'll find out for yourself. Colie loves me! You can't keep us apart now. Colie's decent. He'll do what's right in spite of you. You've tried to keep him a little boy so he'll stay with you. I'll tell you something, Mrs. Colie's a man, and I'm the one who knows, and don't you dare call me trash! I'm not trash. You're mad because I'm taking him away from you!"

187

"Shut up. Get out of my house!" Maggie pulled the door open and pushed Frances outside.

Frances, sobbing hysterically, ran along the path to her house. Maggie slumped against the door, buried her face in her hands, and cried and cried.

The light coming from the kitchen outlined Nora James's boney old frame, clad in a long, white nightgown.

"So, there ye be, sneakin' home in the wee hours, yer rascal gel!" she croaked.

Frances slackened her pace when she saw the cane in her grandmother's hand. Still reeling, but defiant after her encounter with Maggie, she thought, *Granny better not hit me with that cane. I might hit her back.* She decided to brazen it out.

"Granny, why are you doing standing there in your nightie and no with no shoes on your feet? Get back into the house or you catch your death."

"Get in ta house yerself, Janie. Yer've turned into a hussy. Yer thinks yer fool yer old mither, sneakin' about the long night with the laddies?"

She reached out with the cane to strike Frances. Frances grabbed the cane away from her, and led her back into the house.

"No, Granny, dear. You're confused. I'm Frances, and I just stepped out for a breath of air."

"Me supper and me tea—"

"Dear, you had your supper hours ago and your tea. You didn't eat much though, that's why you're feeling a bit hungry. I'll fix some hot porridge for you. It'll help you sleep. Sit here, dear." She led her to a chair by the table and placed the cane beside her.

"Me tea, don't ferget me tea an' a drop a two a gin, Janie gel."

Frances stirred oatmeal into the pot of water, the smell of even the oatmeal made her nauseous, and she was afraid she'd be sick again. She held her stomach, hoping the feeling would pass and her grandmother wouldn't notice. *Granny's mind is wandering*, she thought.

"Who is Janie, Granny?" she asked, puzzled. Nora had nodded off. "Granny, wake up. I asked you, who is Janie? You called me Janie twice now. Who is she?"

Nora looked up, and her old eyes brightened.

"Foolish Gel. Janie's me dotter. Pretty colleen, prettiest one of the lot." Her voice rose to a wail, and she started to rise from her chair. "Janie, gel, get yerself inside, or I'll take the strap ta yer. Yer a bad 'un. I'll 'have ta be lockin' yer in yer room. Yer got the laddies sniffin' 'round the 'house like dogs." Her eyes clouded over, and she stared off into space for a few moments, then, seeming to come back to the present, she stared at Frances and said, "Yer looks just like yer mither. Yer better not turn out like 'er. Yer be a good gel. Yer stay and take care of yer granny, won't yer now, gel?"

Frances stopped stirring the pot and clutched at her stomach. Waves of nausea rolled over her, and she choked back the bile that rose up in her throat.

She went to the sink and splashed water over her face. *Oh, God*, she thought, *I'm going to be sick again. Then, Oh, what is Granny raving about? I look like my mother? How would Granny know who my mother was?*

Unexplained questions that had haunted her all her life, swirled around in her head, and she felt dizzy. She went to her grandmother, sat across from her and took her hand and chose her words carefully.

"Granny, dear, tell me about Janie."

"No, never mind 'bout that one. Was of me own flesh and blood, she was, not one his other's bairns, but bad she was . . . couldn't do a thing with 'her. Used to whip her, I

189

did. Tried to beat the badness out. She run off, ter Halifax, with some dandy fella'. Niver yer mind now, get me tea an' a drop o' two a gin." She drifted off for a minute or two, then, with glazed eyes, looked up and said, "Janie, gel, it's come back yer have." She reached for her cane, lost her balance, and fell heavily to the floor before Frances could reach her.

Frances banged on Maggie's door and shouted.

"Help, help, Mrs. McNeil. It's me, Frances, please, . . . open the door."

Maggie, with Boydie on her hip, opened the door a crack and viewed Frances with suspicion.

"If it's Colie you're looking for, he's not come home. Please go away." She shut the door.

Frances pounded with both fists.

"Please open the door. I didn't' come to cause trouble. It's my granny. She's fallen. I can't get her up. I don't know what to do."

Maggie leaned against the door, closed her eyes, looked up at the ceiling, and said a prayer. "Please, Lord Jesus, I don't need this. My plate is full." She stooped to pick up Boydie, then opened the door, and Frances rushed inside.

"Granny's hurt. I can't get her up. She's heavy, so heavy. I . . . I think she's hurt bad. I didn't know who to turn too. Please come."

Maggie opened the door wide and sighed.

"Why me?" she said. "I've had nothing to do with Nora, ever. It's not my fault if she's fallen. Oh, all right then. Fred MacAllister's the only one with a phone. Get over there and call Dr. Field. I'll . . . I'll go stay with her while you make the call.

"Thank you, oh, thank you, Mrs. McNeill." Frances

reached out but Maggie stepped back to avoid contact, then skirted around Frances, went out the door, calling over her shoulder as she went. "Hurry, make the call before the doctor is called somewhere else."

Fred MacAllister, a widower and retired miner living on a pension, and who the children called "Santa Claus," because of his round, jolly appearance and long white beard, sat in his dark parlor and smoked the last pipe of the day before going to bed.

He heard Frances's footsteps, switched on the lamp by his chair, and got to the door before she had a chance to knock. He took the pipe from his mouth.

"Why, what in the world do we have here? Nora James's young lassie paying me a visit? Well, now, come in, come in."

Frances stopped to catch her breath, then stepped into the cluttered hall with the deer head on the wall staring out with frightened eyes.

"May I use your phone, sir, to call the doctor? Granny fell, and I can't get her up."

"Phone's right there on the table, lassie. So the old girl fell? Hope her hip's not broke. A real Tartar that one. Never liked me after the day I took the switch away from her when she was beatin' the daylights out of one of her lassies."

Frances wrung her hands.

"I don't know how to make a call. I never used a phone before. Will you call the doctor for me? I'm sorry I'm so stupid."

Fred gestured to a bench under the deer head.

"Then, take a seat, lassie. You look like you could use a doctor yourself. Now ain't it the truth; if you ain't never done a thing before, how can you be blamed for not knowing how? Watch how it's done." He started to dial.

Maggie shifted Boydie over to her other hip and pushed open Nora's door. She looked down the narrow hall and could see Nora's bare feet. Nora lay on her left side with her feet under the overturned chair she'd been sitting on when she fell, and the pillow beneath her head rested on one of the stove's clawed feet. Smoke curled toward the low ceiling from the pot of burning porridge.

Maggie put Boydie on a chair, said, "Stay still," and quickly stepped around Nora, grabbed a towel from the rack at the sink, and, keeping the pot away from her, flung it into the basin.

She looked at Nora's still form, and a shudder went through her. She thought, *I don't want to touch her. She looks beyond help.* But she forced herself to bend down, lift the chin, then felt for a pulse on either side of Nora's neck. A sudden rush of compassion swept through her, and she thought, *the poor soul, she didn't lead a happy life.* Then said "Praise the Lord, she's still alive," when she felt a pulse. Then she picked up Boydie and stood ready to intercept Frances, with Fred trailing behind her up the walk.

"How's Granny? Dr. Field is on his way. Mr. MacAllister showed me how to use his telephone. I made the call myself. It was easy." She tried to enter the kitchen, but Maggie held her back.

"What's the matter? Let me pass. Granny. Let me by, I said. I want my Granny!"

Boydie started to wail.

"Hold the baby for me, please," Maggie said and handed her to Fred.

Boydie quieted down, pulled her head back to look at Fred, then began to tug at his beard.

"Frances," Maggie said, "it's best you don't see her

right now. It will upset you and not do your grandmother any good. You take care of yourself. Babies are precious no matter how they come into the world. We'll manage, you, Colie, and me. Come here."

"Oh, Maggie, then you don't hate me after all." She went to her, and Maggie put an arm about her, and over Frances's glossy head, Maggie met Fred's curious look with stony eyes.

Colie leapt from Mike's car as the County Hospital ambulance pulled away from Nora's door.

"Colie, oh, thank God, your back!" Maggie cried. She grasped his arm. "How's Murdy? Tell me. Did he and John fight again? I begged him not to go back. John's turned into a black-hearted monster. We had to run for our lives. He shot at us. I didn't have time to get our things." Then she stepped back. Her hand went to her mouth. She said, "What's wrong? You smell strange, . . . like . . . like smoke. Oh, dear God, what did John do?"

"Nuthin' much," Colie answered, "just set fire to the house. Don't worry, the other one's okay. Nuthin' happened to him. The neighbors takin' care of him. What the hell's goin' on here?"

Franny ran to Colie and flung herself at him.

"Granny's hurt," then she slumped against him.

"Well, pick her up," Maggie said. "Carry her to the house. She's your responsibility now, and there's no getting out of it. Then, for God's sake, tell me what happened at the farm."

A week passed since the ambulance pulled away from Nora James's door. She lived three days, then her heart gave out. Although Nora had shown little outward signs of affection—she'd never cuddled or kissed her granddaughter

193

that Frances could remember—Frances somehow had felt that her granny loved her anyway. Now she'd lost the only security she'd ever known.

No one in town knew how to locate Nora's children. A death notice was published in the local newspaper. Then someone remembered Nora's youngest daughter had run off with a man from Halifax years before. Maybe a notice should be sent to a newspaper in that city?

Dr. Field said he would take care of it.

Nora was laid out in her own home. No luncheon was served, and few Rockhill people or those who were her neighbors on the bluff came by to view the body.

Mabel MacDermott, pleased with herself for being able to outfox Lizzie in town gossip, stretched her scrawny neck and with a toss of her redhead, spoke.

"Who wants to see the old baggage? Good riddance. Now, mind you, if there was a feed put out, I might be of a mind to go." She glanced sidewise at Lizzie, smiled, then stage-whispered, "I betcha I knows somethin' you don't."

"Mabel, yer knows damn well not much goes on on the bluff that gets by me. I could tell a few things if I had a mind to." Lizzie put her hands on her hips and leaned closer to Mabel. "What yer hear, honey?"

Mabel put a hand up to her mouth.

"Young Colie's gone and knocked up the gimp. Ha, will do my heart good to see high and mighty Maggie fall off her high horse. Thinks she's too good to mix with the rest of us on the bluff. Her that comes from a daft family from up county. Heard one of her brothers' set fire to his own house. Burned it right to the ground. He's locked up in the loony bin right now.

"And that ain't the worst of it. Coal company's getting'

ready to throw them out on their arses, you know, since Colie ain't gone back to work."

Lizzie, annoyed, thought, *Mabel ain't never got the best of old Lizzie an' she ain't startin' now.*

She searched her mind, then lifted her chin and sniffed.

"Well, Mabel, don't know how yer heard the gimp's in the family way. I never heard tell of it. Nor any fire either. The gimp sure don't look like she's gone and got herself knocked up. Even though I know the two younguns' been carryin' on for some time—I'd seen him climbin' in her window many a night—if it do be a fact, as I sees it, Maggie still make out well enough."

"How you figure that? Maggie ain't got nothin' but a few pieces of furniture and a pot to piss in, Lizzie. The bullyboys' be 'round to toss her out, and I'll be first to say, 'Good luck to you and kiss my ass, Maggie McNeil.' "

"Sure, Maggie be put out sooner or later. That's the way the company takes care of them that don't work in the pit. Never let nobody live in company houses that get on their bad side. I knows that as well as yer, but I still say Maggie'll do fine. Yer forgets, Mabel, Nora James was well fixed. She owned the house. Was hers free and clear. And . . . she had money from her man's pension, to boot. Never spent a dime neither, 'cept on gin or rum. No kin about to make a claim, so be the gimp's. They'll move to Nora's house once the gimp and Colie marry up, which is what'll happen if the gimp's in the family way, as yer say. Time will tell, eh?"

Then Lizzie glanced up at Mabel and said, "Well, dearie, shifts over. Me old man'll be wantin' his bath. Ta ta now," and she walked away satisfied. She'd outwitted Mabel, after all.

24

It was a pitifully small procession that followed the coffin up the hill, on a morning bright with the promise of a glorious summer day, to the windswept graveyard overlooking the Atlantic.

Purple, yellow, and pink wildflowers dared poke their tiny heads through the rough grass only to be crushed down by the feet of the group standing by the open grave. The people listened as the minister of the Scotch Presbyterian Church delivered a drawn-out prayer, finally ending with "May God have mercy on her soul."

Maggie, Colie, Jenny, Fred MacAllister, and Malcolm (Jessie, his wife, was taking care of Boydie) watched as the coffin was lowered into the earth a short distance from the gravesite of the husband who rested alongside his first wife.

That morning, Frances cried out.

"I don't want to watch Granny being put into the ground. Don't make me go. Please, let me stay here. I don't feel well!"

"If ya don't want to, then ya don't have to, but stay in bed, funny face. Get some rest," Colie said.

Frances tried to stifle her impatience as she lay in bed, and, from the open window, listened to them bickering.

"No, no, it wouldn't be right," she heard Maggie say. "I didn't care for her when she was alive. Now she's dead, I won't pretend any different. I was never a friend to the woman. Jenny, you ride with the body. You were on good terms with her. I've seen you talking to her many a time."

Jenny's head shot up.

"How can you say that? You, of all people, know I choose my friends with care, and having a drunken man to deal with, I'm not apt to seek out a rum guzzler like Nora James! When I'd see her about, I'd speak, sure, only being polite. I'll go to the cemetery, but I won't ride with the casket. Would give me the cold shivers. There was something evil about the woman, might be clinging to the body, ready to pounce into someone else's soul."

Fred took the pipe from his mouth.

"Jenny Gleason, that be fanciful talk for a sensible woman like yourself. Nora was green as grass, come from the old country to marry Bob James, a man she'd never laid eyes on before, and he made a slave of her, never treated her right. I got a good memory of those days. She was a right big bonny lass at the time, let me tell you. True, she got into the rum, but if her man treated her better, she'd been a proper woman. Get in the car, the two of you. Malcolm, you'll join in the last ride with the old dear, won't you?"

Malcolm, laughing hard, could only nod.

Frances had listened until she heard the hearse drive away. Then she'd tossed aside the sheet, rushed to the top of the stairs, and looked down as Mike Monahan handed over the keys to Colie for the ride to the cemetery. She watched the ladies pile inside, then ducked when Colie turned to look back at the house.

When they had driven away, Frances hurried down the stairs and into Nora's bedroom. The air, heavy with the scent of mothballs, made the ever-present nausea threaten to overwhelm her. A steamer trunk under the window seemed to beckon her, and she hurried to it, sat down on the floor, and tugged at the heavy padlock. It held firm.

Desperate, Frances tugged and tugged, thinking, *got to see what's in this trunk before they come back. I'm sure it'll tell me something about my real mother.*

Granny's an old liar. I hate her! I'm glad she's dead. She lied to me. Let me think I was an orphan no one wanted, and she knew the truth. I had a right to know! Why couldn't she tell me the truth about myself? What was there to hide? A throwaway girl no one wanted except Granny is what I thought, when all the time she knew who I belonged to. She was my real grandmother, and I can't ever forgive her.

I know I've got a mother somewhere, and I'm going to find her. Something in the trunk will tell me about her. I know it. She pounded on the trunk until her fists hurt.

She got up and went into the pantry, got down on her hands and knees, and searched the lower shelves until she found Robert James's tool box. She lugged out a heavy mallet, carried it with both hands back to Nora's room, swung back her arms and brought the mallet down on the padlock. Twice she swung until the flattened padlock fell to the floor.

Her hands trembled when she raised the lid and a familiar scent floated up from a pile of clothes inside. She stared for a long moment at a pale-green party dress on top of the pile. She picked it up and held it close to her.

Her eyes became unfocused, and the room started to tilt; she felt dizzy and sat back on her haunches and held the dress close to her face.

Images swirled and danced in front of her closed eyes as she inhaled the scent so familiar to her. Then the sound of music, voices, and a face, a young face, a face that Frances had forgotten but that was engraved on her heart, laughed and blew smoke rings at the man sitting by her side.

Then a little girl cried, tried to climb on the woman's

lap only to be pushed to the floor by the man. Then a sting-ing slap . . . someone screamed . . . shouts . . . the sound of fists hitting soft flesh . . . run . . . run quick . . . get away from the bad man.

Then, held close, the scent! Three-year-old Frances sobbed, Mama, don't leave me, Mama, come back . . . Long-blocked memories rushed at her . . . and she remembered, remembered "the house" and the bad man, a man who ter-rified her . . .

The black night was scary, but not as scary as the bad man chasing them. Her mother held her tight, and they ran . . . , but he caught them, pulled her away from her mother, struck her mother and dragged them back to "the house." Someone carried her away, away from her mother, forever and ever. "Mama, come back. Don't leave me. Mamaaa!"

25

Sammy staggered against Mike Monahan and breathed sour breath into his face until Mike was forced to turn away.

"Come on, be a pal," Sammy said. "Yer sure are a little shit, but yer must 'ave a buck or two on yer for a bottle, important railroad man like yerself. I'll pay yer back. Yer knows I'm good fer it. What the hell, yer me son-in-law, ain't yer?"

Mike, his small featured face stern, shook his head and pushed him away.

"Aw, man, you're drunk. Go sleep it off before Ma Gleason gets back." Then he looked past Sammy and sighed with relief when he saw his own car coming up the road and stop in front of Gleason's door.

Sammy pushed past Mike, rushed to the car, pulled open the back door on the passenger side, and tried to pull Jenny from the car.

"Bitch," he yelled, "get in the house where yer belongs!"

Jenny broke free, cracked him across the face with her pocketbook, and leapt from the car to hit him again.

"Don't you put a hand on me, Sammy! I'll smash your face!"

Sammy staggered a bit, then hauled back a fist and came at her, yelling.

"Yah, that's what yer thinks, bitch."

Jenny ducked, then rained blows on his head with her heavy pocketbook.

"Stop it!" Maggie cried, getting out of the car. She

tugged at Jenny and pulled her away. "That's enough. Come home with me. Don't fight with him. He's drunk, Jenny. Let him sober up."

"That's just it. He's never sober. I . . . I can't live with him. We'll end up killing each other."

Sammy tried to focus his bleary eyes on Maggie.

"Yer a bitch, too. Both a yer, nuthin' but bitches. I'll get yer, Maggie. One of these days, I'll get yer." Colie reached out, grabbed Sammy by the throat, and slapped him across the face until Sammy whined, "Okay, okay, let me go, for cripes sake."

"Ya keep that dirty mouth of yours shut. I oughta beat the shit outta ya, drunk or not! Go on." Colie pushed him toward the door. Then taking a deep breath, Colie lowered his voice and turned to Mike.

"Thank ya for the loan of ya car. Sorry 'bout all this. Ya be a good fella, Mike. Hope I can return the favor someday."

Mike took the keys, started to get in the car, then changed his mind and went over to Jenny, who leaned, sobbing, against Maggie.

He patted her shoulder.

"Come on, Ma Gleason, you're coming home with me. Anna wants you, and now that I've seen for myself how the old man acts, I'm not going to let my wife's mother live with a man like that." He gestured with his thumb to Sammy's retreating back. "I'll drive back tomorrow. You won't have to come. Just tell me what you'll want from the house, and I'll borrow my brother's truck." Mike looked at Colie. "You said you wanted to return the favor? Well, man, help me move my mother-in-law tomorrow. What do you say?"

Colie grinned and shook Mike's offered hand.

"Bet ya life I will. Jenny's the best, salt of the earth. Me and Ma will be that pleased to see her get away from him.

He's no damn good, that Sammy."

A few doors down, Lizzie and Mabel stepped behind the big oak as Mike's car whizzed by.

"Now, what you think of that, Lizzie? The old witch's hardly in the ground and fists starting to fly already. Couldn't hear what they said, could you? What yer s'pose the fools fightin' for?"

"Don't know. Gleason's drunk. Nothin' different 'bout that. Him's always beatin' on his Jenny. Looks like he got the worst of it this time. The young fella's the son-in-law, yer knows . . . works for the railroad.

"Well, will know soon enough. Nuthin' gets by old Lizzie, yer know. Want a cuppa? Come in the house 'fore me man gets home. I'll make us a cuppa, then we'll mosey on past Gleason's place, tell 'em how sorry we is we couldn't make it to the services and we's heartbroken that old Nora passed away, ha ha."

Colie followed his mother into the house and watched, concerned, as she sank wearily into Jock's chair.

"I'll get the baby for yer, Ma. Ya look done in," he said.

"You don't have too, son. Jessie's keeping her for the night. I'm going to lay down for a spell. You look after your girl." Then, she looked up at him, questioning, "She told me she's carrying your baby. Is it true?"

Colie reddened and hung his head.

"Just found out meself. Franny told me last night. Ya, Ma, it's mine right enough. Franny ain't been with no one but me."

"Then you've taken on a big responsibility, and you're still a boy. Have you given thought as to how you'll support her and a baby?"

"I'm goin' back to the pit, Ma. Job's waitin' fa me. Malcolm says whenever I'm ready."

Maggie got up, went to him, reached up to grasp him by the shoulders, and fastened her beautiful green eyes on his face.

"Colie, you know how I feel about the coal mine. The pit has taken almost everything from me. Child and husband and one other who I loved. I won't let it take you, too. Murdy will need help on the farm. He's good and kind. There's a home there for all of us. My brother John will never be back. His mind is gone. God alone knows what will become of him." She shook Colie gently. "You can't even consider going back to the pit, son, I won't allow it."

Colie removed her hands and sat her down in Jock's chair.

"Ma, I knows how ya feel 'bout the pit, but I gotta go back. Ma, I'm a coal miner—it's all I knows. I ain't no farmer, an' I don't want ta be one." He knelt beside her and reached for her hands. "Me an' Franny'll live in her granny's house. Franny owns the house. Her granny told her last year she'd made out a will leavin' the house to Franny 'cause she took care of her and she didn't count on seeing any of her other brood again.

"Franny told me her granny laughed when she told her she made out a will leavin' her the house, and she hoped at least one of her litter would show up at the funeral so they'd find out Nora James was no one's fool.

"And she wasn't leavin' it to chance, in case they did come sniffin' 'round lookin' to see if she left them the house or money or somethin'.

"An', Ma, Malcolm says things better at the pit since the strike. You an' Boydie ought to go live on the farm with ya brother. Be a good place for ya and Boydie, now that he's gone. Murdy's a grand fella', and the country be a fine place for ya and the Boydie. Don't ya think, Ma?"

Maggie didn't answer. She slid her hands from his, got up and walked to the open window and looked out. A few raindrops hit the back of her hands, and she breathed deeply of the moist, salt air and listened to the rustle of the hollyhocks as the brushed against the side of the house.

"Ma, you hear what I just said?" Colie got up and stood beside her.

Maggie turned from the window.

"It's raining . . . planned on doing a wash," she murmured.

"Ma, I'm sorry I brought shame ta ya. I tried to stay away from Franny. She's a good girl, Ma, not like some of the others I fooled with, an' I'll do right by her and the baby when it comes, an' . . . an' we'll be getting' married soon's we can, Ma. Franny an' me . . . we talked it over last night, but Ma, I gotta go back to work. It ain't so bad . . . the pit that is . . . union's workin' for us now. Things change, ma. I can't hang 'round doing nuthin' much longer, and I knows meself, Ma, and ya gotta get this through yer head—farm life ain't fer me!"

Maggie walked back to the chair and sat down. Deep in thought, she didn't speak for a few minutes as Colie stood before her clenching and unclenching his fists.

She looked up at him with blazing eyes.

"That's the way it is, is it? You've made up your minds, you and the girl, shuttle Ma and the little sister off to the country and get on with your own lives.

"You're my son. Why didn't you consult me? Is that the role I'm to play now? Second fiddle to that girl? You say she's a good girl . . . I think not. She slept with the first boy who asked her. What do you know about her? What does anyone know about her? She's a foundling.

"So, you're going back to the mines! What a life your setting up for yourself! God in Heaven, what the matter with your thinking? How do you know you wouldn't like the farm? You've never tried it. No, you'd rather go down the stinking pit than breath the fresh country air. It makes no sense at all!"

Colie took a step toward her.

"I know yer riled up, Ma, and yer has a right to be riled, but don't talk against Franny. She's gonna be me wife. I've no use for ya farm, Ma, and ya can't run me life. I'll run me own in me own way." Upset and angry, he turned and rushed from the house, slamming the door behind him.

Colie went looking for Frances and found her asleep on her stomach across Nora's bed, wearing the green, chiffon dress, and in her hand she clutched a newspaper clipping and the yellowed pages of a letter.

The contents of Nora's trunk were strewn about the floor, and ladies dresses, ones that never graced Nora's big frame, lay crushed beneath Frances.

Articles on top of the bureau had been swept to the floor, dresser drawers pulled out and contents tossed around the room, curtains torn from the window, pictures from the wall, and a chair overturned.

Colie shook Frances awake.

"I just had it out with me ma." He shouted. "Told her I ain't goin' ta live on no cow-shit smellin' farm; pullin' cow tits an' shovelin' manure ain't fer me, and that's final!" Then he stopped shouting, lowered his voice, turned and looked around the room, and said, "What the hell's goin' on? You take a fit? I shoulda' made you go with us to the cemetery. What ya wreck ya granny's room fer? Why ya dressed like that? Where'd ya get the dress?"

Frances rolled over on her back, and, shielding her swollen, red face from Colie with one hand, she thrust a letter at him.

205

"It's my mother's dress. Read, read this. From my own mother to Granny."

"What ya talkin' 'bout? Ya ain't got no ma."

"I did, I did, Colie. I remember her, but she's dead. The bad man killed her. She loved me. I can never get her back. She's dead. Granny was bad, cruel and unforgiving. I hate her."

Colie sat on the edge of the bed and pushed the damp hair away from her face and took her hands away.

"Ya talkin' crazy. Look at me. Don't turn away. Ya musta had a bad dream. Ya awake now, funny face, and ya don't know whatcha' talkin' 'bout."

"Yes, I do, and I'm not crazy. Colie, just listen! I broke open Granny's trunk and found the clothes and letters. Janie was one of Granny's daughters and my real mother. She ran away with a man. Later she had me. The man was bad, and he killed my mother."

"Whoa, slow down."

"No, I'm not dreaming. Listen to me, please, Colie. Carrie, my mother's friend wrote to Granny and told her what happened. Carrie thought Granny would want her daughter's body to be sent home to her, to be buried in her hometown. But Granny wouldn't take her own daughter's body. Janie's friend made the burial arrangements and paid for the funeral. Carrie wrote in the letter that she didn't care about the cost because she loved Janie, and tried to help her get away from that man."

"Naw, this story's too crazy. Ya gone 'round the bend, losin' yer granny an' all. I'll get Ma."

Frances sat up and clutched the front of his shirt and stared wildly at him.

"No. Don't. Not yet. I don't want anyone to know. Shut the door. I'm not dreaming, Colie . . . and I found money . . . lots of money . . . Look!"

206

She raised the pillow and grabbed fistfuls of crumpled bills. "My mother sent money to Granny until . . . until she was killed by that man. Read the letters, Colie. Oh, I remember her, the funny feelings I'd get when thoughts of her tried to work through my mind . . . it wasn't my imagination. They were true, and I thought I was losing my mind.

"She wanted to come and see me. Granny wouldn't let her. Read them. We're rich, Colie. We're rich!"

Colie stared at the money, then at the letter in his hand . . . wonderingly. He put down the letter, picked up the money, smoothed out the bills and began counting.

"Aren't you going to read the letters? They're from my own mother."

"In a minute, funny face—gotta take all this in, an' I ain't much of a reader." He finished counting, then stood up, picked up a chair, and sat down heavily. "There be a thousand dollars here," he said in a choked whisper. "Ain't never seen so much money. Ya tellin' me it's yer money?"

Frances talked rapidly.

"Yes, yes, that's what I'm trying to tell you. My mother sent this money to Granny, but Granny never spent it—it's been in her trunk all this time. My mother wrote she wanted me to have nice things, like pretty dresses. She wanted Granny to take me to a doctor and see if anything could be done about my foot. She came to see me, but Granny wouldn't let her in. And the man followed her, so my mother had to leave me in the church, and then he took her away."

Frances paused to get her breath, then continued, "It was in the newspaper that he finally killed her . . . he murdered my mother," sobbed Frances. "Carrie mailed the clipping to Granny. How could Granny be so coldhearted?"

She got off the bed, stood by his side, and thrust the

letter and clippings at him once more. "This is the first letter. Carrie, her friend, wrote it because Janie couldn't write or spell well enough, Carrie said. It has a date on it."

"Well, that goes for me. I'm 'shamed ta tell ya, I can't write or read good neither. Didn't get much schoolin', ya know. Had to go down the pit when me pa was hurt. I never did learn proper, an' all this got me head startin' to swim; yer read 'em to me."

Frances perched herself on his lap and began to read from the clipping.

June 10, 1920, Halifax, Nova Scotia.

Joseph Pike, age 40, shot and killed himself after writing a suicide note confessing to the beating death of a woman known as Jane Williams.

The body of the 33-year-old woman was found by two boys who were playing in a field behind a known house of prostitution on Carver Street. The house has since been closed down.

Frances leaned her head against Colie's chest and sobbed.

"I'm sure he's the bad man I remembered. My poor mother couldn't get away from him."

Colie cradled her in his arms and rocked her gently.

"She would be 'bout the same age as me own ma. Don't read the letters now; be too much for ya. Ya've had a bad shock, yer knows. I know me own head's spinning. Ain't every day a man finds out he's getting' hitched to a gal come from a pile a money." Colie nuzzled the ticklish spot on Frances's neck and tried to make her laugh.

"Everything's happening so fast. Granny dying, then finding out about Janie, my mother, and the baby. I feel sick all the time and so tired. But I'm glad to find out who I really am, except I don't know who my father was. Please, don't let it be that awful man! I never knew how cruel Granny could be until now."

"Nora was right odd," Colie said with surprising insight, "but maybe she didn't mean ta be cruel. Maybe she wanted to forget? Ya said yerself she was never mean ta ya. She drank the gin to forget, and ta Nora, ya were her girl come back, an' she could raise yer to be the daughter she wanted Janie to be."

Colie carried her to the bed and laid her down. "Listen, now, I wants ya ta go to sleep. We'll talk when ya wake up. Then yer can read me them letters. What yer want ta do with the money? Ya can't let it lay scattered 'bout."

"Hide it in a safe place. It's ours, yours and mine, and a gift from my mother. We can buy a car; then we can go for rides in the country when the baby is born. Oh, I hope it's a boy and that he looks just like you!"

"Naw, don't hide it. Put the money in the bank downtown... naw... that ain't a good idea. There'd be all kinds a talk, ya walk in with a pile a money. Ya'd have ta explain where it came from, and it's no one's damn business. An' I ain't lettin' you buy me no car. I'll buy me own." He picked up the bills. "I'll take care a the money, funny face, 'til ya knows what ya want ta do with it."

"You're smart, Colie, smarter than you realize, and I'll teach you to read, and I never thought of it before, but maybe you're right. Granny wanted me to be Janie, so she couldn't admit to herself the other Janie was still alive. That's why she ignored the letters, money, and everything. To Granny, Janie was dead when she ran away with that man. Granny's mind wasn't right."

Frances sighed. "I... I feel better. Granny couldn't help being the way she was, but... I know she did love me in her own way, and now I know I had a mother who loved me, and . . . and I have you. The baby doesn't seem real to me right now.

"I wonder how my mother felt when she knew she was going to have me? Poor Janie, she had the bad man, but I have you, don't I, Colie? You won't ever treat me mean, will you?" She raised her arms to encircle his neck, and said softly, "Kiss me, Colie."

26

Maggie pushed the flatiron across Colie's shirt, thinking, *that girl's a slack one...does nothing but lay on her back and complain all the long day. You'd think, to listen to her, she was the only girl in the world who'd been in the family way.*

Lord knows, I was sick with Danny, my first, right up until the day I delivered—sick and afraid Jock would find out it wasn't his—but I worked. No complaints passed my lips. Wouldn't have done any good if I'd had, the work had to get done, sick or no, and sewing for the ladies kept food on the table when the mines were shut down.

And where in the world did she get those fancy getups? What in heaven's name is going on with her? I never saw dresses like that except in picture shows. Surely the clothes didn't belong to Nora?

Well, the girl better pull herself together. I know my son. He won't put up with her nonsense for long, baby or no. He's used to hot meals, a neat house, and clean clothes to put on his back. Though, I have to admit, I don't mind the work. I want to keep busy; then I won't have time to think. Oh, Lord, Lord.

Maggie stopped ironing, held the flatiron in midair, and listened as a truck rumbled to a stop in front of the house.

Quickly, she put the iron down, snatched Boydie from her play on the floor, and flung open the door and hurried down the walk.

"Murdy, Murdy, oh, I'm that glad to see you!" She brushed his cheek with her lips. "Did you get my letter?"

Her brother, hatless and wearing navy blue pants and work shirt, his red hair slicked down and neatly trimmed, stopped to wipe his feet against the doormat before grabbing her in a bear hug that took her breath away. His fine-featured, tanned face so like his sister's, broke into a wide grin at the sight of golden-haired Boydie in her mother's arms.

"Come to your uncle, darling."

"Mama, me down," Boydie said, and clung to her uncle's legs singsonging, "Murdy here, Murdy here, baby love Murdy."

He swung her up in the air a few times, while she squealed and grabbed for his hair.

Finally, he answered.

"Got the letter yesterday. Sure is good to see you, sister. You're looking real fine. You'll be the prettiest granny in town. Henry keeps asking when you're coming by. He's all het up, thinking you'll be coming to stay; got courting on his mind."

"That bear of a man? For heaven's sake, what a thought. Please discourage him for me . . . please! Pa pushed him at me so much when I was a girl, I began to hate the sight of him . . . used to run and hide when he'd visit. Pa had him picked out for me to marry. Well, at least I escaped that fate."

Murdock threw back his head and laughed.

"You're right. Hank be too much for a little thing like you. He'd crush you to death in the marriage bed the first night."

Maggie blushed.

"You stop that kind of talk. I can still box your ears, Murdock Beaton." She reached out and tapped him on the side of the head.

"Okay," he pulled his head back and said, "just trying to get a rise out of you, and it worked sure enough. I've been staying with Hank, and he's a bossy son of gun. Would have been here sooner, but old Hank sure keeps at

212

me . . . wants to impress you at how much work is done on the house.

"I'll put a bug in his ear not to get his hopes up where you're concerned. Maggie, I feel guilty as blazes. I know I'm putting Hank and the rest out when they work on the house. It's taking them away from their own chores, and a farmer can't let his work get ahead of him."

"Don't feel guilty. Country people have always helped when there is a need. Ma and Pa were like that. Remember? So the house is up? My, that didn't take long. It's only been two weeks since the fire."

"Just the frame. There is a long way to go before the house is livable. That's what I want to talk to you about."

Maggie glanced down the road and saw Mabel and Lizzie, arm in arm, walking toward them.

"Let's not talk out here. Come into the house. I made a fresh pot of tea and baked a blueberry cobbler, quick, before those biddies are upon us."

Murdock turned and looked at the women, gave them a dazzling smile, then followed her into the house.

"I take it they're not friends of yours, sister. Boy, it sure smells good in here." He sat at the table with Boydie in his lap.

"I remembered you like blueberry cobbler. I baked it this morning in the hope you'd be here today, and, indeed, here you are! Talk to me while I put out the tea things. It's lonely now that Jenny's gone to live with her daughter. Sammy, her husband, gone to God knows where, but that's no loss. No one's heard a word from him.

"Another miner and his family are moving in, and as I wrote in the letter, Colie married the girl. They're living in her grandmother's house . . . belongs to the girl now. She's come up in the world."

Maggie paused in the middle of the room with the

teapot in her hands. "I don't know what to do, Murdy. Colie's gone back to the pit. Says he wants to work in the mines. Can you imagine wanting to work in a hell-hole? He told me I have nothing to say about what he does with his life. He's a changed boy since he took up with Frances James."

Murdock stroked his chin.

"Well, sister, the way I see it, he's a young man who grew up in a hurry, making babies and the like. Soon's I get settled somewhere, I'm finding me a girl of my own to marry and settle down and raise a family. Colie has a right to make his own way. Wish I'd had the courage when I was his age. I'd have gotten out from under John's thumb right enough."

Maggie shook her head in disbelief.

"Are you saying Colie was under my thumb?"

"Now, Maggie, don't put a meaning to an innocent remark. I was referring to myself, not Colie. I don't even know the boy."

"Sorry, I didn't mean to take offense. I don't know what I'm saying half the time. I'm at my wit's end, and I don't understand my son. His father died because of a pit accident. Colie's seen men badly injured. One killed outright. It's insanity to do that kind of work unless you have nothing else. Colie has a choice—the farm, a clean, decent place to raise his child. Surely you'd not prefer work in a coal mine to work on the farm?"

"Sure, I would. If it meant getting away from John, I'd say yes. But John would have come after me, and I was afraid of what he might do. I wanted to come and help you after Jock died, get a job in the mine, but I didn't have the courage."

"I never knew. Oh, Murdy, you haven't had it easy either, have you?" Maggie put the teapot down and went

214

and stroked her brother's hair. "It's not that I can't accept Colie's growing into manhood, of course not." She pursed her lips, poured the tea, and put out plates for the cobbler, then sat down. "It's the mine. I'm deathly afraid he'll be hurt sooner or later. There's not a miner in town who doesn't bear scars.

"The company sent a notice. We were to be evicted unless Colie went back to work. For awhile I thought that's why he did it. I don't think that way now. He pays the rent and tries to give me money. I won't take a cent from him!

"I make my own way. My sewing for the ladies keeps me going, and God knows, the baby and I don't need much."

"It's all Colie knows, sister, and I'd say there's a certain amount of pride in being a miner, even with the risks." Murdock broke off a piece of cobbler, said, "Now, there's a good girl," and put Boydie down. He pushed his plate away and leaned toward his sister. "Listen, I found out we can sell the farm."

Maggie put down her cup, and tea splashed over the rim and into the saucer.

"What do you mean? What are you talking about?"

Murdock got up, stuck his hands in his pockets, and started to pace the room.

"I . . . I . . . went to see John, had to. It was terrible! A godforsaken place. He didn't even know me. They have him tied up in a cell, like a mad dog. You'd never recognize him as the brother we grew up with. Frothing at the mouth, he was.

"One of the doctors told me John's criminally insane and never would be released. Yesterday, I talked with a lawyer fellow in town, and Maggie, listen to this! He told me the property belongs to the siblings, that's us. You, Ned, and me. We can sell the farm. Ned's in Toronto. He got married last year. I wrote to him, and he wants to sell and get his share.

"The lawyer said, since there's no will and John's in the asylum—" Murdock choked up and couldn't continue. He banged his fist on the table until the dishes rattled and spilled tea ran on the floor. Maggie jumped up, and Boydie started to cry. "Sorry, I shouldn't have done that, but man, oh, man, is it ever hard to take, the sight of your brother in a place like that."

Maggie shushed him and rocked Boydie until she quieted down and went to sleep.

"Maggie, the farm's ours, and if you agree with Ned and me, I'll sell the damn place and get the hell away from there."

"I can't believe what you're saying; you're a farmer. What would you do?"

"Sure, I'm a farmer, but never by choice. I'd have preferred something else for myself if I'd had any say. No fun getting up day after day to back-breaking work and looking at the backside of a cow.

"I hate the place. Maybe John's to blame for that. I don't know, and it's an awful thing to say about your sick-in-the-head brother, but a load's been shifted off my shoulders, not having to deal with him anymore. I want a life of my own making, sister, not one foisted on me at birth. If you agree to it, we'd have a stake. Listen, Maggie, we could go to Toronto. You said you wanted to get away from here. What's to keep you? Seems to me, Colie's all set." Murdy got up and started to pace the floor again. He ran work-stained fingers through rumpled hair. "We'd be a family, like before, you, me, and Ned."

Maggie didn't answer but got up, took a cloth from the hook by the sink, and wiped up the spilled tea. She looked at him and shook her head.

"Sit down, brother. Finish your cobbler. I'll get more tea," she said. "You said Ned has a wife, and a baby on the way; that's his family. We can't go back to who we were when we were children on the farm."

She smiled, . . . remembering. "Mama, Papa, John, you, and me. John was all right then, most of the time. We played and laughed together. Don't you remember? The sickness hadn't got hold of him. Maybe I'm to blame for what happened to all of us. If I hadn't . . . if I hadn't got . . . if I hadn't married Jock, oh, what's the use. It's over and done with."

She put Boydie on the cot by the window and went over and placed her hands on his shoulders. "I won't stand in your way if that's what you want to do. You and Ned. You have the right, and I have none. I gave that up, as John was quick to point out, when I married Jock McNeil. I'd hoped there would be a place for Colie on the farm, but he wants none of it."

"Then think about it, Maggie. I'll get the papers from the lawyer fellow for us to sign, put the farm up for sale, and we'll go to Toronto. You, Boydie, and me. We'll do all right, have us a fine old time. There will be no big brother to pick on us, like when we were kids," said Murdock, grabbing Maggie and doing a fast jig around the room.

Maggie started to giggle, lost her balance, fell against the cot, and woke Boydie. Murdock picked up the baby, wrapped his free arm around Maggie and danced with them into the parlor, while Boydie clapped her hands with delight.

Colie, grimy with sweat and streaked with coal dust, took off his boots, cap, and overalls and left them by the tin washtub overflowing with soiled clothes at the back door before entering the quiet kitchen.

He glanced at the stove and frowned. There were no pans of hot water for his washup and no signs of a meal being prepared for his supper.

He sighed, went to the sink, pumped water, and let it run over his head and face, then grabbed a nearby towel and dried himself off before heading upstairs to their room.

Lethargic all day, Frances couldn't seem to will herself to do the much-needed household chores. Instead, she had tried on her mother's dresses and posed in front of the full length mirror, pretending she was Gloria Swanson before finally settling for a long, transparent, gauzy, red gown that she planned to take off before Colie got home.

Then glancing at the clock on the bureau, she thought, *oh, dear, it's late. Colie will be home soon.* She started to make their bed. A wave of nausea hit her, and she moaned, "oh no, not again," and sprawled across the half-made bed. She heard Colie on the stairs and quickly shut her eyes and turned toward the wall.

Irritated and angry, Colie stopped in the doorway and looked slit-eyed at her. Then his eyes widened at the newly developed rounded curves clearly apparent through the flimsy dress, and he hurried to her side, got into bed, turned her to him, and pressed against her.

"Ya looks pretty in that dress, funny face, like Clara Bow in the movies," he said.

"Leave me alone, Colie. I'm sick."

"Ya, but I knows what'll make ya feel better, feel this." He started to breath rapidly. "Come on." He pulled her against him and lifted her dress.

"Ain't it great ta be married? We can make love any old time." He felt her breasts through the thin dress. "Ya tits getting' bigger, too. I can't get enough of ya, Franny."

"No, stop it. I don't want to. Leave me alone. I don't feel

218

like making love." She pushed him away.

He got up, his blue eyes still rimmed with coal dust, and glared down at her.

"Besides, you're dirty. She looked down at her dress. "You got my dress dirty." Why don't you wash when you get home from the pit?"

"Wash? How the hell can a man wash up when there ain't no hot water waitin' for him? Why don't ya take off them silly dresses and do somethin' 'round here? Ya liked me ta touch ya well 'nuff before. Ya liked it then all right," Colie shouted. "Ya always sick. Ya mean ta tell me I ain't to have no more fun 'cause yer havin' a kid? That what ya tryin' ta tell me, Franny? Ya shuttin' me off?"

"Stop shouting, Colie." She got off the bed and shut the window.

"I'll shout, all right. I got a right ta shout when me own wife pushes me away. Ya changed Franny, an' I don't like the way ya been actin'."

"I can't help it. I feel awful all the time. Dr. Field said it would pass in a while. Just don't push at me. Please, Colie. I'll go down and put the water on to heat and start supper. Don't be mad at me. I love you, Colie. I just don't feel like making love."

"Don't worry, I won't be botherin' ya no more. Colie McNeil don't 'ave ta beg for it, I can tell ya that, an' ya can forget the hot water and supper. Me ma will take care a me."

He grabbed his pants, which lay on the chair next to the bed, and slammed out of the room, stopping long enough outside the bedroom to stumble into the pants, then rushed headlong down the stairs and out the door toward his mother's house.

Colie stared, spellbound, as Maggie and Murdock did

a fast jig while his baby sister sat on the floor and clapped her little hands, saying, "Dance. More dance. Me like dance."

"Ya fellas seem to be havin' a good time. I'll be havin' the next dance, Ma, if ya brother don't mind." Grinning, he crossed the room and grabbed her for a fast twirl around the room before he stopped to shake Murdock's hand. "Glad ta see ya, uncle. Glad ta see ya, and it's right good ta see me ma havin' a time. Never knew ya could dance like that, ma. When ya learn how ta do such a fine job?"

Murdock took Colie's hand.

"How are you? I guess we were carrying on some, but it felt fine to dance with my sister again."

Maggie blushed prettily and sank into a chair.

"Oh, my, let me catch my breath." She laughed and said, "Well, guess you've found me out, son. Murdy, Ned, and I used to wait until our parents were away, then we'd dance like demons. Ned would sing, and he could play the harmonica a little. My, he had a grand voice. We were just children after all. I'd almost forgotten. Ma and Pa were straightlaced. We'd get the strap if they ever caught us at the 'Devil's work.' We didn't have much fun when we were children, did we Murdy? But we made our own whenever we got the chance, and that wasn't often."

"That's the God's truth, sister. No wonder I want to sell and get away from the place . . . wouldn't care if I never set eyes on it again."

Colie, a puzzled look on his face, sat down.

"What the hell . . . what ye talkin' 'bout?" he asked. "Ya can't sell the farm. Ma and me baby sister goin' ta live with ya. Ain't yer, Ma? Ain't that what we talked 'bout, Ma? As soon's the house is ready?"

Maggie pushed stray curls away from her face and glared at her son.

"You made your decision, now kindly let me make mine! I didn't say Boydie and I were going back to the farm. That was your idea. And I'll be the one to decide what's best for Boydie and me, and in my own good time, young man." Then in a softer tone, "You look in need of a bath. Go home and clean up. Then come back and visit with your uncle. It's time you got to know each other. Bring the girl back with you if she'll come."

The tension somewhat eased in the room when Murdock got up and clapped his hands against his thighs, with the hearty suggestion.

"Sure, go get her, man, go get her. I've been wanting to meet my nephew's bride, you lucky son of gun, and one of the first things I'm going to do when the farm's sold is find me a girl of my own, you betcha life, before I get set in my ways."

Colie, shamefaced, hung his head.

"Sorry, but now ain't the best time ta meet Franny. She ain't feelin' all that good, and she's cranky as a bi—I mean, all get out. I thought to do me washup here. An' ya knows, Ma, I don't mean ta tell ya what ta do. I thought, since the other one, John, well, is gone to the . . . ya know."

Maggie looked at her dejected son, at the curling, damp hair pasted against his forehead, at his weary face and coal-streaked undershirt, then went to him and put an arm about his stopped shoulders.

"Son, you meant well, I know. I'll heat water, and you have a wash. Then I'll cook supper." She thought for a moment, then added, "Be patient with your wife. Pregnancy is difficult the first months. Her body is changing, and there's a new life growing within her. After awhile, when she feels the baby start to stir, she'll be overcome with joy, like I used to be." Then Maggie prayed God would forgive her for the small lie, for she'd never, when pregnant,

221

felt the joy she described to her son.

Considerably cheered at the thought of a bath and one of his mother's suppers, Colie turned to Murdock.

"Excuse me, uncle, while I 'ave me washup. Hope ya plan on stayin' for a spell." Then, close on her heels, he followed Maggie into the kitchen, questioning, "That the way it is? Ya say it ain't gonna last? I mean the way Franny's been actin'? Long's she don't keep on the way she is, guess I can stand it a bit longer. Ya sure, Ma? Franny's gonna be like her old self when she feels the baby movin'? Did ya really feel happy when I was on the way, Ma?"

"Good grief, son, leave it be. I said I was, didn't I? Now, get on with you. Go talk to your uncle while the water's heating."

"Ma, is he gonna sell the farm like he said?" Colie whispered.

"Well, go ask him, for heaven's sake!"

Murdock put his hand up to his mouth to keep from laughing out loud, then picked up Boydie, put her on his shoulders, and trotted around the room with her.

27

It was dusk when Colie left his mother's house, and as he walked in back of the row houses, he had to fend off Mabel MacDermott's half-starved dog, who growled and tried to nip at his ankles.

"Give way, yer mangy mutt." Colie aimed a kick at the dog's head. "Scram, or I'll kick yer ta hell an' back."

Disappointed, the dog slinked away.

Colie hated to go back to Nora's old home, thinking it a hard house, one that made him feel ill at ease, uncomfortable. He didn't like the horsehair sofa and chairs or the smell of mothballs that still permeated the place, in spite of being thoroughly aired out.

The bare floors, the gilt-framed pictures of Nora's ancient, long-dead Irish relatives that glared down at him from every wall, and he kept bumping into the countless knicknacks and little tables everywhere he turned.

He thought, *soon's Franny has the baby, we're leavin' the bluff ta find a place of our own. Franny can sell the house back to the company or somethin'. We'll move out of town to one of them houses near Jacob's Lake. I can do some fine fishin'. By jingo, just think, me and Franny in one of them swell houses.*

Don't know what to do 'bout me ma. Uncle Murdock sells the farm, what's Ma gonna do? She could live with me and Franny, but knowin' Ma, it ain't gonna happen.

Clean and refreshed, with a good supper in his belly and after a man-to-man talk with Murdock, Colie was in high spirits.

The back door was slightly ajar, and as he entered, he

thought of the comfort of his mother's house, with its soft well-worn chairs that fit his backside, the colorful hooked rugs made by his mother, the starched, ruffled curtains at the windows, and the cheerful pictures on the walls, and always, good cooking smells from the kitchen.

He found Franny carrying a pot of water to the stove.

"Hey, there, never mind the water, funny face. I had me bath at Ma's. Put the pot down and come here." He took her in his arms. "I ain't mad at yer no more. Ma straightened me out. I'll try ta keep me hands off ya 'til ya feels better."

Franny stayed rigid for a moment or two then melted against him and lifted her face to be kissed.

"Cut that out. Whatcha tryin' ta do? Get me steamed up again? Yer a witch, Franny, ya know that?"

"I'm sorry I've been such a grouch, Colie. Oh, I wish we could go somewhere. I'm tired of the house, and no one talks to me except your mother and only when she can't avoid it. I'm restless . . . I want to . . . oh I don't know what I want. Let's buy a car. I've got money, and wouldn't it be grand to have a car? The weather's so beautiful, we could drive along the Cabot Trail. I'd love to see the mountains and the lakes. We could if we had a car. Please, Colie, let me buy you a car with some of the money."

"Aw, I don't want yer buyin' me no car. Save yer money for the baby and a new house. I don't plan on livin' in Nora's place any longa' than I 'ave ta." He stuck out his chin. "An' I'm tellin' ya now, I'll buy me own car with me own money. Fella's down at Miner's Hall been makin' sport a me, sayin' I'm a kept man, since ya granny left ya her house, like one a them gigolos in the picture shows, an' I had ta bust one fella' in the lip for somethin' he said—ain't tellin' ya 'bout that. What ya think they'd have ta say if I came drivin' along Main Street like some company swell? I'd never hear the end of it . . . torment

224

the life outta' me, they would."

Frances moved away from him and, hands on her hips, looked into up into his face.

"What do you care? They're jealous, that's all. She started to giggle. "We're married. You can't be a gigolo. I won't let you. Don't pay any attention to them."

"There're me mates, an' I don't want me mates makin' sport a me. Ya understand? Aw, the hell with it. Come on, I'm tired. Let's go to bed, but keep ya hands offa me, ya hear? An' no more wearin' them see-through dresses!" Then he laughed and smacked her on the bottom.

28

The night, blackish—no moon—the only sound, the surf as it raced up the rocky beach to bounce off the base of the cliff before slipping back into the sea.

Sammy Gleason climbed drunkenly up from the lower, sloping edge of the bluff, grabbing onto bushes and branches for support until he reached the footpath leading to Maggie's house at the tail end.

He stumbled against a geranium-filled planter as he tried the latch at the back door, and muttered obscenities.

"Bitch . . . cunt . . . I'm gonna fuck yer. Me old woman's gone, an' it's yer fault. Turned her against me, yer did, and I knows yer boy ain't livin' wid yer no more. Ha, I'll get yer now."

Maggie sat bolt upright in bed, listening. Gusts of wind had pulled the curtains through the open window, and she scampered from bed to close it. Her heart raced. She hugged herself to stop shivering in the warm room, and her skin broke out in goosebumps. What had awakened her? The curtains fluttering against the house? No, something else. Then the rattling at the back door! *Sammy, he's come back*.

Maggie's hair cascaded about her shoulders like an auburn mantle as she leapt from the bed, grabbed a white cotton wrapper from the foot of the bed, and quickly put it on.

She took Jock's unloaded hunting rifle from the corner of the closet, then thought, *Oh, I've got to calm myself. Chances are it's Colie. He's had a tiff with the girl. But then, wouldn't he call out so as not to frighten me if it was him? He knows I keep the doors latched.*

I'll take the rifle to be on the safe side. I'll not be turned into a nervous Nellie, and I'm ready for Sammy. If he dares show his face, he'll not find me unable to defend myself. I have no fear of Sammy Gleason.

She held the rifle stiffly at her side, walked quickly, but silently, down the stairs, and stood in the dim hall, listening.

"Som' a bitch. Open up!" Sammy pulled back his foot to kick in the door. It swung open, and he found himself looking into the barrel of Jock's rifle, one he knew well, as Maggie stood like an apparition in the lighted doorway.

"Get away from here. Get away from my door. I'm warning you!"

Sammy's eyes flew open and he stumbled back. Then he started toward her again.

"Yer crazy bitch, yer don't know how ta shoot. Let me in, got somethin' fer ya."

Maggie took a few steps out of the doorway and pressed the barrel hard against his chest.

"Oh, I know how to shoot vermin, Mr. Gleason, and that's what you are, vermin. Indeed I do." She started to cock the rifle.

Sammy gave out a frightened *"whoop,"* staggered backwards toward the bluff's overgrowth, turned, and went crashing through.

Maggie held the rifle steady and willed herself to stop shaking in the warm night air, thinking *he's not gone, but getting ready to leap out of the bushes. I...I won't be frightened by the likes of him.*

She pointed the rifle and peered into the darkness. Heart pounding, she waited. Minutes passed, then, after a small eternity, Maggie heard Sammy give a long, drawn out "*A-a-a-a*" that ended with a terrified cry.

Mabel's dog howled.

Maggie's legs started to buckle, and she leaned against the door for support. Then, holding the rifle at her side, she started to walk toward the underbrush, then—

"Mama, mama, baby scared."

Maggie turned and saw Boydie standing in the door-way with her teddy bear held tightly in her little arms. She ran back to the house, dropped the rifle on the ground, and scooped her up.

Colie came running.

"Ma, yer all right? We heard a scream . . . somethin' outa' hell. Sounded like it came from here!"

Frances stood behind Colie and held fast to his shirt-tail as Tom and Mabel MacDermott hurried toward them.

Maggie, pale and trembling, pointed toward the spot where Sammy had disappeared. Finally she found her voice.

"Sammy . . . he tried to break into my house. He . . . he was going to attack me. He . . . he tried to once before. I got Jock's rifle. It isn't loaded. Sammy ran. He must have fallen over the bluff. Oh, I didn't want him to get hurt, just to . . . to go away."

Colie raised his fist and shouted.

"The dirty bastard. I hope he broke his rotten neck, 'cause if he didn't, I'm gonna' do it fer him, the stinkin' old goat!"

Tom put a calming hand on Colie's shoulder.

"Get a grip on yourself, boy. Got a flashlight handy? Let's get down to the beach, see if there's any breath left in him, then you can beat the crap out of him, heh?"

It took them twenty minutes to find Sammy. He lay face down in the water while the surf washed over him, slowly pulling him along the rocks to the water's edge. Blood from his battered face flowed past his outstretched hands and blended with the tide.

Tom reached him first. He knelt down and rolled Sammy on is back, then pressed his fingers against the side of his neck and hollered over the roar of the surf.

"I found him. Shine the light over here. Can't feel no pulse. Phew! He smells like he fell into a bucket of shit...must have crapped himself. Face looks like raw meat. Got to pull him out of the water!" Tom lowered his voice when Colie reached them. He said in an awed tone, "I think...I think he's dead. Grab hold of his legs, son."

Tom, a big man, got his hands under Sammy's sodden body and lifted him by the shoulders.

Colie pocketed the flashlight.

"I wish I didn't 'ave ta touch him," he said. "God, he stinks." He knelt down and shouted near Sammy's ear, "Good thing yer dead, 'cause I was gonna kill ya myself for botherin' me ma!"

He grabbed Sammy's legs and pulled and dragged him up the side of the slope until he was out of the water, and left him spread-eagled in the underbrush.

Out of breath, with the roar of the surf ringing in their ears, Colie and Tom climbed the steep bank to the footpath.

Fred MacAllister, Mabel, and Lizzie stood close to Maggie's door, while other people from the row houses kept their distance, waiting.

Mabel grabbed Tom by the arm.

"Well, didja find him, Sammy? Dead, ain't he." Tom shrugged her off.

"Aw, shut up. Go home to the kids."

Colie looked around.

"Where's me ma?"

Lizzie gestured to Maggie's door.

229

"Inside. No manners a'tall. Slammed the door in me face when I enquired afta 'er. Tried to shoot poor old Sammy, she did." Lizzie pointed. "There's the rifle right there. Call the Mounties, Fred. Maggie tried to do murder, yes, she did!"

Outraged, Fred MacAllister shouted.

"Maggie had every right to defend herself. Shut that mouth of yours, Lizzie, or I'll shut it for you. Go on home!" He turned to Colie. "Don't be listening to that one. Doc Field will know how to handle this. I'll call him right off."

Tom started to chuckle.

"Sure, and that will be a waste of time. Sammy needs an undertaker." Then, to Lizzie, "Shut your trap about Mounties. No one wants the Mounties sniffing around here. Sammy got drunk and fell off the bluff. No more to it than that."

A gaunt old man staggered toward them.

"Look, Lizzie, there's your man with a snootful in him. Get him home before he falls off the bluff, and no more talk 'bout Mounties, you hear?"

Mabel started to protest.

"It ain't right a'tall. We seen the rifle. Maggie was goin' ter shoot—"

Tom shoved a balled fist under her nose.

"Get home, woman, or you'll feel this."

Mabel pulled her head in and backed away.

"Don't hit me, I'm leavin'. You ain't plannin' on beatin' me, are yer, Tom? I ain't done nuthin' ter get beat over."

"Aw, shut up, and get your scrawny arse *home*."

"Thank ya, Fred and Tom, fer stickin' up fer me ma," Colie said. "That old rifle of Pa's ain't loaded. Ma tried ta scare Sammy. Ma wouldn't hurt nobody."

"Sure and we all know it, even that one," Fred said and pointed to Lizzie. "I'll call the doctor. He'll know what to do." Then, to the waiting people, he hollered, "Sammy Gleason got drunk and fell off the bluff. Go back to bed, folks. The doctor is on his way."

Flossy Matherson yelled out.

"I've some nurse's trainin'. Sure an' shouldn't someone be lookin' after the poor soul?"

Her husband nudged her painfully in the ribs.

"You're daft, woman. How in hell yer plan on getting' down there to the bugger? Yer'll fall an' break yer own neck, yer will." He pulled her away, shrugged, and said, "Looks like more trouble for Maggie McNeil, an I says, keep it from our door."

The people wandered back to their houses in the darkness, whispering amongst themselves.

Mabel hurried past her husband, sorry she'd angered him and hoping he wouldn't beat her, and filled with hatred for Maggie McNeil. It would be Maggie's fault if she got a beating tonight.

Dr. Field arrived soon after, pronounced Sammy dead by accidental drowning, signed the death certificate, and that was the end of it.

Sammy was waked at the Russel Funeral Home on Main Street, merrily attended by his drinking cronies and most of Rockhill's coal miners.

Maggie knew she'd done the right thing in frightening Sammy away from the door that awful night; still, traces of guilt lingered—a man had died because of her. She didn't want to go to Sammy's funeral.

Dr. Field said he thought she should go. He would drive her to the cemetery, and it would comfort Jenny to see her there.

29

Maggie chewed her bottom lip, while Boydie played on the floor with a few wooden blocks.

Downstairs, a door slammed, and Frances called out from the foot of the stairs.

"Maggie! Maggie!"

"I'm up here, Frances, in my room. I can't come down. I'm trying to make up my mind about something."

Dimples showing and eyes sparkling with good health, Frances burst into the room.

"Guess what, Maggie? I feel real good today, and I'm not sick to my stomach anymore, and look, my belly's getting big." She placed her hands on her swelling abdomen and turned sideways.

Maggie suppressed a smile.

"My, my, you are beginning to show. Soon, you'll feel the baby begin to move, and it will feel like the fluttering of butterflies at first."

Frances put her hands up to her glowing face.

"Really? So that's what I've felt when I'm sitting still, the baby, my very own baby. Oh, I've never been so happy. I cleaned the house and cooked Colie's supper, his favorite, beef stew with dumplings. Will he ever be surprised when he gets home from shift." Then her eyes lit on the scarf and dress draped across the bed, and the smile left her face.

"Oh, you're going to that man's funeral, after all. Why, after what he tried to do?"

Maggie shook her head.

"It's hard to explain, girl. Jenny's my friend, and he was

her husband and father to her child. The doctor said he'd drive me to the cemetery. I haven't seen Jenny since it . . . it happened. I don't want her to think I'm avoiding her."

"Well, can I take the baby to the beach? She can play in the sand. I've got nothing to do the rest of the day. Please?"

"Of course, dear. Boydie would like that. I intended to ask you to mind her, anyway, and it will be cooler at Black's beach."

Frances pouted.

"I still think you shouldn't go. That mean Lizzy and the rest will be thee, and she said terrible things about you. I hate her."

Maggie shook her head.

"Don't talk like that. Hate is a strong word. Lizzie's just an ignorant, frustrated woman, like most of the wives on the bluff. She doesn't know any better. Don't hate her. Pity her."

"Pity her? How can I pity someone that hateful? Lizzie and that Mabel MacDermott, mean, spiteful women. They made fun of Granny and me. Lizzie spied on Colie and me. She didn't think we knew, but we did. I'll never have pity for her. Maybe for the other one, her husband beats her, but never old Lizzie!"

"Yes, dear, I know it's hard, but it's the Christian way."

"I can't be a Christian then. She tried to hurt you. Why do they hate us? What did we ever do to them?"

"I don't know. Maybe because I kept to myself. Who knows? I didn't join them in gossip and backbiting. I supplemented Jock's wages with dressmaking and such. God knows, the money was needed. I didn't have time to socialize even if I'd wanted to.

"Jenny told me, oh, this was years back, that the women on the bluff said that I thought I was too good to mix with them. What nonsense! You better not be different in this town, or they will eat you alive for it."

Frances looked thoughtful.

"Well, that explains why they don't like me. Does Colie know you're going to Mr. Gleason's funeral? He won't like it, I know."

Maggie sat on the edge of the bed and sighed.

"No, he doesn't, and you're not to tell him, understand? Maybe no one will notice me if I stay in the background until the services are over. It's amazing how many will turn out for a funeral for the likes of Sammy. Makes one wonder? Would they if there wasn't a spread put out at Miner's Hall afterward?" Maggie got up, went to the dresser, picked up a silver-backed hairbrush, and started to brush her hair. "Believe me, I don't want to go to that man's funeral, but Jenny's been a dear friend for a longtime."

Frances frowned and didn't speak for a few moments, until Boydie held out her arms saying, "Uppy—uppy," then, Frances scooped her up and hugged her.

"Oh, you're my sweetie baby, yes you are. Come to Auntie Frances."

Maggie watched them, noticed how Frances's smooth dark hair gleamed against Boydie's red-gold curls, and wondered, *What color hair will the new baby have. Most certainly, chestnut, like Colie and Frances's. Would the baby look like Colie? He was a beautiful child.*

She felt a sudden chill and folded her arms in front of her. Five months, in five months, Colie will be a father. Her boy, a father. *Well, we won't be here. I've made up my mind. Boydie and I won't be here when the baby is born.*

I've good use for the pittance the company gave me when Jock was killed, and, thank goodness, I was able to put aside a few pennies a week for the insurance policy. Hard to come by were those pennies, but I managed. The Lord was guiding me.

It's enough to live on until I get work. I'm a good dressmaker. A big city like Boston will have many in need of my skills.

If the child is a boy, I'll not have to watch him grow up only to dig the company's rotten coal and have the cycle start once more. No, I'll not go through that again.

She reached out to smooth down Boydie's hair.

"Don't forget her bonnet and take a few crackers and a jar of tea in case the sickness comes back. The day is overcast, still, you'll get sunburned if you don't cover up. It's almost time for her nap. Here, take this." Maggie took a blanket from the foot of the bed and handed it to Frances. She kissed them both and said, "Now be off with you."

Maggie, dressed in a somber print dress, covered her hair with a black scarf, then, tapping her foot, sat down on the wooden bench in the foyer to wait.

Earlier, she'd hung clothes out to dry, and the air, thick and humid, made every breath she drew seem like an effort, and the hovering fog, like dirty, gray wool, made Maggie think, *what a wonder,...we've had glorious sunny weather for weeks until today, almost as though God Himself doesn't think Sammy deserves a bright sunny day for his funeral*.

Dr. Field had been Larry the barber's first customer that morning. Now, unruly hair neatly cut and off his brow, face shaved and smelling strongly of bay rum, he leaned over to open the car door and looked closely at Maggie.

"You're pale. Are you taking the tonic I left for you? It's important you take care of yourself, young lady." Then he reached for her hand and clutched it, as if it were a lifeline, when she settled into the seat. "I care about you . . . I hope—"

He cleared his throat. "Dear, dear, Maggie, I know this isn't the right time, but I hope you will take what I'm about to say, and will give it considerable thought before answering. I've watched you through the years and grown to love you. I want to take care of you, dear. Marry me. You have courage, beauty, and grace. I've loved you since I delivered your first baby and heard you cry out the name of the baby's father over and over."

Unbelieving, Maggie stared at him for a long moment, then withdrew her hand from his sweaty grasp.

"Doctor, what are you saying? I—no—it's not possible."

He reached for her hand again.

"I knew James Boyd. He was a fine young man, and no one but me heard you call out for him. Jock was in a state, wringing his hands and crying. I sent him to his mother's to get him out of the way when you were in hard labor. Your secret's been safe with me, dear girl." He reached for her. "Call me George, Maggie. You'd be Mrs. George Field, my beautiful wife."

Maggie crouched in the corner of the seat.

"All this time, you knew? Oh, I'm so ashamed." She covered her face with her hands.

He leaned over and tried to pull her into his arms.

"I shouldn't have told you. I don't know why I did. Forgive me. I didn't want to upset you. It doesn't matter. I want to marry you."

Maggie pushed further into the corner.

"Not upset me? What did you think it would do? I can't look at you. I feel such shame. Why do you bring up something like that after all this time? What kind of man are you? *You knew.* You said it to bring me down, hold it over me." Maggie sat up and glared at him. "I'll tell you this much, Dr. Field, if I did marry again, it wouldn't be to a man who'd bring up something that happened years ago to make a woman feel cheap and dishonored. *Let me out of this car!*"

236

Dr. Field held onto the door handle.

"You're even more beautiful when you're angry, Maggie, and the only woman I ever wanted. I'm sorry I hurt you, but I never intended to bring you down. I admire you too much to do that, and . . . I've kept your secret, haven't I?"

Maggie sat back and rubbed her hand over her forehead.

"I won't give you any credit for that. Isn't a doctor supposed to honor his patients' confidences? Would it have made you happy to spread it all over that Maggie McNeil was a loose woman? The baby was not her husband's?"

"Stop that kind of talk, young lady. I want to marry you. Will you marry me? I've waited a long time for you, Maggie."

She picked up the scarf that had slipped off her head.

"No, I thank you for the offer, especially knowing what you do about me."

He rested his hands on the steering wheel and looked out.

"I'm too old for you. That's it, isn't it?"

"No, no. Age has nothing to do with it. It's me. I'm going to be in charge of my own life from now on. I'll not depend on anyone. My little girl and I are going to make a new start, in the States—Boston. I'm leaving soon. Colie's married and back working in the mine. He doesn't need me. It's me and the little girl left to me."

Dr. Field moved away, leaned back in his seat and looked sharply at her.

"That is nonsense! What would you do in the States? Maggie, you're a country girl, used to a small town. You don't know what you're saying."

Maggie looked down at her hands then up at him, a defiant look on her face, her eyes, green slits.

"It's not nonsense. What's there here for me? I hate this town, and the farm belongs to my brothers. They can do with it what they like. If Colie had wanted any part of the farm, things would be different. But he made it clear, he's quite content with his lot, now that he has a wife, house, and soon a baby."

Dr. Field scowled.

"Maggie, it's insane. You can't up and leave. Do you know anyone in Boston?" Then he scratched his chin and started to smile. "Boston is a big city. Better give up that idea and marry me. I'll take good care of you and the baby."

"Don't patronize me, doctor. I'm not an idiot. I know Boston is a big city."

He patted her knee.

"Of course, my dear, and I don't mean to sound patronizing. Of course, you've looked into it, done your research. Please, don't be angry."

Maggie gently removed his hand from her knee.

"Boston, Boydie and I are going to Boston to live. It's an industrial, cultured city with good schools for Boydie, museums, churches, libraries, and plenty of jobs.

"You ask who do I know in the States. Well, doctor, Marion McNeil, Archie's widow is there now. Two weeks after Archie's funeral, she packed up and left with her two boys. Marion has a flat in a building owned by a relative of her father, and she's getting along quite nicely."

The smile left Dr. Field's face.

"Well, then, guess you do know what you're doing. No hope for me. Don't know what I'll do without you, Maggie . . . when I can't see your lovely face. But you're still here, and I'll try to wear you down." He lifted her chin and kissed her lightly on the lips.

Maggie didn't object.

"I do like you, doctor," she said softly, "but you deserve

a wife who could return your love. That I could never do. I'm sorry."

He cleared his throat once more.

"Don't be sorry. You can't help how you feel, can you? I had to speak up, find out if I had a chance, and I thank you for being honest with me. Now, we'd better be off. I'll have to leave you at the cemetery gate as I have calls to make."

Maggie touched his arm.

"Doctor, you're a good man and a valued friend."

He forced a smile.

"And I will stay a valued friend, as you so nicely put it."

She reached over and kissed him on the cheek as he started the car.

Maggie pulled open the creaking gate and looked about. Overhead, seagulls screamed a protest that mingled with the cawing of crows as they fought over the carcass of a rabbit.

The entrance led to several paths with leaning, aged tombstones on each side, and Maggie cringed when she saw the large crowd gathered around Sammy's gravesite and heard Pastor MacMillen's loud, sorrowful voice in the humid air. She noticed the twitching, the foot-shuffling of the uncomfortable people as they seemed to urge him to "get on with it."

Quickly, she ducked behind the one large granite monument with the name "DILLON" etched across the surface and waited for the service to end. The coffin was lowered into the grave.

The women kept their heads lowered and dabbed at their eyes with dainty handkerchiefs in feigned sorrow as they walked away.

Maggie waited until they had passed by before stepping out from behind the monument.

Jenny, wearing a low-waisted, pleated, dove-gray dress and matching cloche hat, and black shoes with a buttoned strap over the instep, spied Maggie when she stepped from her hiding place. She flung her arms around her.

"Oh, Maggie, it's that good to see you! I didn't think you'd come, and why in heaven's name should you? God forgive me, but I'm glad he's gone." Then she whipped off her hat. "Look—my hair—I had it bobbed. It was Anna's idea. I don't feel like me anymore."

Maggie held her at arms' length.

"You look so stylish, Jenny, your dress, and the hat. I wouldn't have known you. Wonderful!"

"It's Anna. She's making me into a new woman. Oh, Maggie." She started to cry. "You remember, don't you? The early days, when I first married him? Wasn't he a good man then? Kind to me and our little Anna? Not cruel and mean. It was the drink made him evil. You should have told me he was bothering you in that way. I'd have put a stop to it right enough!"

"I don't think so, Jenny. No one could control Sammy when he was . . . well, anyway it's not the sort of thing you tell your best friend. I felt ashamed. Besides, I thought I could handle it myself. Well, he won't be bothering me or anyone else ever again, God rest his tormented soul. Then a smile started to curl around Maggie's lips. "Malcolm told Colie about the wake. The miners will be bragging about it for years to come."

"Yes, it was something awful. I loved Sammy once, and because of the good days, I wanted to give him a nice funeral, for the man he used to be. Some of the miners got drunk at the wake. Must be all over town by now. Dear God, it's hard to believe, but they lifted Sammy right out of the coffin, stood him in a corner, and put a drink in his hand, . . . said he'd need it for where he was going—the scoundrels!

"Anna and I were in another room when it happened. My, my, the screaming that went on! Daisy Moran and Pauline Jenkens fainted dead away. I almost passed out myself when I saw Sammy upright in the corner of the room. The undertaker rushed everyone out and put Sammy back in the coffin.

"Then Mike got into a scuffle with the two devils that did it and knocked one to the floor. He's right strong for a little man. The men brought it with them, the drink, I mean. I'd never have provided the drink, not on your life. All I wanted was a nice send-off for a once-decent man, and I hope dear Jesus has mercy on him."

Jenny wiped her eyes with a lace handkerchief, then linked arms with Maggie as her daughter and son-in-law approached. "Anna and Mike treat me like a queen, and the little one is precious. Anna is expecting again. Why do I feel guilt for being happy? Was it my fault that Sammy got into the drink so heavily? Don't know what more I could have done to please him. I tried not to make him angry."

Anna and Mike greeted Maggie warmly as Lizzie and Mabel sauntered past and Mabel uttered under her breath, "slut," as she passed Maggie.

Maggie could feel the heat rising in her face. She thought, *Oh, my God, what did that woman call me? Did I hear right?* She ran after Mabel, pulled her by the arm, and swung her around. The scarf fell from Maggie's head, and her eyes tore into Mabel like twin green flashes of fire.

"*What—what did you just say? What did you call me?*"

"Take yer mitts offa me!" Mabel, one eye swollen and bruised, tried to outstare her. She looked at the ground, then at Lizzie, and gained confidence when Lizzie nodded her head toward Maggie as if giving permission. Then

Mabel shouted, "Slut, yer be a slut, Maggie McNeil. Yer were carryin' on with Sammy behind Jenny's back. An yer were goin' ta shoot him 'cause he was fixin' ter tell on yer. Made him run fer his life. Ya killed him. Everyone knows yer did it!"

To Maggie, the world turned over, and she was spinning in a deep black tunnel, and at the end of the tunnel, Mabel waited hands on hips, uttering that hateful word over and over.

Mike, sensing what was about to happen, reached out to stop Maggie—too late. Maggie let out a primitive, guttural snarl. Her feet left the ground as she leapt, got her fists in Mabel's hair, and pulled her down.

Lizzie, pleased at what she'd brought about, covered her mouth to hide the smirk.

Jenny wrung her hands and cried, "Oh, dear, Oh, oh . . . "

Mike grabbed Maggie by the waist and pulled her away from Mabel. Eyes wide with fright, her face scratched, hair in disarray, dress dirty and rumpled, Mabel tried to get to her feet.

Lizzie helped her up, cooing.

"Niver yer mind now dearie, yer bring charges agin' that one." She pointed a bony finger at Maggie. "I see it all. I'm yer witness, dearie. Don't yer worry, assaulted yer, and yer mindin' yer own business, too."

Maggie clenched and unclenched her small fists, breathing heavily, still in a temper, wanting to tear Mabel apart, thinking, *how dare that creature in human form call me such a terrible, foul name. Lies, all lies, that, that . . . !*

But Mike held her firmly until her temper ebbed and she went limp.

"I'm sorry. I'm sorry. You can release me now, please," she whispered.

Mabel pushed back her tangled hair and brushed the dirt from her skirt, then took Lizzie's offered arm, and they scurried away. And, when at a safe distance from Maggie, Mabel turned and shouted the hated word.

"Slut!"

Maggie wrapped her arms about herself and fought to stop the trembling that shook her from head to foot. Anger, shame, indignation welled up in her, and she bit her lips, determined not to cry, as curious onlookers were passing by.

Jenny, Mike, and Anna gathered round her in stunned silence, not knowing quite what to do next. Then, Anna, a plain-faced, younger version of Jenny, put her hands on Maggie's shoulders.

"Look, look at me," she demanded. "You're not to cry. Don't give them the satisfaction. We'll take you home."

"You sure got some temper on you, lady," Mike said, "not that I blame you. She got what she deserved."

"No, she didn't. Oh, my God, what's wrong with me? I've lost control of myself. Please, let's go quickly. I feel like I'm going to faint."

Mike grabbed her before she hit the ground and carried her to the car.

Mabel and Lizzie shook their fists at them as their car whizzed by them on the road.

Maggie recovered quickly from the fainting spell, and when the car stopped in front of her door, she sat up.

"I'm all right. You go along. They will be waiting for you at the hall."

"No, I won't leave you. All this is Sammy's fault, mine too. I had misgivings that I shoved aside. I'd noticed the sidelong glances he'd give you and how he'd put his hands on you when he thought I wasn't looking. But, God help me, I didn't think Sammy'd try to—Mike, you and Anna go to the hall. Make some excuse for me, and if Lizzie and Mabel are at the hall, toss them out on their backsides!"

"Please, Jenny, I'll be fine," Maggie protested. "I'm going to lie down for awhile. Go to the hall. Don't give them more fuel for gossip. God knows I gave them plenty today, and Mabel will surely press charges. I'll face up to that when the time comes. I shouldn't have set foot in that cemetery today, but I didn't want you to think our friendship was at an end because of what happened. I didn't want you to think I wouldn't still be your friend."

"I know, I know, but I'll not hear another word. I'm staying here with you, and if Mabel dares to go to the police, I'll tell them a thing or two, how she shouted an obscenity, provoked you, blackening your good name." Jenny took off her hat and put it beside her on the seat. "I won't be missed. All the lot of them want to do is fill their faces. Anna, Mike, will look after things for me, won't you, dears? Bless your hearts."

She put an arm around Maggie and helped her out of the car and up the path. Anna followed.

"Mother is right. And, Maggie, I think you should come back with us and stay awhile, at least until my father's death isn't news. Let things die down a bit. Will you do that? We'd love to have you and Boydie. You've never been out to the house. Mike and I are proud of it. Please come. Pack a suitcase for you and the baby, and be ready to leave with us when we get back from Miner's Hall."

"Well, I don't—Colie will—"

"No buts, you'll come," Jenny said. "There is no reason not to, is there?"

"No, no, no reason in the world, and thank you for asking me. I'll be glad to get away from the bluff, but what if Mabel goes to the police, brings charges against me, shouldn't I be here to answer them? I did knock her down, God forgive my temper."

"Don't worry," Jenny sniffed, "her man will beat her if she tries that, and she knows it. Tom MacDermott doesn't want anything to do with the Mounties . . . he makes boot-leg liquor."

After the car drove away, they went into the kitchen, still fragrant with the smell of bread baked that morning. Maggie felt restless and had tossed and turned most of the night. Then, knowing sleep would not come, got up and put a batch of bread to rise.

Jenny fell into a chair.

"Glory be," she said, "I can't stand these shoes a minute longer. My Anna means well an' all, buying me styl-ish dresses and sending me to the beauty parlor, but she's trying to make a silk purse out of a sow's ear. How I long for my old comfortable shoes and a loose housedress to put on my back." She gave a short laugh and waved her hand. "Oh, listen to me complaining, when I've a wonderful daughter who wants me to look nice." She glanced around. "Where is the little one?"

"At Black's beach with Frances," Maggie answered. "The girl is fond of my baby, though she's but a baby her-self—babies having babies—God help her!"

Jenny wiggled her toes and sighed.

"Ahh, it feels that good to have them darn shoes off. Maggie, put the kettle on, and let's have a good talk. It's been a longtime, and though I'm happy with Anna, Mike, and the wee one, oh, Maggie, I've missed you."

Maggie spoke over her shoulder as she filled the tea kettle.

"And I've missed you, dear Jenny."

"Have you? With all you've had to deal with, a person wouldn't think you'd have the time to give your old friend

245

a thought." She padded over to the sink and looked into Maggie's face. "Just listen to me go on, when you should be resting after that fainting spell."

"I'm fine, really. Don't fuss over me. Sit down and rest your feet while I slip upstairs and change my dress." Then, tea kettle still in hand, Maggie paused, her lower lip starting to tremble, and she whispered, "Dear Jesus, but I've known trouble since I left my parent's farm and married Jock McNeil. But this dreadful year! In eight months I've lost my dear Catherine and now my son. I have no say in his life. He all but told me to my face. And . . . and the pit will get him. He'll be hurt, maybe die. I know it."

The tears welling in her eyes finally spilled over and ran unheeded down her cheeks. She put the kettle on the stove, turned and flung her arms around her friend in a tight embrace. "Oh, Jenny, I shouldn't be burdening you with my problems after you've laid your husband to rest, but I'm glad you're here, and do you forgive me for what happened to Sammy? I . . . I had to defend myself, yet I feel guilty for the way he died."

"Hush now." Jenny patted her on the back. "Drunk, he was drunk and came after you. No one's fault but his own. Stop thinking about it, Maggie. And as for forgiving you, there is nothing to forgive. You and I both know I'm well rid of him.

"He'd taken to coming out to Anna and Mike's place. You know, drunk and making a pest of himself. He was a good man at one time, but there are those who never should drink, for it changes them and turns them into beasts. Sammy was one of those beasts. Don't shed a tear over him. My tears over that man would fill a lake. I've cried enough for both of us. You need to rest," Jenny soothed. "Never mind the tea. Let me take you upstairs and tuck you in. Then, when you're rested and the baby is back from the beach, you'll come home with us."

Maggie wiped her eyes with the back of her hand and swallowed. "I can't," she said. "Much as I'd like to be with you, it would seem I was running away, and how they'd gloat. No, I'll stay and face whatever comes from my knocking Mabel to the ground."

"Nothing a'tall will come of it. Let's go upstairs. You have to rest. You're trembling, dear." She took Maggie by the arm, led her up the stairs, then started to giggle. "You should have seen yourself as you went for her. A red-headed fury. No, you won't have trouble with Mabel; she's scared to death of you."

Maggie slipped out of her shoes, then stretched out on the bed. Jenny started to leave the room.

Maggie bolted upright.

"Don't go yet. I've something to tell you. You'll never believe it. Dr. Field asked me to marry him. Can you imagine?"

Jenny went back and sat down on the edge of the bed, causing the mattress to plunge under her weight.

"He didn't? I don't believe it, why the old devil! Old doc." She mused, "Well, I suppose you could consider it, though he's a bit long in the tooth. Always thought him a born bachelor not interested in women a'tall. Well, you never know.

"What you tell him? Would you? Would you marry the town doctor?" She threw back her head and laughed. "Would get you off the bluff and into a big fancy house. You'd be one of the town mucky-mucks, Maggie."

"You know me better than that. Of course I won't marry him. He's old enough to be my father. Though he's a good man and I am a bit flattered at the attention, I've other plans, dear friend."

She leaned closer to Jenny and put both hands on her

shoulders. "I've got to tell you or bust. I'm going to Boston. There, I've said it, and it sounds strange to my ears. Boydie and I are going to Boston . . . soon, Jenny. I've our papers in order, and I can't wait to get away from here. At last I'm going to leave this miserable town." Jenny's mouth hung open, but no sound came out. Maggie laughed and shook her. "Say something. Didn't you hear me? What do you think of that?"

"I . . . I don't know what to say," Jenny stammered. "You . . . Boydie . . . in the States? Why would you want to go to the States? I'll, I'll never see you again."

"You will, Jenny, you will. When I get settled, you will come to visit often. Boston isn't that far away. Don't cry. Be happy for me. You see, when Colie went back to the pit and married the girl, I realized it was time for me to act, to do something to change the way my life was headed.

"I took the ferry to the city and found my way to the Immigration office, and believe me I was nervous when I applied for our papers. I shook like a leaf. I'd never done anything like that before in my life. They asked me a few questions and such, but were ever so nice and kind."

"But what about your brother's farm? Colie and the girl and the new baby on the way. Are you telling me you're just up and leaving? Just like that? Without a by-your-leave? I don't understand, Maggie. I thought you'd live with your brother on the farm, now the bad one's out of the way?"

Maggie sighed deeply.

"Now, I know John wasn't a bad man. He's sick in the head and can't be held responsible for his actions. Murdock and Ned have my blessings to sell the farm if that's what they want to do. I don't deserve a share in it, and I don't want any. My two brothers have worked hard, and it belongs to them."

"But Colie—" Jenny started to say.

Maggie interrupted her.

"No, Jenny, Colie made his choice. If he'd wanted the farm, Murdy would have held onto it. But Colie intends to go on being a coal miner, and Jenny, . . . I can't stand to watch him wear himself out in the dirty pit, to be hurt, maimed, or worse. I've come to the end of my rope. I have to leave here. Don't you see? I owe it to my little girl."

Jenny took the wisp of handkerchief from the sleeve of her dress and wiped her eyes.

"But Boston, of all places! Why, that's another country, and so far away. Where will you live? You don't know a soul there."

"I'm getting around to that. Marion is there now. Seems she has relatives in a place called the North End of Boston. She and Archie planned to live there before he was killed. Living with her mother and brother didn't work out, and that didn't surprise me, for I know Marion's ways. So you see, dear friend, I will not be alone. I'll have Marion and the boys. I'm pleased for that. And I admit, it will be frightening for me to be on my own in a big city, but the Lord is with me and He will guide me."

Jenny frowned.

"Well, praises be, and I guess Marion's better than no one. It eases my mind to know you will have someone to turn to, even Marion, the half—I didn't think you got on that well with her?"

"Yes, well Marion's a bit rough around the edges, and we've had our differences, but she's a good soul and means well."

Jenny looked skeptical.

"I suppose so. Have you enough money . . . oh, of course, you must have; you've always been a good manager. When will you be leaving us?"

"I planned on going to the city next week to see about train tickets. That's changed now, since I let my temper get the best of me. Mabel will surely bring some kind of charge against me."

Jenny twisted her handkerchief in knots.

"Believe me, she'll do no such thing. She's a coward, that one, and lets old Lizzie lead her around by the nose. What does Colie have to say about your leaving?"

Maggie's face hardened.

"He's upset. We had quite a go around. It surprised him. He thought he knew his mother pretty well." Her mouth thinned into a tight line. "But then, he's pulled a few surprises on me of late.

"As to where we will live? Well, I wrote to the chamber of commerce in Boston, and they mailed me information about jobs and such, and we'll stay with Marion for a short time until I find a place of my own."

"I'll worry about you. Let me give you some money. I haven't had to spend a nickel at Anna's . . . .I've money put by."

Maggie put her hand over Jenny's.

"Please don't worry about me. I know what I'm doing and I have more than enough for our needs. I've been saving for a long time. Don't distress yourself. You've had a difficult time of it, . . . and . . . and your life is taking a better turn, too. Be happy for both of us. But Jenny, I've these mixed feelings. Scared, but excited, and I get all tingly and goose-bumpy when I think of leaving Rockhill.

"I prayed and prayed and asked God to send me a signal to let me know that I'm not running away from my problems—angry at Colie and the girl, losing Catherine, my whole life. Then, on my knees one night, I felt His presence as never before and felt wrapped in a warm, comforting glow. I felt such peace in my soul that I'm confident

God is with me and telling me it's all right to go ahead with my plans."

Maggie wrapped her arms around Jenny, and they rocked back and forth on the bed.

Then, a series of sharp, screeching blasts brought them to their feet.

"The mine! Jenny, oh!" Maggie cried. They flung on their shoes and raced down the stairs and out the door as other frantic women and children spilled from the row houses.

"Get in, ladies!" Dr. Field braked to a stop as Maggie and Jenny reached the road. He leaned across and flung open the doors, and Maggie and Jenny climbed inside.

"God save us all. Wait for us." Lizzie and Mabel rushed up to the car. Lizzie pulled open the back door and jumped beside Jenny in the backseat. Wild-eyed, hair streaming down her back, Lizzie cried.

"It be a bad one. Knew it were comin'. Saw a forerunner last night, a skull, a death head stood grinnin' at me by the side a' me bed."

"Shut up, Lizzie," yelled Dr. Field. Then lowering his voice, said, "It's no. 9, the man-rake . . . cable broke."

"Colie. Oh, sweet Jesus, Colie," Maggie murmured.

Mabel started to whimper.

"Jesus save our menfolk," Lizzie prayed loudly.

"Be calm, ladies, be calm. No hysterics. You've all been through this before. The men will need your support and courage. Stay calm. We'll be there in a few minutes." He reached for Maggie's hand and squeezed it tightly.

"Please, not Colie, too. Oh, please don't let him be on the rake," she called out.

"Me man be on the rake. He be on it," Lizzie sobbed. "He be on it. I saw the death head. Me man be dead."

Speeding ambulances kicked up road dust, and screaming sirens mingled with the blast of mine whistles and horns. A white and blue ambulance speeded up to the rear of the car, crowding it, then zigzagged past on narrow Main Street, past the post office, movie house, Woolworth's Five and Dime, the Presbyterian Church, and the waterfront. Then with wheels squealing, it rounded a corner and headed down a long, barren road to the stricken mine.

Suddenly blinded by road dust, Dr. Field leaned into the windshield, then brought the car to a spine-jolting halt that threw the women forward.

"Oh, me poor back," groaned Lizzie.

At the bankhead, grim faced miners' wives stared at the roped-off pit entrance, waiting and seemingly oblivious to the shouted orders of dirty-faced men, mining officials, and rescue apparatus. They moved their lips in private prayers while holding tight to the hands of too thin, somber-faced children.

More ambulances raced up the road to the bankhead. Rear doors flung open and attendants carrying stretchers hurried to the mine. Dr. Field grabbed his medical bag, and, long legs striding forward, joined the rescuers as miners, some on foot, and others, battered and bloody, assisted by seemingly uninjured men, staggering out of the pit.

"Colie McNeil. Colie!" shrieked Jessie, slapping at the hands of the little boys who clutched her skirt. *"Malcolm, my Malcolm, where is he? Tell me he's alive!"* She ducked under the rope and plucked at Colie's arm.

Dr. Field and an attendant took the injured man Colie half-carried and lowered him to a stretcher, wincing when the man screamed out.

"Where's me own man? Why ain't he with you? Tell me, you be his mate," Jessie cried.

Maggie reached them and tried to speak, but coherent words didn't come from her shock-dried throat, just a soft crooning as she patted her son.

Mabel and Lizzie glared at Colie and his mother, unconcealed hatred gleaming in their eyes, then they linked arms and stood with the other miners' wives.

Colie leaned down and put his hands on Jessie's shoulders. Coal dust rimmed his bloodshot eyes. He said,

"I couldn't do nuthin', Jessie. He wouldn't jump. I yelled jump, for the love of God, jump 'fore we hit the curve in the slope. *Jump, man!*

"Malcolm froze. He froze. I jumped clear 'fore it hit the slope. The rake, it ran wild, crazy fast, I knew I had to jump. Some jumped when I did. Oh, Ma, Jessie, it be somethin' awful in there. Saw one a me mates' head roll at me feet. Couldn't find Malcolm, Ma." Colie let out a cry and pressed his head against Jessie's gray-streaked hair.

Jenny spoke up.

"Don't lose hope. Malcolm's an experienced miner. Maybe thought his best bet would be in stayin' with the rake; whereas, you, Colie, took a big risk when you jumped. If you'd hit the cable, you wouldn't be standing here now. Malcolm knew the risks. He's a careful man. Probably thought his best chance was to hunker down. Jessie, take heart . . . see? There's men walking out right now. Don't look like they've a scratch on them."

Colie swiped at his eyes with his sleeve.

"Goin' back in, Ma. Ya gotta let me go. He pried her hands loose. I gotta' help me mates."

Rescue workers began to emerge from the pit. Some carried tarpaper-covered stretchers, other stretcher bearers carried bloody miners. A temporary morgue was set up in the colliery washroom, and beneath two of the tarpaper-covered stretchers lay the broken bodies of Malcolm McGee and Gordon MacKinneon, Lizzie's husband.

Dr. Field approached Jessie McGee, grief and pity etched like stone across his face. Jessie stared at him as if

253

mesmerized. Maggie moved quickly to her side.

Jessie sobbed quietly while her young sons buried their faces in her skirt.

"I'm sorry. I'm so sorry," murmured Jenny.

Then, a young man, new tweed cap on his head and dressed in a navy-blue suit, gaudy red tie and shiny black shoes, approached.

"Mrs. McNeil, my buddy, Colie? Was he . . . is he . . . was he on the rake?" he asked, hesitantly.

"Alex Campbell, is that yourself?" cried Jenny, swinging around to look at him. "You're a sight for sore eyes, I must say. Yes, dear, he was on the rake, but he's all right. Colie's not hurt. He's down the pit with the rescuers. It's terrible . . . terrible!"

Dr. Field, sweat-soaked and harried, rushed up to them and shook Alex's hand.

"Glad you're back, young fellow. We can use you. Can you drive?"

Alex looked puzzled.

"Sure, used to drive Da's tin lizzy 'til it fell apart."

"Good, take my car over there." He gestured with his thumb. "Take the women and children home. Get out of those glad rags, then come back. We need able-bodied men here. It's bad, the worst yet." He grasped Maggie's shoulders, said, "Go with the boy . . . you, Jenny, go with Alex. This is no place for you."

Maggie twisted away from him, protesting.

"No, I'm not leaving without Colie. I can help!"

"Jumping Jehovah, woman! Take the other ladies, and go home. There is nothing you can do here, unless you're a trained nurse." Then in a softer voice. "There will be plenty for you to do in the days to come. Go on now. Go with Mrs. McGee. Help her if you can." He dashed away.

Soon, off-duty shift miners and more women and children arrived at the scene. The miners quickly joined rescue workers, while the women and children merged with the hushed group who surged against the ropes and stared as each stretcher appeared at the pit entrance. Few spoke, only soft gasps and murmurs as each tar paper-covered stretcher appeared, and no one seemed to notice when it started to rain.

Alex lost no time in herding the women and children into the doctor's car.

"Come on, ladies, let's go. Doc is right, this is no place for ya, an' yer getting' wet."

"Jessie and the boys will come home with me then. She shouldn't be alone right now," Maggie said.

Jessie lifted a wan face.

"But I ain't alone. I have me boys here, an' I feels a need ta be in me own place. Malcolm's waitin' fer me there, waitin' fer me ta bring him his slippers an' pipe and brew him a pot a tea. Me an' me man, we'll 'ave a last talk. You understand, Maggie? Malcolm's spirit is waitin' fer me at home . . . hurry, get me home. Quick, take me home."

"All right, Jessie. I understand. We will take you and the boys home, but I'll come by first thing in the morning," said Maggie. "You will need support to get through this terrible ordeal. Believe me, I know. You can't do it alone. When Jock passed on, I don't know what I would have done if it hadn't been for his mother, Archie, and Marion, and my dear friend Jenny." She reached over and pressed Jenny's hand.

Jessie nodded and looked up.

"I clear forgot 'bout yer man passin' away." She whispered. "I'm sorry fer yer trouble, Mrs. Gleason." She glanced quickly at Maggie before turning away.

Maggie felt as though she'd been pieced through the heart. She thought, *even you, Jessie McGee. You're wondering about Sammy and me. It's started, rumors . . . gossip. Well, what did I expect from this town? I have few friends here.*

Jenny was quick to notice the glance.

"Humph," she started, "Malcolm was a good man, Jessie. I know it's an awful thing to say about my husband, but Sammy's no loss to the world. He was a brute and a drunkard and unknown to me, he tried to shame and torment my dearest friend in the world."

Alex listened as he searched his mind for something nice to say about Sammy before giving Jenny his condolences, and thought better of it and said nothing. Instead, he brought the car to a stop, leapt out, and opened the door.

Maggie started to get out. Jessie waved her back inside.

"No need fer ye ta get wet. We be all right now, and I thank ye for the ride."

They watched the mother and sons trudge up the rain-soaked hill to the solid gray house.

"God be with you, Jessie McGee, with you and your sons," Maggie murmured, with a catch in her throat. Then a feeling of elation swept over her. She thought, *Colie is spared...he has been spared.*

The rain slackened off as Alex brought the car to a jerking stop in front of Maggie's door.

"Out yer go, ladies, gotta change these duds an' get back ta the bankhead."

"Thank you for the ride," Jenny said over her shoulder as she started to get out of the car. "You're home for a visit, eh? Must say you're looking prosperous, Alex. You must have a good job in Halifax, then?"

Alex took off his cap.

"Naw, don't let the suit fool yer," he said sheepishly, "I spent me last money on new duds. Ain't no good jobs in Halifax for a fella' like me. I got some work on the waterfront, loadin' an' unloadin'. Lots of men lookin' for the same jobs. Got into fights, worked in a diner washin' dishes for a spell. Got the odd job here and there. Da's getting' on an' Mum's ailin'. She needs help since me sister married.

"Heard things better in the mines, so high-tailed it back to town. Ha, that's a hot one; same old pit killin' off miners."

He looked at Maggie. "Good ta see ya, Mrs. McNeil. Glad to hear Colie's still in one piece. Better get back 'fore doc thinks I took off with his car." He tipped his cap, then jammed it on his head, and the car took off with a series of jerks on the wet road.

Pale and frightened, Frances stood in the door, with Boydie at her side.

"Colie, Oh, tell me he's not dead! Everyone is rushing around and crying. No one will tell me anything. Oh, please, what's happened?"

"He's alive, child," Maggie answered, grim-faced. "Colie's not hurt. He's one of the lucky ones, . . . this time. He is at the mine helping with the rescue. Malcolm McGee is dead. Lizzie's husband, too. Many more badly hurt who will die of their injuries."

Frances went limp and sagged against here mother-in-law. Maggie braced her and grasped her shoulders.

"Stop that! Didn't you hear me! Colie's alive. Give thanks to the Almighty . . . the other poor wretches . . . Colie has seen some terrible sights today."

Sandy and sweaty, Boydie grabbed her mother's skirt with a grubby hand.

"Baby hungry. Me want cookie."

Jenny picked her up.

"There's my sweetheart. Come to Jenny. I've missed you, wee one."

But Maggie took her from Jenny's arms.

"I'll take her. She'll soil your nice dress. Look, there's Anna and Mike now. I'll make us all a cup of tea and a bite to eat."

Frances turned a sickly gray. She hurried to the sink and vomited.

Late Afternoon

Haggard, indescribably dirty, and aged beyond his years, Colie stumbled up the walk. Frances dashed down the path and flung herself at him, sobbing against his shoulder, while he smoothed her hair.

Then with fire in her brown eyes, she looked up at him.

"Colie McNeil," she ordered, "you will not work in a coal mine ever again. You hear You don't have to. We have money. A gift from my mother. We can sell the house and go to the States. Maggie and I . . . we . . . we . . . talked about it. You have to listen to us!"

Maggie stepped up and lightly touched his arm. Tears welled up.

"My son, my dear, Frances told me about her mother, the letters and the money. It's a gift from God himself and His message. You must heed His message. He wants this family to leave Rockhill and the mines. Your father, your brother, they gave their lives to the pits. Are you going to let the coal company take your life too? Do you think the company cares how many miners die or are injured so badly the might as well be dead?"

Colie grunted and pushed Frances away. He went into the kitchen and slumped in a chair.

"Get off me back, the two of ya. I ain't had nuthin' to eat all day. Ya suppose ya could stop yakin' long 'nuff to fix a fella some supper?"

Maggie and Frances bumped into each other in their haste to obey, while Boydie tried to climb into his lap.

"No, baby. You can't come up. In a while after I have a

washup." He rested his head on his hands for a few seconds, then looked up at his wife and mother, and a shadow of a smile flitted across his face. "I can't fight the two of ya, since ya linked up, joined forces. Anyways, I'm through with the pit . . . it . . . got Malcolm, me mate, best mate ever. I'll go—Franny and me—we'll go the States. Didn't know what to do with the money, anyways, did we, funny face?"

Released by Colie's words, some of the anxiety of the past months melted away. Maggie breathed a sigh, sat next to him, took his face in her hands, and kissed him over and over again.

"My boy, my dear son, you've made me happier than you will ever know!"

"My mama got dirty face like brother," Boydie chuckled.

They looked at Maggie's coal-streaked face, and the tension and grief of a long, terrible day broke, and they started to laugh until their sides ached and they could laugh no more.

Then, sobered, Colie thought, *Why'm I laughing like a hyena when me best friend and me pit mates dead, all dead,* and sobs shook his body in spasm after spasm—neither his wife nor his mother could console him.

When the man-rake ran wild, twenty-eight coal miners lost their lives. Men crippled for life, men who would never again enter a coal mine to dig the black gold that made the coal company rich.

Back-to-back funeral services for twenty-eight miners crowded Rockhill's two churches, Saint Ann's and the Scotch Presbyterian.

Dry-eyed, Jessie McGee held tight to her sons' hands and stared rigidly at Malcolm's coffin, while Lizzie's wails echoed through the church's vast walls.

All of Rockhill's mines remained closed while company investigators descended on the town, seeking someone to blame for the accident and absolve the coal company from failure to keep equipment in safe-working order.

Wiping her eyes, Lizzie sidled up to Maggie when services for six miners ended and mourners were leaving the church.

"I'm sorry for your loss, Lizzie. Please let me know if there is anything I can do for you."

"Ain't likely. Yer can't do nuthin for me. I'm goin' ter stay with me son and his missus for a spell. They'll take care a me now me man's gone to his reward, thank yer. Hear yer leavin' town for the States? When yer fixin' to go? Just as well yer leavin: Yer never fit in with the rest of us on the bluff. Yer won't be missed . . . good day ter yer, come 'long, deary."

Mabel, with her husband close at her heels, kept her head down as she skirted around Maggie, while Tom tipped his cap to Maggie, then nodded to Colie and Frances.

"See, Ma? Didn't I tell ya? Mabel ain't goin' ta do a darn thing 'bout the fuss ya got in with her. Ya can get ya train tickets and stop worryin' 'bout her."

"Please, I wish you wouldn't bring up that unhappy affair, especially at a time like this when so many are burying their loved ones, and I'm quite ashamed of what I did to Mabel MacDermott."

"Ya right, won't say no more 'bout it. Ya got a letter from Aunt Marion? What she 'ave ta say?"

"Not too much. Marion' isn't adept at letter writing, but I gather from the tone of her letter that she's lonely and anxious for Boydie and me to arrive. She writes that she has furnished the front bedroom for us and is appreciative of the indoor plumbing and big bathtub. Really, the wonders of her bathroom have impressed her more than the whole city of Boston, it would seem, and—"

"But has she made any friends?" Frances cut in. "How are her children? Do they like where they are?"

Several people nodded to then, and some of the men paused to talk with Colie as they walked along, and it was a few minutes before Maggie could reply.

"Marion said Kevin and Sammy have been accepted by the neighborhood children, and the bullying has finally stopped. At first, the poor boys had a bad time of it. They are in school now, and she wrote she's having a fine time investigating the city without them tagging after her. She made friends with the family who live on the first floor of the building—Italian people—sounds like they helped her adjust to her surroundings, good church-going people, she wrote.

"It's curious, though. Marion doesn't say anything in her letters about her kinfolk, the woman who wrote to her and the person responsible for Marion being in Boston in the first place. Marion told me how this Moira had written to her and Archie quite a while ago, informing them of the death of Marion's father's cousin Joe. She was Joe's wife and owns the building Marion is living in. Oh, well, that's Marion for you."

"Can't see ya and me aunt livin' together, Ma. But it won't be long 'fore me an' Frances gets ta join ya. Then I'll get a place for all of us McNeils'. The company's buying back the house, and they can have it. Can't wait ta get away from the spot. Ain't spent a peaceful night. Think old granny's hauntin' the place." He nudged Frances and winked at his mother.

"Don't tease, Colie. The poor soul is resting peacefully,

261

not haunting houses. Don't talk of ghosts and haunting, not a good subject on a day such as this. It gives me cold chills. The sooner we leave Rockhill, the better.

"I'm fortunate to have Marion to go to in Boston. We understand each other and know each other's faults. I will get along just fine with Marion, and it's only temporary. Boydie and I will soon find a place of our own when I get work."

"Ma, ya will live with me and Franny, and that's the end of it!"

"Well, we're jumping ahead of ourselves, aren't we? First things first, my dears. Let's get to Boston, then we will see. There is much to do and much to discuss before we talk about living arrangements." Then Maggie thought to herself, *Mmm...Colie is so young...he knows nothing...he and the girl will have their own row to hoe when we get to the States...Boydie and I will have ours.* She linked arms with Colie and Frances, and they picked up their pace. Maggie's voice had a young girl's lilt as she raised her chin and said gaily, "Tomorrow, tomorrow, I will take the ferry to Sydney and buy train tickets to Boston for Boydie and me."

Unbelieving, euphoric, Maggie thought, *It's happening. It's really going to happen. I feel as though I could take wings and fly. Boydie and I, we are going! Me and mine will leave Rockhill forever.*

Murdock is coming later today, must get home and prepare dinner and bake a pie or two. Oh, Lord, you have blessed me! I'm delighted with Murdock's decision not to sell the farm, now that Ned and his wife want to move back. A wise decision. It's a good farm; the will make a proper living out of it.

I will answer Marion's letter tonight after everyone has left and Boydie is asleep.

My dear little Catherine...Danny...it grieves me to leave you, but your memories are engraved on my heart and in my soul for all time. Your sister's so much like you in looks, but not temperament, Catherine. Boydie will, with the Lord's help, have the chance in life that you and Danny never had.

30

September 1922—Aunt Marion in Boston

Kevin and Sammy hung back, ashamed to have their mother take them by the hand, afraid the might be seen by hard-won, newly made friends. But Aunt Marion hung on tight and pulled them up the steep hill.

"Stop hanging back. You want to see your ma drop dead in her tracks?"

The thought of his Ma stretched out dead on the pavement was too much for Sammy.

"Ya ain't gonna die, are ya, Ma? Ma, Pa died . . . don't die, Ma, don't die!" he cried out, frightened.

"Aw, 'course I ain't going to die. Don't take every little thing I say to heart. Things going to be all right now that dear Maggie's coming. Thanks be to God, Maggie's coming. Now stop yelling." Them people across the street looking at us. Come along now. Be a good boy."

Finally they reached the crest of the steep hill and stared at the big, ugly red brick structure with two huge chimneys. The building, surrounded by a tall, black iron fence with sharp arrowlike points at the top, seemed to loom down at them, and Sammy felt icy chills creep over his small body that made him shake.

Aunt Marion felt his tremble before he tried to free himself from her grasp.

"Come on, you young devil, it's to school you're going, like it or not!"

Her once coal-black hair, now streaked with gray,

flowed past her shoulders and down her back. She wore a drop-waisted, pleated red dress to mid-knee, black pointed shoes with buttoned straps over the insteps, and a black patent leather pocketbook hung from her right arm.

When Cousin Moira had strongly suggested that Marion cut her hair to a fashionable bob, Marion felt like smacking her one, and thought to herself, *what the hell does that skinny bitch know?*

Marion thought back to the times when Archie would say "I hates them damn braids, makes you look like a squaw. Wear your hair loose. I like it that way, woman . . . me own Indian princess, you are." Her Archie had loved her hair, and by damn, no skinny rag of a woman was going to talk her into cutting it and having it plastered to her head, like a man's.

Kevin and Sammy, scrubbed clean, miserable in new shoes, shirt, sweater, and cap, eyed the red building ahead of them and the shouting children playing just beyond the fence.

Sammy darted ahead, put his face up against the fence, and stared. A few stopped their play to stare back at him with open mouths. Soon they were joined by others, who ran toward the fence to gape at the little boy wearing the funny cap that was too big for his head and fell to his brow, covering the tips of his stick-out ears. Visible were tow round, sky-blue eyes, a snub nose, freckled cheeks, and a mouth minus its two front teeth.

A little girl started to giggle. Soon, all the children were pointing and laughing.

Aunt Marion yanked him away and put her own face up against the fence and yelled.

"Boo to the lot of you! What's the matter with you. Ain't you ever seen a boy before? Well, this here's a fine

Cape Breton boy, and don't you be laughin' at him! Get away!"

Dejected, and thinking, *now I'm gonna get beat up some more*, Sammy plopped himself down on the step of the white-framed parsonage next to the steepled, stone church, where, from her pedestal in a niche in front of the church, a statue of the Virgin gazed down with sorrow-filled eyes at his bent form.

"I ain't goin' in there, Ma," he cried. "They's starin' at me an' laughin'. I ain't goin' ta school. I hate it here, hate Cousin Moira. I want to go back home to Grandma. Please, Ma, let's go back home. Please, Ma." His nose started to run, and he wiped it on the sleeve of his new shirt.

"Get up, you little bugger." Marion swiped at him with her pocketbook.

Tired and winded from the climb up the steep hill and her feet hurting from the tight shoes, she felt as miserable as her boys. Nothing seemed to be turning out right. From the moment they landed at Boston's North Station, she'd had a nervous, uneasy feeling at the pit of her stomach. That was a month ago, and it hadn't left her.

No one in the bustling, vast, train station had paid the least attention to two little boys wearing caps, knickers, and boots in the September heat or to the big, dark woman, hair flowing down her back, who wore a red dress and looked around, uncertain what to do next.

Until the landlady, Moira—for that's how Marion now thought of her, not a relative who cared, but a landlady with her hand out—showed up to rescue them.

Wearing a navy blue dress that reached the middle of her knees and flattened her already small bosom, bobbed hair with spit curls plastered to her cheekbones, she'd held her head to one side and her nose in the air as she looked them over, then started to approach, holding out a hand.

Marion never dreamed the woman who had been writing to her would look like the person coming toward her. She'd pictured a motherly sort with graying hair. Confused thoughts raced through her mind . . . *ah, no, she ain't a'tall like I'd pictured.* But she whipped the caps off the boys' heads and pasted a smile across on her face.

There were no glad greetings from Moira, no hugs, no kisses for the boys. A real cold fish she turned out to be.

"How ah you?" she'd said in a rich Boston accent, "I do hope you had a pleasant trip. Sorry my husband couldn't be here to greet you, but he is out of town. His work keeps him quite busy." Then she beckoned to a black man dressed in some kind of uniform and said, "The porter will take your luggage. He will expect to be tipped. Hurry along, I have a taxi waiting, and the meter's running . . . " and then she rushed in front of them and out the wide open doors into a frightening broad street with crowds of people, all seeming in a great rush to get somewhere.

Marion thought, *so this is Boston? Eh? It will take some getting used to* . . . then . . . bewildered, they hurried after Moira, afraid to lose sight of her in the crowd while the porter gathered up their bags and grinned from ear to ear in a display fine white teeth.

Marion wondered, *what she mean "expect to be tipped." And what in the hell's the big hurry? That woman's like greased lightening.*

Sammy looked up at the tall porter.

"I ain't never seen a chocolate man before. I likes you."

The porter threw back his head and gave out a booming laugh.

"Where you come from, boy? Lots of us chocolate folks 'round 'bout, an' some of us be sweet 'nuff all right, 'specially lady ones." Then he bent down and pinched Sammy's cheek.

267

"Ma, a tip means ya gotta give him some money for carryin' the suitcases," Kevin whispered.

Marion tapped him on the side of the head.

"I know what it means. I ain't entirely ignorant, you know." She reached into her bag, brought out a Canadian dollar bill and handed it to the porter. He looked at it, started to say something, then shook his head and stuck the bill in his pocket.

Moira hailed one of the yellow checkered cabs lined up at the curb and got in beside the driver. Aunt Marion and the boys climbed in the back of the cab. Moira hadn't even looked back at them, and Marion felt dread in her heart at what she had gotten herself and her boys into.

As the cab drove through the streets of Boston, the boys pressed their faces against the windows and gazed out.

"Lean back from them windows, young fellows," the cab driver said, not unkindly, "I just cleaned them." He then nodded to Marion, saying, "Sorry, Missus, I don't own this cab, you know. Gotta keep it clean."

In a few minutes, he'd brought the cab to a stop in front of a street lined with dingy gray tenement houses, and while Moira paid the fare, Marion held tight to her sons' hands and looked about.

Dirty-faced young children played in the street and dark-haired, sturdy looking women pinned wash to lines on front porches while laughing and shouting to each other in a queer foreign language.

Garbage cans stood against curbs, cars honked, milk wagons and delivery trucks drove by. Across the street, a grocery, with a green and white striped awning, displayed fruits and vegetables on stands in front of the store, along with a fat man who sat with his buttocks overflowing a small wrought iron chair as he chewed on a hunk of salami and bread and waved to passersby.

On the same side of the street, a few doors from the grocery, the swinging doors of a tavern flew open, and a drunken man found himself shoved into the street. He lost his balance, fell, got up, brushed himself off, then staggered back through the swinging doors.

Dogs barked and chased each other through littered alleyways, and mixed odors filled the September air: garlic, cooking of food, dog feces, and exhaust fumes.

The women stopped their jabbering long enough to point and stare at Aunt Marion and her boys.

The cabdriver deposited their luggage on the sidewalk and tossed Moira a dirty look.

"I wish you and your kids the best of luck, ma'm," he said. "I've a hunch you're going to need it." Then he got back into the cab and drove away.

The trio gazed longingly at the back of the cab as it disappeared up the street. Then Aunt Marion shrugged her shoulders, thought, *well, we're here. Got to make the best of it*, and hugged the boys to her.

"Well, come on now, little chums, cheer up. I knows you're hungry and tired, but we'll soon get settled in." She pointed to the two smaller suitcases at the curb. "One for each of you," then picked up two large, bulging ones and said, "You'll like living in the city—look there." She pointed to a group of children playing kick-the-can in the street. "Lots of kids to play with, once you're acquainted an' all."

Moira, hands on hips and tapping her foot, waited for them to climb the stairs, then turned and took a string of keys from her handbag. The door swung open before she could fit the key into the lock, and a fat woman with a pronounced mustache filled the doorway.

Startled, Sammy took a step back and almost fell down the stairs before Kevin caught him. Behind the woman, a little girl with big, brown, eyes, peeked curiously at them from behind her grandmother's skirt.

"Oh, there you are, Mrs. DeLucci." Moira smiled. "I want you to meet the new tenants for the third-floor flat, Marion McNeil and her two sons. They've just arrived from Canada. I do hope you will help them get acquainted with the neighborhood. I am sure they will find living in the city quite different from where they are from." She put the keys back into her bag. "Would you do me a big favor and take them upstairs and show them the flat? Here is the key. I've an appointment at the beauty parlor, and I'm already late."

Moira smiled at Marion and the boys for the first time, revealing prominent front teeth, and said, "I went to the trouble of having the flat outfitted with the things you will need, dear. So there will be no need for you to bother yourself about furniture and such.

"Of course, a furnished flat costs more, but then, I'm sure you will appreciate the convenience of being able to move into a place ready for you with no fuss or bother on your part. Don't you agree, dear?" She bent down and patted Sammy on the head. "My, my, you're a real carrot head aren't you, sonny?"

"Me name's not Sonny, and I ain't a carrot head!" scowled Sammy.

She ignored his remark and looked at Kevin.

"You, too, young man. You won't find many redheads in this neighborhood, but you will get along fine. Now, I must run." She turned to Marion. "I will come by tomorrow morning to take you to my bank. You will need to exchange your Canadian money and open an account, dear. The rent is due the first of every month."

She started down the stairs, then said over her shoulder, "Speaking of rent, Mrs. DeLucci, this is the fifth of the month, your rent is overdue, and you know I have expenses to meet. Please, have the money for me tomorrow."

Aunt Marion started after her.

"Wait just a damn minute there, Mrs.—Moira—I don't know what's going on here. Don't you live here? Ain't this here your house? What about all the nice letters you been writing me? You actin' like me and the boys nothing a'tall. We come all this way, don't know no one but you. I thought we'd be kinfolk, livin' in the same house?"

Moira's laugh was high like a horse's whinny.

"My dear, I'm sorry if you came to the wrong conclusion. You're not my relatives but my late husband's. I'm sure I never wrote that we'd be living in the same house. But, of course, this *is* my house, and five others on this block—but *live* here?" she tossed her head, "my husband and I live here? Heaven forbid. No, dear, I live in the Back Bay, and, of course, I intend to help you."

She patted Marion's hand. "Go with Mrs. DeLucci now. There's milk, eggs, butter, and cheese in the icebox and bread and groceries in the pantry. I will see you in the morning. We will reconcile what you owe me then, and don't worry, you will soon get to know your way around. This is an Italian neighborhood, very friendly." She then hurried down the stairs to hail a passing cab.

Marion had stood motionless, rooted to the spot until Mrs. DeLucci touched her shoulder and spoke to her.

"You comma 'long, missus. I showa you place, uppa stairs." She drew a fat finger across her neck and said, "Land-a-lady no good. Comma 'long. Donna worry, I, Carmela, I looka afta you."

The little girl, Rosa, dashed out from behind her grandmother, stuck her tongue out at the boys, then raced ahead up the stairs while her grandmother scolded and tried to slap the child's thin brown legs. They reached the landing, and Mrs. DeLucci unlocked the door. Marion and the boys entered the kitchen of their new home for the first time. Kevin pointed to a fat cockroach making its way across the shiny new oilcloth on the kitchen table.

Marion didn't like to think back to that awful day, but they had lived through it. Now she could get on a street car, subway train, or elevated train in a city that had nearly scared her out of her wits a month ago.

At least once a week, kind-hearted Mrs. DeLucci would lumber up the stairs with dishes of hot pasta, reeking with the hated garlic.

And Tony DeLucci, Carmelia's kind-hearted, good-looking son had driven the boys and Rosa, his daughter, to an amusement park. The boys talked of nothing else for days after.

Rosa's beautiful young mother had hemorrhaged and died shortly after her birth. Grief stricken, Tony disappeared, to reappear a year later and open a tiny cobbler shop and become a devoted father to little Rosa.

They were good people, but their ways were strange to Marion, and she longed for her own kind. But she kept a cheerful face for her boys, who were having a rough time of their own with neighborhood bullies who regularly beat them up. Kevin got the worst of it when he stood up to them and protected his little brother.

But a week ago, the Italian kids, impressed with Kevin's courage, finally accepted them both and allowed them to play in street games.

And when Marion received Maggie's letter saying she and Boydie would be arriving at South Station in two weeks, Marion felt that with Maggie by her side, together, they'd make a life for themselves and their children away form the coal mines, after all.

Marion had a hunch that Moira was cheating her but couldn't be sure. She couldn't figure out the checking account she'd opened at Moira's bank or the queer American money, but dear Maggie would know.

Her head began to ache with all the thinking, so she sat down beside Sammy. Kevin looked at them with disgust.

"We ever gonna go into that school and sign up? Ain't that what we came here for, Ma?" He punched Sammy on the shoulder. "Stop bawling, brat."

"Don't be hittin' your brother, or I'll smack you silly!" Marion reached for Kevin, but he quickly stepped back.

A woman wearing a white apron with a blue-checkered scarf tied about her head came out on the front porch of the house with a broom in her hand.

"You people there," she cried out, "get along with you. Don't be loitering in front of the parish. You can't sit there. What do you want?" Not waiting for an answer she went on. "Is it the Father you're looking for? He ain't in . . . you can wait in the parlor. He'll be along soon for his noon meal."

The boys jumped up, and Marion and brushed off the back of her dress and took the boys by the hand once more.

"Thank you, missus," she said. "We was on our way to the school, to sign up me boys, here, you know. The damn hill nearly did me in . . . was sitting here getting my second wind, so's to speak."

"This is a decent neighborhood. Folks don't sit on the steps of the parish." Then she waved before going into the house, and said, "That's a Cape Breton tongue if I ever heard one. Sister, get on with you now, and good luck to you."

As they walked toward the school, Kevin took off his cap.

"Sammy's cap is too big for him," he said. "Why'd you buy him a cap too big?"

"Sammy weren't with me . . . had to guess his size.

Home sick, he was. Mrs. DeLucca looked in on him. You was playing baseball in the park that day . . . did a good job picking out your duds, didn't I? Your cap fits."

"Sure, mine fits. The kids was laughin' at Sammy 'cause of his cap. Take off that friggin' cap, Sammy, or they'll start laughin' at us again."

Marion said, hurt, "Guess your ma don't know a thing no more. Don't know what's the right duds for my boys to start school in. Thought you both looked right smart in your new clothes."

"I likes me shirt and pants fine, Ma. Shoes, too." Kevin stuck his out his lower lip. "But make Sammy take off that damn cap."

The school bell started to clang as they walked through the iron gate to a brick-laid walkway.

Marion pulled open the massive black door, and they entered a wide hall, painted a nauseous shade of green, with huge portraits of two white-bearded, cross-looking gentlemen, one on each side of the glass-fronted principal's office.

Kevin thought, *smells like school back home, chalk-dust, Ma's egg sandwiches, and kids*. A youngish woman with honey-colored hair pulled into a tight bun at the back of her head and glasses balanced just on the tip of her nose sat with bent head behind the desk in the office. To the left and right down the oiled wood-floored hall were classrooms for grades one through six. The bell stopped clanging and children filed out of the classrooms. The woman looked up and saw Aunt Marion and her boys standing in the hall. She smiled, got up from the desk, and walked toward them.

"She be a pretty teacher, huh, Kevin?" whispered Sammy and pinched Kevin.

Kevin blushed.

"Shut up, you brat, she'll hear ya."

31

Boston—Thanksgiving Day, 1922

A gentle falling snow fell on Sammy's bare head as he sat on the front stoop with reddened cheeks and dripping nose.

"Wipe yer friggin' nose, fer crying' out loud, an' put yer cap back on." Kevin sat down and thrust the cap at him.

Sammy stuck out his lip but, afraid of getting smacked, put the cap on without further protest.

"Don't see why Tony couldn't take me to the station. I'm small, I coulda' crunched up. I wanted to go, too."

Rosa, dressed in a frilly pink dress, her dark hair pulled to the back of her head with a matching bow, stuck her head out the front door.

"Come look at the turkey," she cried. "It's all cooked and the biggest turkey I ever saw!"

Delicious odors radiating from the open door reached the boys and made their empty stomachs growl and rumble.

Kevin pulled Sammy up.

"Stop cryin'. Tony didn't 'ave no room fer us in the car, ya dummy. Yer think he got to take us every time he goes somewheres? Besides, Aunt Maggie'll 'ave suitcases and stuff. Where yer think Tony gonna put us, on the roof, fer cryin' out loud? Come on, let's go look at that turkey. Boy, it sure smells good in there. I'm puttin' in me dibs fer a turkey leg."

Maggie sat on the bench under the big clock with Boydie asleep in her arms. Blue shadows ringed the child's eyes, and Maggie, dressed in a moss-green wool suit that made her eyes look like emeralds, watched stylishly dressed women with bobbed hair walk by and felt envy stir in her. She thought, *I look dowdy, should have had my hair bobbed, like Jenny's. Well, at least my shoes look nice.*

She looked down at the black T-strapped shoes on her slim feet before snatching the matching tam off her aching head, then sighed deeply as she thought of Rockhill and those she had left.

Murdock and Ned had come by with the truck and carried away the few pieces of furniture, dishes, pots, and pans. The linens, rag rugs and curtains to be stored at the farm until she had need of them.

The minister and a few friends from the church had come by to wish her well.

Alex Campbell, Jenny, her daughter Anna, Mike, Fred MacAllister, Tom MacDermott, Ned, his wife, and Murdock came to the going-away party thrown by Colie and Frances.

Maggie had felt a sad tugging at her heart when not one of the women on the bluff stopped by to say good-by and maybe, wish her the best.

"I never did them any harm. Why do they dislike me so much?" she had remarked to Jenny.

Jenny laughed, then hugged her.

"Jealous, the lot of them, and full of misery. They're here to stay, and they know it. It takes gumption to change your life and they, poor souls, don't have any to speak off. The fight's gone out of them.

"I would have left Sammy even if he hadn't done me the favor of dying first. I'd made up my mine to that on the last night he tried to beat me and I whacked him with a vase and knocked him flat...eh...but it felt good to

276

defend myself. And you know, after I went upstairs, I wanted to go back down and finish him off. Lord forgive me."

Maggie choked up as she thought of Frances and Colie and how they looked as they waved to her when the train pulled away. She watched their figures grow smaller and smaller until she could see them no more.

The train ride had been exhausting. Boydie, fretful and hard to manage, had hit out with her small fists at the kind ladies who tried to give her chocolate candy. Little did they know that she'd never tasted chocolate in her young life.

Oh, where is Marion? If she doesn't get here soon, I'm going to bawl like a baby.

Marion leapt out of Tony DeLucci's car before he could bring it to a complete stop, and bounded across the busy street toward Boston's North Station, heedless of the traffic's honking horns and the curses and the shaking fists as drivers slammed on their brakes to avoid hitting her.

"Crazy squaw," screamed a taxi driver leaning out the widow. *"Go back to the reservation!"*

Marion felt like going back and pulling him from the cab and beating the hell out of him . . . no . . . she didn't have time. Maggie was waiting, and they were late.

Tony's car had had a flat tire. He didn't have a spare, and pumping air into the flat had made them late for the two-thirty train's arrival.

So Marion, a bundle of nerves, kept her temper and ignored the horns and curses. "Frig em," she muttered under her breath. "Maggie won't know what in hell happened to me."

Dressed in the rich-looking black coat Maggie had made for her, hair damp from the falling snow, she looked anxiously at the throngs of holiday travelers carrying valises of all types as they surged in a noisy swell, the sounds bouncing and echoing inside the terminal.

Then she spied Maggie, looking forlorn and near tears on the bench under the clock and hurried over to her.

"So you're here, dear heart. I'm that sorry I'm late, but Tony's damn car got a flat. Oh, I'm glad to see you. You look worn out. Come give your sister-in-law a hug. Was it a terrible trip? Never get me on a train again, I'll swear to that. Oh, I've so much to tell you, but when it's all said and done, Boston's a right grand place to live, dear heart. Wait 'till you see me, I mean my, bathroom!"

Maggie smiled in spite of her fatigue.

"Marion, you haven't changed a bit, thank goodness. I don't think I could stand it if you had changed in the few months you've been in Boston, and I am glad to see you!" She wiped her eyes with a gloved hand. "I was starting to worry and haven't the slightest idea what I would have done if you hadn't come for us, dear."

Tony DeLucci stood by the door and searched the crowd for Marion. He wore his good navy-blue suit and soft gray felt hat. After a few minutes, he walked toward the information booth on the right side of the clock. He saw Marion and Maggie with Boydie (still asleep on her lap) and abruptly came to a halt.

"Watch where you're going, buddy," snarled a man who did a quick side-step to avoid crashing into him.

Tony turned and tipped his hat.

"Sorry, sir," he apologized, then continued to gape at Maggie in amazement. His heart raced as he thought, mama mia, she's beautiful, like a Madonna, like my Marie, with red-gold hair. His look drifted down to Maggie's slender calves and ankles to her well-shaped feet in the new shoes. He took off his hat and walked up to them.

Marion nudged her sister-in-law.

"There ... there's Tony now, dear heart. Ain't he a handsome one? Nice as they come, too. He's been a god-send to my boys, he has—so you found us. Come over and meet pretty Maggie. I like the look on your face. Eh? Surprised, ain't you? I failed to tell you how pretty she is. Did it on purpose, too. Knew you'd be pleased as all get-out when you saw her."

Maggie raised her head and looked into Tony's face. Her color deepened, and her heart did flip-flops. She thought. *Jim...Jim Boyd. Why, he looks like Jim. Now I know I've lost my mind.*

Tony, his dark eyes glistening, smiled.

"Welcome to America, pretty lady," he said softly.

And when he picked up her hand and kissed her gloved palm, Maggie felt the heat of that kiss course through her weary body like an electric shock. Long forgotten warm, tingly thrills brought her to life, and she felt safe and at home at last.